She Fell in Love with a Real One

Tamara Butler

**Lock Down Publications and Ca$h
Presents**
She Fell in Love with a Real One
A Novel by *Tamara Butler*

Tamara Butler

Lock Down Publications
P.O. Box 870494
Mesquite, Tx 75187

Visit our website
www.lockdownpublications.com

Lock Down Publications
Like our page on Facebook: Lock Down Publications
@
www.facebook.com/lockdownpublications.ldp
Cover design and layout by: **Dynasty Cover Me**
Book interior design by: **Shawn Walker**
Edited by: **Lashonda Johnson**

Stay Connected with Us!

Text **LOCKDOWN** to 22828 to stay up-to-date with new releases, sneak peaks, contests and more…

Submission Guideline.

Submit the first three chapters of your completed manuscript to ldpsubmissions@gmail.com, subject line: Your book's title. The manuscript must be in a .doc file and sent as an attachment. Document should be in Times New Roman, double spaced and in size 12 font. Also, provide your synopsis and full contact information. If sending multiple submissions, they must each be in a separate email.

Have a story but no way to send it electronically? You can still submit to LDP/Ca$h Presents. Send in the first three chapters, written or typed, of your completed manuscript to:

LDP: Submissions Dept
Po Box 870494
Mesquite, Tx 75187

DO NOT send original manuscript. Must be a duplicate.

Provide your synopsis and a cover letter containing your full contact information.

Thanks for considering LDP and Ca$h Presents.

Acknowledgments

I would like to express my gratitude to the numerous individuals who saw me through this book; to all who provided support, read, presented constructive criticism, edited, and assisted in design. I would like to thank my mother Carolyn who bought me a typewriter at such a young age, which sparked my interest in writing, and I would like to thank my friends and family for encouraging me. Last and not least I would like to thank LDP for publishing my book and leading me down the right path to become a bestselling author.

Tamara Butler

Chapter 1

Heaven

I caught a glimpse of myself in the mirror, then jumped back a bit, after looking at, my appearance. There were dark circles under my eyes, covering my flawless caramel skin. My face was very wet and stained, with tears.

My naturally, curly dark brown hair, normally came a little past my shoulders, but today, it was matted, due to neglect. To say, I was having a bad hair day, would be an understatement. My body, which I took pride in, looked like a work of art. My wide hips, and Coca-Cola shaped body, was luckily given to me by my mama, as well as my C-cup perky titties. I had crimson, stained pouty lips, doe-like eyes, and an ass big enough to sit a cup on, but even that wasn't enough, to keep my man from stepping out on our marriage.

I was a beautiful woman, but I didn't feel beautiful at all. In fact I felt like the scum of the earth, every time I thought about what he did.

My soon to be ex-husband, Naheem, who'd committed adultery, was the cause of my lack of sleep, with his lying ass. Although he'd apologized, he could shove, that apology up his ass. He wasn't thinking about, how I'd feel once I found out. He didn't think about, how his actions would affect me.

"Get yourself together, girl. Don't let that fuck nigga, get the best of you." I whispered, to myself after seeing how ugly I looked.

I grabbed a napkin from the napkin dispenser, wet it, and quickly began cleaning myself up. My eyes were puffy, with a hint of redness and my hair was covered by an ugly ass beanie, that I got from the dollar store.

Giving myself a once over, I let out a sigh, exiting the faculty restroom. Spring break had just ended, and although I definitely needed more time off, to deal with my stupid ass life. Being at school with my students, always seemed to help get my mind off pretty much anything. Dancing was always an outlet for me, hence the reason, I'd become a dance teacher in the first place.

I walked into the dance studio and glanced at the clock. The bell would be ringing in a few minutes, and although I wasn't looking forward to being here, I put a fake ass smile on my face, to mask my pain. Today would definitely be a long day, I could already feel it.

Ring—ring!

My class filled up pretty quickly, with the exception of a few late comers, but that was nothing new. Some of these little heifers loved testing my patience. I watched all of the girls mingle, for five minutes, until the late bell rang and in ran a few more students.

"Okay ladies, before we get started, I need you all to stretch for ten minutes. I also need thirty push- ups, jumping jacks and burpees, because half of you were late, and you know I hate tardiness. There's no I in team, so if one of you is late, you're all late." I heard a lot of groans throughout the room, as a few of the girls complied, and got down to begin their push-ups.

I glanced across the room and saw, two students in the back of the dance studio talking and snickering, as if they hadn't heard, what I'd just said. That was unquestionably, one of my biggest pet peeves. I smirked, before I got up, and walked towards the back of the studio. They were so immersed in what they were doing, they didn't see me coming. I cleared my throat, which caused them to jump apart from one another.

"You all know my rules about not being on your cell-phones in my classroom. Who does this phone belong to?"

The two girls stared at me blankly, as if I wasn't speaking English. Neither of them said a word.

"If no one speaks up, you're both getting detention." I threatened, although my threat was an empty one. I just wanted to make an example out of the situation.

"Okay fine—it's mine." Cynthia spoke up first. She was a sassy student, with a nasty attitude. She rolled her eyes. "But I'm not giving you my phone, and I for damn sure ain't going to detention." She sneered, popping her gum.

"Oh—" I chuckled. "Is that right? This is still my class, either you follow the rules like everyone else, or you can get out of—"

She held up her hand, cutting me off mid-sentence. I really tried to figure out, who in the hell this little girl thought she was talking to. She always gave me a hard time for no reason at all, and I hated it.

"I can what, huh?" She paused, looking around the room, trying to make sure she was the center of attention. "You gone choke me, the same way you did Shania?"

My eyes grew wide in shock, as the entire classroom gasped. I felt like the wind had been knocked out of me.

"W—what?"

I tore my eyes away from her momentarily, and looked around the room, just as I suspected, all eyes were on me.

I turned back around to face her, she smirked, and then someone yelled out, "C'mon Cyn, that wasn't even called for! That's a rumor, we don't even know if that's true or not!"

I felt my eyes begin to water. How did this get out?

"Oh, trust me it's true." She twirled her platinum blonde rope twists around one of her dirty fingers, as she snorted, shrugging her shoulders. "Shania is my girl—we cheer together. She told me all about it. Mrs. Holmes choked her, after she found out, Shan, was carrying Coach Holmes's baby. She's just mad, because she couldn't keep her man satisfied, and he had to sleep with a student to satis—"

"Okay, that's enough!" I yelled, my voice echoed throughout the studio, as she stood there with a cheesy grin on her face. "You need to get out of my cla—"

My words trailed off as the door opened, everyone, including myself, looked back. The principal and two security guards appeared at the door. I hastily spun on my heels, and walked over to the door, to see what was going on. The principal motioned for me to step into the hallway.

"I uh—need to see you in my office." Principal Greer muttered to me, avoiding eye contact with me.

"Okay, no problem." I glanced at my watch. "I'll come, as soon as this class is over in about forty-five minutes."

"No. You need to come to my office, right now." Her body language said it all. I knew something was wrong, as I scoped out her fidgety behavior.

As she turned to walk away, I noticed one of the security guards, was blocking the doorway to my dance studio. I had no idea what was going on, but it definitely raised a red flag in my mind.

I followed behind her, as the other security guard, trailed behind me. I sighed heavily, as I entered her office. I attempted to sit down, and her eyes widened.

"Uh, there's need to sit down, Mrs. Holmes. This won't take long at all."

My stomach was doing back flips in anticipation of what she was about to say. I swallowed the lump in my throat.

"I don't know how to say this, but—we're going to have to let you go."

My eyes practically bulged out of my head. I started looking around, hoping, and wishing someone would jump out, and say I was on an episode of Punk'd.

"What! You have got to be kidding me. I haven't done anything!" I shrieked, angry that I was losing my job.

She exhaled, before finally looking me in the eyes.

"Shania's father is pressing charges against your husband for uh—for impregnating her." She played with her fingers nervously, avoiding eye contact.

"So! Excuse my French, but—what the fuck does this have to do with, me?" She was about to bring the hood out of me, and I didn't want to take it there.

"Well, her father also mentioned, that you'd gotten into an altercation with, Shania, and we can't allow you to continue working here. He's not pressing any charges against you, but we think it's in our best interest, to let both you and Mr. Holmes go. I'm sorry."

I stepped closer to her desk and the fat ass security guard stepped closer to me.

"Don't fucking touch me, Fred. I ain't gone hit her—back yo' fat ass up!"

He looked at Principal Greer, looking for confirmation from her first. He backed away from me soon after.

"I have been here for four years, my students love, my dance class! I've never been in any drama, I've never missed any days, and I'm always on time. So, because my husband can't keep his dick in his pants, I have to be punished because of it? Shania isn't fucking innocent, okay. She was grown enough to lay down, and fuck my husband, over and over again, but because, I acted on impulse, after hearing such devastating news, I have to be punished?" I was out of breath, by the time I'd finished talking.

"I'm sorry, but I'm going to have to ask you to leave, Mrs. Holmes." Principal Greer suggested. I felt Fred's fat ass stubby fingers wrap around my arm.

I yanked away from him.

"Get the fuck off me, I know, my way out."

I stared at her for a few more seconds, wanting her to see the fury in my eyes. I raked my hands across her desk and knocked every photograph and trophy to the floor. That dumb bitch, could kiss, my ass. I never liked her. She was always fake and phony. I always knew she had a crush on my husband, because every chance she got, she was always calling him into her damn office. She'd probably fucked him, too.

I stormed out of her office, and tried to hold back my tears, as I finally made it outside. I felt like breaking down. I'd lost my husband, and my job all within a matter of a week.

"Hey, Heaven—are you, okay?" One of my nosey *used to be*, co-workers said to me, but I brushed past her and practically ran to my car. Once inside, I broke down, and started thinking about how all of this shit started.

****

The loud bangs on the front door, began to get louder, by the second. Whoever was out there, was definitely determined to get inside, as they continued to pound on the door, like a drum.

"Open up the muthafuckin', door!"

I clenched the covers tightly to my chest, with my trembling hands, as my breathing amplified. Something wasn't right, I could sense it.

"I know, you're in there!"

The disturbance wasn't hard to hear, in our tiny confined, one-bedroom house. I could tell, that it was a man on the other side of the door, after I'd heard his deep and very livid baritone voice, but the question was, what did he want?

"Babe." I kept my voice just above a whisper, as I shook my husband of the last three years, hoping he'd wake up from his deep slumber.

"Babe!" I continued to shake him, until he annoyingly snatched away from me, and sucked his teeth.

"What Heaven? I'm trying to sleep, baby—why you shaking me?"

He rubbed his eyes and looked over at me, with his eyes half open.

"S—someone is at the door."

He sighed deeply. "What time is it?" He asked groggily, grabbing a pillow and putting it over his face.

I gazed over at the clock, on the bedside table.

"It's 2:32, baby." I'm sure, he could hear the shakiness in my voice.

When he didn't respond, I grabbed the pillow from his face, and threw it across the room, as the banging continued. I was two seconds away from just calling the police, because Naheem wasn't helping and I was afraid they'd break the hinges off the door, with their intense banging.

I reached over and shook him more before he finally agreed to go see who was at the door. He stood up, as naked as the day he was born, and drug his feet all the way across the room to throw on some sweats. He then flipped on the bedroom light, to look for his Nike slides. We both quickly, squinted our eyes, as they attempted to adjust to the light.

He turned to walk out of the room, but then turned back to make eye contact with me.

"Stay right here, okay?"

I shook my head, but didn't bother saying anything, because my voice was caught in my throat. I just gripped the covers tighter around, my naked body. Time seemed to stop, as I heard him unlock, and swing open the squeaky door. I swear my breathing stopped, when I heard lots of shuffling and my man, yelling at someone, to get out of our home.

I quickly hopped out of bed, with the sheets wrapped around me, and almost slipped when my legs got intertwined in the sheets.

"Shit!" I hissed, as I grabbed my house robe, and rapidly threw it on, as I looked around the room for a weapon.

I couldn't find anything other than a stiletto high-heeled shoe. Whoever this guy was, I planned, to put a hole in his muthafucking head with the heel of my shoe.

I crept slowly into the hallway, careful not to make, too much noise, as my heart began to beat wildly, ready to practically, jump out of my chest. My legs felt like noodles and shook like a stripper, as I got closer.

I saw, Naheem wrestling, with some guy and I noticed a light-skinned, curly haired girl, with a tear stained face, trying to break up the fight. I wasn't able to get a good look at her face, until I got closer. I instantly recognized her as Shania, a student that goes to the high school, where both, Naheem and I, teach at. Why was she at our home?

"Stop it! Please Daddy, just stop!" She yelled, which caused my eyes to grow wide, as I threw the shoe to the ground instantly. This shit wasn't adding up and someone had better get to explaining.

I quickly ran over to the two and jumped in between them, the best way I knew how. The two men stood before each other, as their chests heaved up and down speedily. They mean mugged each other in silence, as I observed her running up to the guy, who I assumed was her father.

I looked back at Naheem, who stood behind me glaring infuriatingly at this mystery guy, like he wanted to kill him. He then wiped the tiny droplets of blood from his busted lip.

"What is going on, Naheem?" Naheem tore his eyes away from him, and looked me in the eyes as his rigid, ominous glare, turned into a soft one. He didn't say a word.

"Yeah, Naheem, why don't you, tell her?" Shania's father exclaimed, as his words slurred. He was definitely drunk.

"Okay, that's enough! Let's just go, daddy. We shouldn't be here." Shania replied, which caused my eyebrows to rise.

"Shania, what's going on?" Although she goes to Dillard High, the only time I saw Shania was in passing. I'd only had her as a student once, her freshman year. Never had she ever been invited to my home, so this whole ordeal, had me confused, as to why she was here, with her dad of all people.

She nervously looked over at Naheem, then back over at her father, yet she still said nothing.

"She's pregnant." Her father blurted out, confusing me even more.

"Wait—what?" I questioned him.

I'd figured out, who he was, but not why, he'd showed up to fight, my man.

"Let's go, dad—you're drunk, and just talking. Let's go home, okay." She tried to grab his hand, but he pulled away, and stepped closer to me.

"Ask her—ask her, who the baby daddy is." His breath smelled horrible, and the whiskey smell crossed paths with my nose. Unexpectedly he hauled off, and started punching, Naheem, in the face.

"Stop! Get off of him!" My pleas landed upon deaf ears. "I'm going to call the police if you don't get out!"

He let go of Naheem and turned to me with a smirk on his face. By now his wife beater was ripped in three, he also had a busted lip, a scratch underneath his right eye, and a bloody nose. He chuckled, then pointed at, Shania.

"Like I said—she's pregnant. You'll never guess, who she's pregnant by."

He reached deep into his pocket and pulled out a bunch of folded up papers, then threw them at me. The papers scattered all over the floor.

Unsure of what to do, I went with my first instinct. I bent down and scooped up one of the papers.

"Read that shit, out loud!" Her father, yelled, causing me to jump, as his voice echoed.

My eyes scanned over the crumpled paper in my hand, that looked to be a love note, with hearts all over it, and smiley faces.

"I am in love with you, Shaina—" I began reading the letter out loud, just as he'd requested. "Meet me in the parking lot during lunch—I miss you. I know you're mad at me, but I promise, I'm leaving, Heaven, soon you just have to give me some time—"

The letter fell from my hands unhurriedly, the same way leaves fell to the ground, during the fall. I didn't know what to do, or think about what was going on.

17

"You're going to jail, you bastard, you got, my daughter pregnant!" her father, shouted.

I looked over at, Naheem, who looked like; he'd seen a ghost. Due to his high yella skin complexion, his cheeks were cherry red in embarrassment. His beautiful freckled face was now hideous to me and I couldn't even stand to look at him any longer. This man was drop dead gorgeous and the epitome of a pretty boy with amazing broad shoulders, and a body that you'd see in body builder magazines. Naheem's hazel-green eyes, big full lips, full beard and amazing dress code drew me to him originally. Although he was fine as hell, rocking a baldhead and all, he still managed to look like to ugliest person in the world to me right now.

"I'm so sorry, Mrs. Holmes." Shania sobbed. "We didn't want you to find out like this, but, Naheem, and I are going to be together. We—."

Everything Shania said, went into one ear and out the other, as I charged at her, and wrapped my hands around her little neck, as tight as I could. Her eyes grew wide, as she tried her hardest to pry my hands from her neck. I could feel her father, yanking at my robe roughly, with all of his might, trying to pry me, off of his daughter, with the little bit of energy he had left.

"Heaven! She's pregnant, stop!" Naheem bellowed, which caused me to let her go, and direct my attention, to him. I could hear her, over my shoulder as she wheezed and coughed.

I punched, kicked, and scratched him, with all of my might, as he attempted to block my hits, but failed miserably. I hated him, and wanted him to feel, how hurt I was.

By now, my tears had begun to cloud my vision, halting me from beating his ass. How could this happen, to me? Why me?

"How could you do this to me?"

He dropped his gaze towards the floor. His fuck ass couldn't even look me in the eyes.

18

"I'm sorry." he murmured.

"Fuck your sorry, you sorry, muthafucka!"

I reached up to wipe the tears, that cascaded down my face repetitively. My chest felt heavy, and I felt like the room was spinning. This was surreal. My head was aching unbearably, and my hands continued to quiver.

"Fuck you!" I screamed, at the top of my lungs. "I hate, you!" I managed to say, through clenched teeth.

Though my vision was blurred, I managed to grab my purse, and keys from the kitchen counter, and stormed out of the apartment, in just a robe with no shoes on. I had to get out of there. I knew that, I'd do something I would possibly regret.

Once inside my car, my hands wouldn't stop shaking long enough for me to put the keys into the ignition. I just kept envisioning them in my mind, sneaking around behind my back, and probably even fucking in our bed. How else, would she know where, we lived? How could he do this to me, and with a fucking seventeen-year-old, who probably still had got damn, Similac, on her breath.

I used my hands to dab my tears and snotty nose, as I struggled to pull myself together, but it was no use. My life was officially over, and I'd squandered three years with this man, time I could never ever get back. I was officially, heartbroken.

Tamara Butler

Chapter 2

Banks

Somewhere on the other side of town

"Carter!" I jumped out of my sleep, when I felt someone shaking me, frantically and yelling my name. I must've fallen asleep. I opened my eyes sluggishly, and saw my beautiful girlfriend, of two years, with a scowl on her face, and her arms folded.

"You need to get up, right now!" She yelled, loud and extra, for no fucking reason. She knew, I hated that shit, yet she still did it. I watched, as she swung her long, platinum blonde weave over her shoulder. She sighed deeply, walking over to the light switch, and flipping it on.

"Look at this shit—the fucking lights are off, again!" She rolled her eyes, so hard, I was sure they'd fall out of her head.

I knew there was something, I'd forgotten to do.

"Baby I forgot to—."

She cut me off mid-sentence, something else she did, that I hated.

"Save your bull shit ass excuses."

I got out of the bed and walked over to where she stood. She looked away, then blurted out, "I'm leaving, you. I can't live like this anymore."

"Leaving?" My eyebrows rose and my eyes grew wide, at the mention of her leaving, me. "The fuck is you talking about, Lakenya?"

She tried to brush past me, but I snatched her ass up by the back of her shirt and threw her down onto the bed gently.

Her eyes grew wide in astonishment. I was tired of her running away every time we had an argument, or disagreement.

"Like I was saying—I won't have the money to pay the lights until, Friday."

She chuckled like shit was funny.

"Friday? It's only, Monday! You have got to be fucking kidding. So, we're supposed to just sit up in here, in the dark until, Friday? Is that really what you thought we were going to do?"

When I didn't answer her, she nudged me to the side, with her foot and scooted to the edge of the bed, until she was able to get up.

"Baby, I swear things gone get better. You just gotta give me some more time."

"No—absolutely not, I'm done."

She walked out of the room and into the living room, with me hot on her trail. There was a big duffle bag sitting by the front door.

My heart started beating so fast, I didn't know what to do. We'd gotten into arguments plenty of times, but she'd never tried to leave a nigga, before.

She grabbed her purse and keys from the couch, then she slung the duffle bag onto her shoulder.

"Lakenya." I paused to gather my words. "Baby, I can borrow the money from someone to get the lights back on."

She turned around to face me, with tears running down her face.

"It's not just about the lights, Carter! We are struggling, we have been for two years. You say shit is going to get better, but it never does. We can barely pay the rent, the lights are always off, and there ain't shit in here to eat! We don't have any money for groceries. Why would I want to stay here, with you? Huh? I haven't been happy for a long time."

I swear at one point, I opened my mouth to say something, but nothing came out. I had no words. I didn't know what to say, because she wasn't lying. After she went back to school, we decided her working while in school was a hassle. So, we went from having two sources of income, to only one. I tried my best to take care of her, but I guess my best, just wasn't enough.

"Bae chill. I can get a real job and—"

"Where? You never completed school, so you don't have a degree. You're twenty-five years old, with nothing going for yourself. You think this music shit, is going to blow, but it's not, I wish you could see that. You spend all of our money at the studio."

She was right, I did spend a lot of money at the studio, but I was always able to make the money back, by doing shows at local clubs, rap battles, and slanging a lil' weed on the side.

We gazed at one another for a few moments. I watched as she shook her head from side to side.

"I just can't do this, anymore."

Lakenya gripped the bag on her shoulder, tighter before she walked in the direction of the front door. Just as she twisted the knob to open the door, I called out to her, hoping she wouldn't leave.

"Lakenya!"

She sighed, before she countered, "What Carter?" She only called me by my real name, when she was mad, so she must've really been pissed at me, right about now.

A look of confusion washed over my face. "So, you really tryna make a nigga, beg and shit?"

"No. I just—I think it would be best if I left."

We held eye contact, as I got closer to her, and I got all up in her personal space. My six-foot, three stature, towered over her five-foot, seven-frame. I looked down at her, with pleading eyes. I wasn't ready to end our relationship. Her face was scrunched up, as she smirked at me, speculating what the hell I was about to say.

As I gathered my thoughts, the two of us stared at one another and I took that time to really reflect on her beauty. Lakenya was slim thick with thighs thicker than some left over grits. She had high cheekbones that complimented her face, a smooth honey complexion that looked like it was kissed by the sun, and A-cup breasts that were the perfect size for her frame. Her juicy succulent lips and almond shaped eyes drew me in immediately when we first me.

I softly grasped her chin and leaned down to kiss her on the lips. She turned her head from side to side, trying to avoid my kisses, but she reluctantly allowed me to kiss her on the lips.

"Please—don't—go." I begged, in between pecks.

I placed my other hand around her waist and pulled her soft body closer to mine. As I deepened the kiss, she let me slip my tongue inside of her mouth momentarily, but I felt her hand on my chest. She firmly pushed me away, ending what might be our last kiss.

"You know, I love you, right?" I needed her to know that, I wasn't just trying to give up on us.

She shook her head, but looked away when she countered, "But love can't pay these bills."

I watched as, Lakenya, walked out of our home and probably, out of my life for good. She threw her things into the backseat of her red 2009 Camry, then she hopped in and sped off faster than the speed of lightening.

I stood there for a moment, in the doorway and stared at the spot, she'd just pulled off from, before I sucked my teeth, and turned around to head back inside. She'll be back, I'm sure of that.

A letter taped to my door, caught my attention. I ripped it from the door, and brought it close to my face, just to make sure I wasn't imagining the words on the paper.

It was a got damn eviction notice.

"Fuck!"

Now what are you going to do? I thought, today just wasn't my day.

Chapter 3

Heaven

5 days later

I poked my head from underneath the covers, momentarily to look at the time. It was early as fuck, and someone had the nerve to be banging on my door. Whoever it was, they obviously had a fucking death wish. I was about to kill them for disturbing, my sleep.

I sucked my teeth, when I noticed they weren't going to stop. My eyes shut tightly, once I fully pulled the covers from my head, because the sun hurt my eyes. I hopped up to throw on some shorts, underneath my over-sized, *'Fuck Love'* t-shirt. I was wearing this shirt, so much, because I believed the words scribbled across the front in big red letters. I'd gone shopping to get my mind off of things and had to grab it when I saw it in this little boutique by, my house.

"I'm fucking, coming!" I yelled, and the banging came to a halt. I drug my feet across the floor and took my slow ass time getting to the door.

I looked through the peephole and sucked my teeth when I saw who it was. This bitch stopped by without an invite, but she was lucky, I wanted to get this shit over with.

I opened the door for, Naheem's mother, Shelby, who stood on the other side of the door. She had her mouth twisted up, and a stern look on her face. She knew not to say shit, though.

"Here." I picked up a black bag and practically shoved it into her arms. "Hurry up and get all of his shit before it's too late. I can switch up from, Heaven, to Bernadette, real quick! Grab his stuff, before I throw it into his car and burn it." I replied dryly to Shelby, who practically begged to come get his things.

She'd been on my trail, since he'd gotten locked up a few days ago, although I originally planned to cut his shit up into little pieces, she begged to come get his stuff. I packed a majority of his shit, into big black garbage bags, and had all of his shit sitting right by the door.

"Don't talk to me that way I—"

I cut her off. "I don't care what you have to say. You never liked me. You gave me a hard time our entire fucking marriage. If I didn't know any better, I'd say you probably knew he was fucking, that girl." I stated with a smug look on my face and my arms folded. "You never cared to get to know me, as my mother-in-law, and you used to talk all that shit about me to them old hoes at the hair salon."

Her eyes grew wide, as she opened and closed her mouth several times like a fish out of water.

"I never said a word about you." She lied, which caused me to laugh. Her nose was longer than Pinocchio's.

"I know, everything you said about me, courtesy of my aunt, who gets her hair done at the same salon." I shrugged. "You said your son could do better and that you didn't know, what he was thinking marrying me. You even had the nerve to say that I used my job at the school as a cover up for actually being a stripper! To be honest, it's me that deserves better. You clearly failed at raising him, to know right from wrong."

I could tell, she was at a loss for words when she turned her nose up.

"Well—I certainly don't have to stand here and take this."

I scoffed and threw my hands up. "You're right, so take his things and go good riddance, to you and your cheating ass son."

We starred at one another, before she turned, and begin putting his bags into her car, one by one. After about seven trips back and forth to her car, her old ass was finally done gathering his things.

"I'll be back for his car sometime this week." She was all out of breath, as she stood in my door way trying to regain her composure. "I just need to find a tow truck to tow—"

I put my hand up. "Listen, let's cut this short." I handed her his keys. "Do whatever you want with his car. I don't have the energy to care anymore."

"Well you don't have to be so rude, I was in the middle of talking." She jeered, she had to be joking.

This woman gave me pure hell, from the time she met me because, she thought I was trying to steal her only child away from her, which is childish as fuck. I never tried to complete with this woman. She barely ever spoke to me, and when she did, she'd say some slick shit. Shelby gossiped about me and practically shut me out, whenever I tried to hang out, or when I'd invite her to events I thought she'd enjoy. She was just too damn jealous and never wanted me around, so I was sure she was glad, I was out of the picture.

"My door will be closing in three—two—one." I counted down, slamming it in her face once I got to one.

I drug my feet across the floor, slowly, until I was back in my room. I wasn't sleepy anymore, so I just laid in bed looking up at the ceiling.

I groaned at the fact, that people wouldn't stop bothering me, when my phone vibrated. I grabbed my phone to check the time. It was 10:00 a.m., still too damn early for anyone to be texting me. It was from my sister.

Twin: You shouldn't be alone right now—come over.

She was right. So, after brushing my teeth, taking a much-needed hot shower, and throwing on some clothes. I headed to my sister's crib.

****

The sun shinned through the windowsill adjacent to me. I silently stared at the wall in front of me, just thinking about my life, and how it got so bad. My eyes were burning, due to my lack of sleep, but sleep was the furthest thing from my mind. I tossed and turned so much at night, I probably only accumulated a good three hours of sleep. How could I sleep peacefully, knowing that my husband slept around on, me? I couldn't help, but to think about the things, I may have done wrong to practically push him into another woman's pussy.

I thought, I'd done all of my wifely duties perfectly. I didn't nag, I cooked, and cleaned every fucking day. I washed and ironed his clothes, gave him sex, whenever and wherever he wanted, yet he still cheated. I kept myself looking, and smelling good for him, yet he still fucked another, bitch.

"I don't know why you're tripping, Heaven. You know, men ain't shit!" I mumbled to myself.

Don't even get me started on, Principal Greer's ugly ass. That bitch was lucky, I didn't come across that table to smack her damn glasses off. Now I was husband-less and jobless, just great!

"Here—you look like you could use some coffee." I looked up, my eyes locked with my twin sister's eyes.

I'd been at her place for the past two hours, trying to clear my head, and get away from all of the chaos in my life, mainly, Naheem. Thankfully, he'd already been arrested for fucking that young ass girl, but the thought of still living in our apartment was one, I hated thinking about.

"Thanks sis."

"No problem. You know, I got your back." She smiled, sweetly.

Nevaeh sat across from me, on the couch adjacent to the one, I'd been sitting on.

"Did you get any sleep?" She questioned, blowing her coffee, to cool it down a bit. I followed suit, blowing the hot liquid, before sipping it.

"Yes and no. I can't sleep, Vaeh." I frowned.

She sighed. "You can't mope around, blaming yourself, for what that fuck nigga did. He didn't deserve you, babe."

"I know but—"

"No buts, Heaven—you are beautiful, you have so much going for, yourself. You don't need him. He will see, he lost the best thing, that ever happened to him. Now please, do me a favor, and get some rest."

My eyes had already started to water, and tears slowly fell. I used my free hand, to cover my face. I was tired of crying, but I just couldn't stop. I loved, Naheem, with everything in me. I never sensed, our marriage was going downhill, not even once. Boy, I was a fool. How could I not have known, he was screwing around on me? Why hadn't, I seen the signs?

My sister sat her coffee down on the coffee table, and quickly came to sit next to me. I felt her arms wrap around me, as she began to console me.

"I hate him!" I yelled, as she continued to rock me back and forth.

"I know—it's okay. Let it all out." she countered.

"How could he do this to me?"

She said nothing, she just continued, consoling me and rubbing my back. Nevaeh was always there for me, no matter the circumstances, and I loved her for that. She truly was more, than just a twin sister, to me. She was my, best friend.

She lifted my head from her shoulder, for just a moment to look me in the eyes.

"Let me go get you some tissue, okay?"

I shook my head, as she swiftly got up, and headed towards the back to get some tissue from the bathroom. When she returned, she handed me the tissue, flashing me a reassuring smile. She took her same-seated position, next to me on the couch, as my head gravitated towards her shoulder yet again.

"Listen Heaven, you're my twin, and I love you, so much. I don't expect you to get over this situation any time soon, but I don't want you blaming yourself, or second-guessing the things, you did, or didn't do to make him cheat. It's not your fault, babe. I promise, it's not your fault. Please do me a favor and get some rest."

My nose was stuffed up from crying and my throat was scratchy, but I managed to say, "Okay."

"A'ight. I'm going to try and get some rest, myself. I'm a little tired from work." She worked late nights at the strip club as a bartender. She got home around 6:00 a.m. that morning, but barely got any sleep, because she was up thinking about me.

She stood up and leaned down to give me a kiss on the cheek. I gave her a small smile, before she walked away. Moments later, I heard Vaeh 's room door open, then close.

I adjusted the pillows on the couch, to my liking and covered up with the blanket, Nevaeh, gave me to stay warm in her cold ass house before I laid down.   It didn't take long for me to drift off to la-la land and momentarily forget, about my fucked-up life.

Nevaeh

After talking with my sister and taking a long much-needed shower, I plopped down on my bed. I smirked at the nasty text messages, Lance, left me while I was at work last night. I sent his ass a quick text and told him to slide through, but to be careful, not to wake my twin on the couch. He had a key, so he could just let himself in. I was beyond tired, but I knew he'd fuck me so good, I'd probably be sleeping for the whole day.

Lance: Be there shortly. I want to talk to you about something when I get there, too—

To be honest, I didn't care what he needed to talk about, as long as he was slanging that dick. He arrived about twenty minutes later and walked into my room wearing a white V-neck shirt, some cut up dark blue jeans and beach looking flip-flops. Some white boy, shit. He still looked good, though.

Anyway, my mood was instantly ruined, when I threw his ass down on the bed and started snatching his clothes off. I was already butt ass naked, but once I got to his boxers he stopped me.

"What? Why'd you stop, me?" I was hot, horny, and ready for him to slide inside of me.

"I want to talk first." he declared.

I'm sure, I had a confused ass look on my face, because I was fucking confused, about why he wanted to talk instead of fuck.

"Umm okay."

So, I've been thinking about something." I looked over at my, on again off again fuck buddy, Lance, as he stared lovingly into my eyes. I smirked at him, already knowing what he was about to say.

I gave him a fake ass, smile. "Yes, what's up?"

"I was wondering if we could take what we have to the next level." Lance implored, as the room got very silent. "I want to leave, my wife, for you."

I released a deep sigh, before responding. The reason we were on and off again, was because Lance, desperately wanted to be in a relationship with me, but I was not interested. Yes, I cared for him, yes, he had good dick, and yes, he treated me right, but I liked what he could do for me without the strings attached.

It was silent, for what felt like eternity. I released a breath I didn't know I was holding when he finally spoke up.

"Maybe, I should go." Lance replied, knocking me from my daydream.

"No—you just got here, and we didn't even have sex yet."

He shook his head. "So, that's all you're worried about?"

I stared at him, wondering what the hell he was sniffing this morning, because he was acting different. Normally, I wouldn't have been able to keep his hands off of me.

"Yes—I mean no—I don't know."

He scoffed, before he tried to get up.

I released another sigh, then grabbed his arm before he got off of the bed.

Lance Regis, was different from all of the men, I had ever been serious with, or close to being serious with. Lance was half black and half white. He was fine as hell. His kept the sides of his hair shaved down but left a little hair on top. His dark brown hair was curly and he often times wore it up into a man-bun. His green eyes were mesmerizing, and I loved how he kept his goatee and mustache, well-trimmed. Although he was half white and black his skin complexion was mahogany. Lance had several tattoos on his arms, a nose ring and the most beautiful pink lips I'd ever seen. They reminded me of pink starbursts.

He was an A&R rep for The Money Group records also known as TMG Records. One of the hottest record labels in the fucking world, so money was never an issue, for him. I loved his money and what he could do for me, but I wasn't interested in being tied down. I really wasn't trying to be his girl. Hell, he was already tied down to his wife, but that didn't stop him from dipping out on, her ass. The nigga paid my car note, rent, lights, and gave me spending money whenever I asked. Like I said though, I wanted things to stay on a no strings attached basis.

Although he knew, I wasn't ready, he was willing to wait, until I was ready to commit to him. He kept saying he wanted to divorce her and marry me, but I wasn't with that shit. I wasn't intentionally, trying to fuck with his married ass, but it's not my fault, he never wore his ring. I'd already put this pussy in his face but once I found out, he showered me with gifts and money to keep me. I could get any man I wanted, but when a nigga was paying my bills, and I didn't have to work as much, of course, I was going to stick around. I hated bartending and he gave me enough money, so I'd never have to work.

Standing at five-feet, four-inches, I was far from slim thick like, Heaven. I was a little on the chubby side, with my thick thighs, full C-cup breasts, caramel complexion, and fat ass. My stomach wasn't that big, but I did have a pudge. I was a little overweight for my height, but that never stopped me from getting men. I was gorgeous, nonetheless. My doe-like eyes were my best feature as well as my long curly blonde hair that I took pride in. I didn't believe in getting my ends clipped so my hair was practically touching my butt when it was straightened. I kept it blonde so that people could differentiate between my sister and I. I liked to express my self differently than my sister. I wore my hair in box-braids often.

"No don't leave like this, all mad and what not."

His nose wrinkled, and his nostrils flared. "I mean, I'm not mad, I'm just fed up."

My eyes bored into him. "What are you fed up with? Me?"

"No—the situation. Like we have amazing sex and we enjoy each other's company. You know I lo—"

I cut him off. "No don't say it."

His eyebrows snapped together. "Vaeh I lo—"

I hopped out of the bed and said, "Stop Lance, don't say the 'L' word."

"What the hell is so wrong with me, loving you?" He stood up as well, and made his way around the bed, to stand near me. He took my hands in his hands and pulled me closer to him. I tried to look away, but he grabbed me by the chin, and made me look at him.

"Your wife is what's wrong with this whole situation." I blurted out.

He sighed. "I know, I'll handle that, but, right now I wanted to talk about us taking things to another level. What do you think about that?"

I pursed my lips. "I think that's a bad idea, Lance."

"Oh yeah, how so?" His mouth twisted, I knew he was pissed, but trying to play it cool.

"Why fuck up what we have? Shit is all gravy, right now, we shouldn't be trying to do unnecessary shit like being in a relationship." I watched, as he gritted his teeth.

I managed to get out of his grip then I walked over to the other side of the room and retrieved a pair of panties to place on my bare bottom. He followed me to the other side of the room and I discreetly rolled my eyes. I really wasn't in the mood for this conversation, early in the morning. Hell, I even hated arguing on an empty stomach.

I invited him over this morning for some good dick, that was it. If I knew, he'd try to have this damn talk again, I wouldn't have invited him.

"Why is me loving you unnecessary?"

I tried to ignore him and grabbed a bra to cover my exposed breasts. He grabbed my arm and I softly pulled away.

"Because Lance, I don't feel the same. I'm sorry, I like you and I like the sex, but that's about it."

He somewhat laughed.

"Okay say less." Lance quickly grabbed his belongings and attempted to leave the room.

"Wait Lance, why are you leaving?"

"I just don't need to be here anymore, since it's so damn, *unnecessary*. But let me tell you this, Vaeh—you had your chance."

I released a deep sigh, as he stormed out of the room. I was upset, that he left without giving me some morning dick. I was also upset, about the fact that he kept bringing this topic up, which kept causing us to be on again off again, fuck buddies. I just wasn't looking for a relationship.

Chapter 4

Banks

I looked around my apartment and saw nothing, but big ass brown boxes, scattered all over the damn place. I packed all of my shit, by my damn self, so I needed to take a break. I collapsed on the couch momentarily, then put my head on the armrest, and stared up at the ceiling. A nigga was tired as fuck, sweaty and hungry. I wasn't able to come up with enough money to continue living here, so unfortunately, I'd be back at my mom's crib from here on out. The Eviction notice said, I needed to be out, by today, so that's what the fuck I was doing.

Just as I was about to close my eyes, my cell phone vibrated in my pocket. I wasn't in the mood to talk to anybody, but I saw that it was my boy, Lance, so I answered.

"Yo." I answered awaiting his response. I already knew what he was going to say.

"My muthafuckin' nigga!" He bellowed into the phone.

I chuckled at his lame ass. "What's up, bruh?"

"Nothing nigga, I called to check on you, since you forgot all about me and shit. I'm back in Miami."

I sucked my teeth. "Now you know, you're the one that forgot about me, after you started working over there at TMG. I be seeing yo' ass on Instagram, and all over the blogs in pictures with these rich ass, niggas. You be all over the world in Hawaii, Paris, Haiti and shit. You really doing it big."

I sat up and leaned forward, to grab my lighter from the coffee table in front of me. I sparked up my blunt and took a hit, as I listened to him tell me all about these model bitches and rappers, he'd recently discovered. Lance was that nigga.

We met in high school, we used to play basketball together. Man, the ladies used to go crazy over us. They had the best of both worlds. At the time, I was the tall dark chocolate nigga, with dreads, tattoos and swag. Lance was the mixed nigga, that was more in touch with his black side of the family. We ran trains on a few girls back in the day and ran the streets together, until, Lance, decided to get out of all that shit. I should have followed in his footsteps.

I used to run the streets a lot slanging dope and selling weed, my mama knew about it, but she knew it was nothing she could do to control me. With my daddy, being locked up, she knew I was bound to follow in his footsteps. I was young and dumb. I fucked around and got shot in my leg, because some niggas set me up. Then I lost my scholarship to college, I couldn't play ball anymore, due to my injury.

"Banks." Lance knocked my ass out of my little day-dream and brought me back to reality.

I blew the smoke out before responding. "Yeah."

"I said, what have you been up to and how's Lakenya?"

I scoffed, at the mention of her name. I had been calling her non-stop, she'd blocked my fucking number, so I really wasn't in the mood to talk about her ass, right about now.

"Shit is still the same. I'm in the studio every chance I get, but shit ain't really shaking around here, like it should be." That was the honest truth, hence the reason, I was moving out.

"Man, you know, I always tell you to hit me up if you need some money. You're my brother and—" I cut him off.

"Nah, man, I can't take your money." I neglected mentioning my eviction notice, because I didn't need him feeling sorry for me and shit. "I'm good, bruh, trust me I'm good."

"A'ight. Well the reason, I was calling you is because, I saw your video on Instagram, that new song, '*Bitch I'm tryna make it*', is fire."

I took another puff from my blunt and smiled a little at his words.

"Thanks man. You see how many views that video got, though? One million views and that was only a snippet—shit crazy, bruh."

"Yeah, I saw that, and guess what? I played it for Rod-C. He wants to meet with you, a.s.a.p."

I took another puff from my blunt, but instantly started choking after hearing, that the owner of The Money Group records wanted to meet with me. Rodney fucking Chambers, wanted to meet with me. A nigga had to be dreaming, because nothing had been going right for me, lately. I almost wanted to pinch myself, just to fucking see if I was in fact sleeping.

Lance chuckled. "I told him, you were my boy, and that we go way back. He wants to hear more of your music, so I told him, I'd call to set some shit up." He sounded excited, as hell to tell me the news.

"Wait—hold on." I managed to say in between coughing. "Rod-C, wants to meet me? You not fucking with me, are you?"

Nah, I'm serious. I know, I joke about a lot of shit, but this time, I'm dead ass serious." he confirmed.

I started cheesing unbeknown to myself, until I felt my face begin to hurt. "Damn, good looking out."

"You my, brother. You know, I got you. But listen though, I'm going to hit you back, I have to go, but clear your schedule for, Monday, be here at one p.m."

"A'ight bet."

After we ended our conversation, I swear, I damn near jumped off of the couch, like it was on fire. My heart was beating fast as hell, and I didn't know how to control it. I was happier than a, muthafucka. My mind was racing with so many thoughts. I felt like dancing, so I did just that. I don't know shit about dancing, but I was in my living room doing the damn Crip walk, Dougie, Stanky leg, and the Nae-Nae, like my life depended on it. I looked like a fool dancing to no music, but I didn't care.

Rod-C could possibly sign me. I knew, it wasn't a guarantee, but I had a strong gut feeling about this shit. I couldn't contain the smile, that was practically glued to my face, as my mind continued to wonder.

When I first put out, '*Bitch I'm tryna make it*' I received so many messages and comments on social media from people, I didn't even know, asking me where they could download the song. I even had a few hoes, in my DM, asking if they could be in the official video for the song. I never thought, I'd get so many views or that, Rod-C, would want to meet with me.

Nothing could ruin my good ass mood, today not even the fact, that I was being evicted, or that my damn lights were still out. The only other thing that could make this day better, would be some pussy, but, Lakenya's ass was tripping.

****

I'd just made my fifth trip into my mama's crib carrying a few cardboard boxes and I was all out of breath. Luckily, I'd put all my furniture out by the road, so the only shit I was bringing over here was personal belongings, like my clothes and shoes, pots and pans, rags and towels, you know shit like that. I made a mental note to fix a tall ass glass of ice-cold water when I was done. The scorching hot sun didn't help much, and this South Florida heat was no joke. It was only five p.m. a nigga was drained.

"Carter, what are you doing, here?" My sixteen-year-old little brother, Camden, asked as I walked into the house toting a few boxes. I wasn't trying to hear his mouth, right now, I was still on cloud nine, about the news I'd gotten from the homie, Lance.

"Minding my own got damn business, lil nigga. This is my mama's house, I can come and go as I please." I brushed pass his short fat ass and made my way into my old bedroom.

"Why you got all them boxes?" He was nosey as fuck, that's one thing I always hated, about my brother, but I loved that, lil nigga, till the death of me. He was overweight, wore glasses, got straight A's and played video games all day. None of these lil thots gave my brother the time a day, so he never really had shit to do, other than being in my business anyways.

I placed the boxes next to my old bed and looked over at him.

"Stop asking so many got damn questions and go get the rest of my things from outside, punk." I declared and tried not to laugh, at his facial expression, as he used his short stubby fingers to push his glasses back up onto his chubby face.

He sucked his teeth. "I'll go get the boxes when I feel like it."

I shook my head and watched him wobble away, just as I suspected he came back five minutes later, with my last two boxes.

"Thanks."

He threw his hand up. "Yeah whatever."

After he left my room, I was just about to close the door when, my mama stepped inside wearing a halter-top, that showed her midriff and some booty shorts. I fucking hated how my mama dressed, but couldn't tell her shit. She still looked young as fuck, because of that, she dressed like she was twenty instead of forty-eight.

I sucked my teeth.

"Man—the fuck you got on, ma?"

I looked her up and down, she placed one hand on her hip, before scolding me.

"Don't even start, Banks. I just came in here to tell you, that I'll be back a little later, and dinner is on the stove if you want some. I know, you told me, you'll only be here temporarily, but don't have no fast ass hoes all up in my shit like you used to do."

I sized her up. "Ma—"

She rolled her eyes and neck. "Don't ma, me. I don't want to be hearing no moaning or headboards knocking. Do not smoke any weed in my shit, and make sure you pull your weight around here. Clean up behind yourself, okay?"

I lay back on the bed and closed my eyes. This is why I didn't want to move back here. I had been on my own since I was twenty, I never thought, I'd be moving back in with my, mama. It was like being in prison.

"A'ight."

A few moments later, she was out of my room. I ended up saying, fuck that tall glass of water, I wanted. I fell asleep a few minutes later.

Chapter 5

Banks

Monday

I was standing in the full-length mirror, in the living room looking over my outfit, to make sure, I wasn't over doing it. I had on a navy-blue Armani Collezioni suit, baby blue button up underneath, and a burgundy tie. A nigga, looked fresh as hell, like I should've been getting married today or something.

I could hear my mother's feet from a mile away, as she dragged them down the hallway. "Oh snap, look at my baby, all dressed up."

I turned around to see my mama in her pink house robe, with a cigarette and ashtray in her hands.

"Where are you going, baby?" She placed the cigarette and ashtray, down on a nearby table, then stepped closer to me.

"I gotta go meet the owner of TMG Records today, remember?" My mama never remembered anything growing up. I always had to remind her, at least three to four times about something, so she'd remember. Funny thing is, she never forgot, when she had an ass whooping for me, though.

She just gazed at me silently, but her eyes lit up when she remembered.

"Oh yeah! I remember, now. What time did you have to be there, baby?"

"Well I'm 'bout to leave now. I wanna make a good impression, by showing up early."

"Come here." I took one last look in the mirror, before walking over to where, my mama, was standing.

She reached over and pinched my cheeks, kissing me on them in the process. Something she had been doing since I was a child.

"Ma—" I sighed frustratingly.

41

I tried to push her off of me gently, but that didn't work. I then watched her lick, her thumb, and attempt to smooth down my eyebrows. "Stop with all of that, ma."

"Oh, hush up. You my baby, I can kiss on you. You just look so handsome, I am so proud of you, baby." She smoothed down my tie and readjusted it for me. I never knew how to put them shits on, she knew that.

Lance, against my will, sent some lil' pretty ass chick over to my mother's crib on Saturday, to take my measurements. She returned Sunday evening and after trying on every suit, button up, tie, sock and shoe that she had, we both agreed on the suit, I'm currently wearing. Lance said, I needed to look professional when meeting, Rod-C.

"Thanks ma."

"Now, you listen to me. You got this so don't even sweat it. You have worked so hard, it has finally paid off. I want you to go in there and give it your all. Just be yourself, okay?"

I shook my head, as my mama pulled me into a hug.

That's what I loved about my, mama. She was like my best friend, we could talk about any and everything. No matter what, she was always very supportive. If I wanted to plant trees for a living she'd be understanding, and right there next to me helping. My brother and I had two different fathers, who never did a got damned thing for either of us, but my mama held the family together, and did the best, she could. That's another reason, why she was so willing to let me move back home. I always made sure my mama was straight, I gave her money for her bills whenever I could, which sometimes resulted in my lights and rent not being paid on time. I never told, Kenya, any of this, because it wasn't her business.

I pulled away from the hug and kissed her on the cheek. She smiled, sweetly.

"I got this, ma, now watch me work." I spun on my feet and walked towards the door like a male runway model, causing her to laugh.

"You so silly, baby." She shook her head, then she headed back into her room.

I grabbed my car keys off the kitchen table and headed out. I had to squint my eyes, because of how bright it was outside. I was nervous as hell, but I hopped into my car, then got right on I-95.

About thirty minutes later, I was parking my car outside of TMG Records.

****

"My muthafuckin', nigga. You looking fresh in that suit." Lance exclaimed, as we pulled away from a brotherly hug.

I chuckled. "What's good, bruh? It's been a while since I saw you. Yo' fat ass done put on some weight." I said to him, as I took a seat on one of the couches in the studio

"Man." He sucked his teeth. "Fuck you. My wife ain't complaining." I looked at him confused.

Yeah, we used to run trains on girls in high school together, but Lance, changed his ways. Hell, I did too, but this nigga changed way before I did. He got married about three years ago to a chick named, Imani, that he fucked around and got pregnant. He was trying to do the right thing, which is why he married her, but not too long ago, he told me, he met some girl, that made him want to divorce, Imani. I told him that was a bad idea, and that he shouldn't leave his wife for some random bitch, but he wasn't trying to hear all that.

"Hold up. I thought, you were trying to be with the other chick?"

He shook his head from side to side. "Nah man."

"Word? What happened with the chick you were telling me about? I think you said her name was, Vaeh?"

43

I didn't know what had gotten into, Lance, since the last time I saw him, which was probably a year ago. We'd always kept in contact, but, with him being this big time A&R rep, we didn't kick it like we used to. Imani was a good woman for him, I didn't really condone that cheating shit. He was going to do whatever the fuck he wanted do anyway, so my opinion never really mattered.

"Thank you, baby." I said to some woman, who walked in and handed Lance and I, a flute glass of wine. I sipped on it, as I awaited his response.

"Nah, I ain't fucking with her no more. She played too many got damned games for a, nigga. I'm sticking with my wife."

"Shit—I feel you." Lakenya was playing more games than Hasbro. So, I definitely knew what he was talking about.

"But anyways what I got going on ain't important, right now." He pointed at me. "You are what's important, right now. This nigga, Rod-C, has been talking about you non-stop since he heard your song. I also forwarded him the music you emailed me, he been vibing to yo' shit real talk." He smiled widely, that shit was contagious because I'd immediately started doing the same thing.

I reached over to dap him up. "Good looking out."

"You my brother from another, you know, I got you."

The door opened interrupting our conversation.

"Uh, excuse me." We both turned to see an older woman, who looked to be in her late forties, dressed up like she was going to a, Yolanda Adams, concert.

She smiled sweetly, before continuing. "Rod-C is ready to see you now."

"Okay, thank you."

"Follow me."

I stood up and Lance gave me a reassuring look, before I exited one of the studios, we were currently in. The woman led me down a very long hallway. That had gold and platinum plaques on the wall, from a few of the other artists that were signed to the label. It made me feel good seeing all of the labels accomplishments on the wall.

She opened two double doors, that had the words '*The Money Group*' written on them in cursive. Inside Rod-C was sitting at a long conference table, smoking a cigar.

"Please—come in." He put his cigar out, then stood up and adjusted his suit.

All of a sudden, my legs felt like noodles and my heart started beating wildly. It seemed like it took me, forever to get to the other end of that long ass table.

"Hi, how're you doing, sir?" I put my hand out for a handshake, but he pulled me in for a brotherly hug, instead.

"I'm good young, man. Have a seat."

The both of us sat down and my stomach started doing back flips, feeling like I had to take a shit, or something.

"You doing good, today?" he asked.

I shook my head, "Yes sir, I'm having a great day."

Rod-C was an older guy, who looked old enough to be my, young grandpa. He was a bald dark-skinned man, that dressed like a black, Hugh Hefner. I never under stood that part, but everyone respected him, because he had his shit together. He knew what he was doing and had changed the lives of, so many people when they signed to his label.

"You don't have to be so formal." he chuckled. "Call me, Rod."

"My bad, Rod. I'm just a little nervous." I admitted.

"Don't be, today is your lucky day."

I watched as he stood up and walked over to an intercom on the wall.

"Julio bring in the contract." He spoke into the intercom.

Then a man with a very heavy Latino accent, responded. "I'll be right over, sir."

Once the contract was brought in, a few moments later, Rod slid the contract over to me.

"So, to my knowledge, people call you, Banks, right?"

"Yes sir—I mean yes. You can call me, that, but my real name is, Carter."

I stared down at the contract, then back up at him, waiting to see what he'd say next.

"Banks—I am very impressed with your music. I want to do nothing more than to take you to the top. You have a talent young man, but I can't push you in the right direction, unless you're ready to work. You have to be dedicated to this. I need you to eat, sleep, and shit in this studio. You feel, me?"

I chuckled a bit. "Yeah, I feel you."

"Okay good. Now, I'll leave everything else up to you. If you want to be famous, sell out arenas, go on tours, be on T.V., and count more money, than you could ever imagine, then the choice is up to you. I'm talking endorsement deals, girls throwing pussy at you every night, and traveling all around the world. Make sure you take a look at the contract with your lawyer, or whomever you choose to go over it with. Just make sure you give me a verdict, by Friday. I'm sure, you'll make the right decision."

Nothing could stop the big ass grin on my face, as I reached over, and stuck my hand out. "You got it, Rod—I'll definitely review the contract and keep in touch with you."

He shook my hand, with a knowing look on his face, as if he already knew, I'd sign with him. Hell, he was ninety-nine percent right, because it was a very big possibility, I would sign after looking over the contract.

"I'm glad to hear that, son."

The two of us stood up and I bid him, goodbye.

My life had been in shambles the last couple of months. Lights always off, rent late, barely enough to eat. I wasn't constantly struggling. But, after deciding to quit my call center job to pursue music full time. I wasn't always able to make ends meet. Deep down inside, I just knew, life would be different once, I signed this contract. I walked out holding the key to my future, tightly in my hand.

Chapter 6

Nevaeh

2 weeks later

"Your phone has been temporarily disconnected. Please make a payment of—"

I threw my phone down onto the bed angrily. Lance hadn't paid my bill for the month, and I was highly upset about that.

I hadn't heard from Lance's ass in two weeks. I was pissed beyond belief. I didn't need his ass to be cutting me off, when he was my main source of income, right now. I called him practically every day, and he ignored all of my calls. He even read all of my messages foolishly forgetting, he had his read receipts on. I was fed up with this bullshit ass game he was playing, so I pulled up to his crib. I would've pulled up to TMG Records, but he'd kill me for causing a scene at his job.

I hopped up and threw on some clothes, so I could pay him a little visit. On top of my phone being off, rent was due pretty soon, so I'd need money for that and the lights. The club was barely paying me enough, business was slower than usual, lately.

Lance had gotten mad at me before, but never to the extent of completely ignoring me. He must've really been fed up with my, bullshit. After getting dressed, I grabbed my purse and car keys, then stormed out of my room like a mad woman. I made it halfway to the door, before my sister startled me.

"Where are you going?"

She was lying on the couch in her pajamas, stuffing her face with Oreos and popcorn. I kept forgetting that she was here, because these days she barely said anything. She often times slept here, instead of at her own place.

"To handle some business." I answered shortly. "I'll be, right back."

She replied softly. "Okay."

She diverted her attention back to the television, as I left my place, and damned near ran to my car. Lance was playing, I knew all I needed to do was put this pussy in his face to get him to act right, again.

I threw on my shades once inside the car and hopped right on the highway. I got to his house in twenty minutes, due to the roads being clear. I parked across the street.

Lance gave me a key to his crib to use for emergencies only, I felt this was a got damned emergency, so I let myself in. He had a bitch like me fucked up, if he thought, he was going to keep ignoring me.

He was blasting music, so he didn't even hear me when I came inside. I walked through the living room and was headed up to his room, until I spotted him in the kitchen making a sandwich. The only thing he had on was a pair of black polo boxers and some black socks.

He was fine as hell, I must admit as he danced around the kitchen, singing along to Drake's '*Nice for what*'. He'd put on some weight in the past month, but it looked good on him, he was built. His six-pack abs was now a four-pack, but I wasn't complaining. His mahogany complexion always looked good enough to lick. Don't even get me started on his soft pink lips and piercing green eyes. I wanted to kiss his lips; I actually missed him more, than I thought, I would.

I laughed, as I watched him hump the air, like he was having sex.

"Wow—it's nice to know, what you do when you're alone." I yelled over the music, startling him.

He for sure had a scowl on his face, as he quickly walked over to his surround system and turned the music off. He turned around to glare at me, as I walked closer to him.

"Nevaeh, what the fuck, are you doing, here?"

I smirked. "You're a little feisty today, I see." I tried to touch him, but he smacked my hand away.

I looked at him, like he was crazy. I knew he was upset, but he was acting like a little bitch.

He shook his head, as he walked back into the kitchen to finish making his sandwich. "Don't act like that, Lance."

"I'm not acting like anything. You ain't tryna be with me remember? So, don't be touching me, then." He warned harshly. I could tell, I'd hurt his feelings, so I knew what I needed to do to get back on his good side.

He focused on putting mayonnaise on his ham and cheese sandwich, as I just stood there silently trying to figure out what to say. He looked up at me for a moment.

"Why you, pop up over here unannounced? That key is only for emergencies. What if my wife was here?"

I hated when he brought her up. "She ain't here, so we don't even need to be discussing, her." I rolled my eyes. "Plus, you turned my damn phone off, so what else was there to do other than pop up on, your ass?"

He smirked and crossed his arms with furrowed eyebrows.

"Whatever Vaeh, I did that for a reason." He chuckled. "I thought we were done anyways."

I stepped closer to him, this time he allowed me to touch him, without pulling away. I gently wrapped my arms around his neck, as he stood there with his arms still crossed.

"I know you're still mad at me, but—"

"Ain't nobody mad, Vaeh—I'm just not about to chase yo' ass, anymore. That's what the fuck you want me to do anyways."

I leaned in real close to his face, so that our lips were almost touching before I responded.

"I don't like it when you're mad, at me." I pecked his lips a few times, before I started nibbling on his bottom lip. He tried to turn his head away from me, so I grabbed his arms and pulled them apart, then wrapped them around my waist.

"Boy—you better wrap your arms around, me!" I demanded jokingly, causing him to crack a smile and wrap his arms around my waist.

"You don't miss me? I know you do." He was slowly falling under my spell, I was happy as hell because, I'd be getting some money soon.

"Nah, I don't, sorry." He reached around me and grabbed his sandwich after breaking free of my embrace.

"Oh yeah?"

He started walking off towards his bedroom upstairs, of course I followed. When he plopped down on the bed, I stood in front of him and started removing my clothes.

He sucked his teeth. "Man, Vaeh, what are you doing?"

"You'll see."

I shook my head, because that was way too easy. I didn't have to put up a fight, I knew it was because, he was missing this good ass pussy.

"Lay yo' ass down" I demanded.

He took his time and grinned, but he did exactly what I'd told him to do. He laid back, but he propped himself up on his elbows and watched me, wondering what was going to happen next.

"Now pull that dick out, baby. You know I missed him." I climbed up on the bed next to him.

He pulled his dick out so fast, I almost laughed at his behavior. I tooted my bare ass up in the air and threw my hair over my shoulder, then spit on his dick. His eyes were on me, as I wrapped my lips around his shit, and went to work. Lance wasn't with that slow, sensual head, so once I was sure his dick was wet enough, I bobbed my head up and down at a fast past.

"Suck that dick." Lance moaned, as he lifted his hips to pump in and out of my mouth, the same way he does when he's inside of me.

She Fell in Love with a Real One

I released the dick from my mouth, with a loud popping sound, then stuck my tongue out and slapped it against my tongue.

"You like the way I suck this dick, baby?" I swirled my tongue over the tip of his dick.

His breathing was erratic, and his eyes were low. I spit on it, before slurping it up, spitting it out, then slurping it up again. I continued to suck and move my hands in a circular motion.

"You know, I love that shit." He managed to say in between groans. I reached down and began to fondle with his balls, before taking them into my mouth. I took turns sucking on his balls, while I jacked his dick.

"Suck them balls, baby."

I smirked. I wanted the dick too, so I spit in my hand before I rubbed it on my bare pussy. Lance sat up.

He grabbed me by the hand and bit his lip. "Bring yo' sexy ass over here."

I bit my lip too, in anticipation for his amazing dick, I was about to receive. "You want this pussy?"

Lance grabbed me by my shirt and pulled me in closer, until our lips connected.

We were tonging it down, then he pulled away and said, "Take this shit off."

I licked my lips seductively. "No—you take it off, for me." I moved my hand in a come here motion, he leaned up to pull my top over my head. I was fully naked underneath.

"Let me get a rubber, baby." He said, before he tried to lean over and grab a condom from his stash.

"No. We don't need it."

I positioned myself in the face down, ass up position, ready for him to enter me.

The moment he was about to slide into my fat, wet pussy, we heard the sound of the front door opening and closing.

"Shit!" Lance practically threw me off of him.

I smirked. "Oh, that's ya, bitch?" I questioned him.

He quickly got up in search of his boxers. He hurriedly put his clothes back on, as I just sat on the bed looking at him.

"What the fuck, Vaeh? Get in the closet or something." he whispered.

I put my hand out. "What?" He looked like he was going to shit on himself.

"Give me some money." I whispered.

"You really gone do this shit, right now?" He whispered, harshly.

I didn't say a word. I sat comfortably on his bed, naked, and waited for him to give me what I was asking for. I knew him, sometimes he liked to play around and not give me the money when he was mad or wanted to teach me a lesson.

"I want three racks."

"What?" He countered starkly.

"Either that, or she's going to catch me on the bed naked."

"Okay, fine now get in the closet!" He whispered, harshly.

When I stood up he grabbed my clothes off the floor and threw them at me, then he shoved me in the closet. I watched, as he ran over to his nightstand and pulled out three bands. He practically tripped over his own two feet.

"Here!" He murmured right, before he slammed the closet door in my face. Once inside the closet, I threw on my clothes, careful not to make any noise.

A few moments later, his wife came strolling in.

"H—hey, baby." What are you doing home so early?" This fool was stuttering, making matters worse. He walked over to her and tried to kiss her, but she curved him.

She scoffed. "I was off today don't you remember, me telling you this?" She paused to look at him, but when he didn't respond, she continued. "Anyway, why haven't you called, or texted me back in the past hour?" His wife sat down on the bed and took off her heels. She winced in pain and began to massage her feet.

"Oh, I didn't see it." He lied.

She laughed. "Wait, why are you sweating so damn bad?"

"The AC was off, I just turned it on baby." He sat down on the bed next to her and began to fiddle with his fingers.

She looked at him weirdly."

"How was your day?" he changed the subject.

"Oh, my God, it was horrible. I got a fucking flat tire on my way home, that's why I was texting you and calling you like crazy."

Lance grabbed her sore feet, put them into his lap and started massaging them. "Damn, I'm so sorry, I wasn't there for you. My phone been acting up lately, I didn't get any calls or texts from you."

She waved him off. "It's okay, babe."

He leaned over and kissed his wife on the forehead. "I'm going to make you a hot bubble bath, since you had such a long day."

He scooped her up wedding style and she giggled. "You better not drop me."

"Oh, I know you did not just try me. Your man is strong, you know this." he joked.

"Yeah yeah—just don't drop me, Mr. strong man."

Their voices trailed off and eventually, I was no longer able to hear them, because they were in the bathroom. I wasn't sure if I should make a run for it, or not but, I definitely wasn't trying to be trapped in the closet like R-Kelly.

"What are you doing?" I heard Lance yell from the bathroom, as his wife ran back into their bedroom.

"I forgot my phone. I wanted to play some music!" She yelled back. I watched through the closet door, as she dug through her purse a few times. "Oh shoot, where is it?" She said to herself, as she looked all over for her phone.

She yelled back, "I forgot my phone in the car, can I use your phone to play music?" Once he agreed, she picked up his phone and skimmed through it.

"Come here real quick, baby!" She bellowed, with a confused look on her face.

Lance came back into the room, with wet hands and he wiped them on his pants.

She pushed the phone very close to his face, that he jerked back a little to avoid, her hitting him in the face with the phone.

"So, what the fuck is this?" She questioned him pointing to the phone.

I started to sweat a little, I was nervous, plus it was hot as hell in this damn closet. I hoped she didn't read any of the messages, I'd sent him.

"What's what?"

"Why did you just lie to my face, and tell me you didn't get any of my calls or texts, when I seem them, right fucking here?"

They stared at one another for a few moments before he responded. He blurted out, "Why are you going through my phone? I told you about doing that." He snatched his phone from her hands and she glared at him with wide eyes.

"I know you did not just snatch your phone away from me. What the hell is in there, you don't want me to see?" She crossed her arms awaiting his response, as her left leg started to shake violently.

He pointed in the direction of the bathroom. "The water is still running. Do you still want that, bath?" He tried to change the subject, but it was far too late for that.

His wife literally lunged at him and started hitting him, anywhere she could with all of her might.

"Quit it, Imani." She latched onto his man bun and started punching him in his head. She was definitely throwing some hands.

"Imani stop!"

He shoved her off of him, she fell flat on her ass. She hit the floor with a loud thud.

They stared at one another, both out of breath, as her eyes began to water. "What are you hiding from me, Lance?" She sniffled, as she looked up at him, with hurt in her eyes.

"Nothing baby, I'm sorry. I didn't mean to push you, I was just trying to get you, off of me. Let me help you up." He tried to help her up, but she pushed his hands away.

"What's this?" she quizzed.

She grabbed a high heel that was slightly underneath the bed, when she stood up, she showed him the shoe. My breath got caught in my throat, when I realized she was holding up my shoe.

He scratched the back of his head. "That's a shoe."

She stared at the shoe. "I know, it's a shoe, Lance. I wear a size five, this shoe is a size eight." She nervously bit her lip. "Are you cheating on me or something?"

He shook his head from side to side. "No. You tripping for real."

"So, how'd it get—" Her words trailed off, as she began to look around.

My fucking phone chimed signaling, that I'd received a text message. Although my phone was off, I could still receive messages on Wi-Fi. I wanted to punch myself, for not putting my phone on silent.

"Hold up. Is there someone in here, with us?"

By now, I was sweating horribly, I wished, I'd stayed my ass home.

"Nobody is in here. Let's just go downstairs and watch some T.V. or something."   He tried to pull her out of the room, but she yanked away from him. She stared at the closet for a moment.

She began to walk closer to the closet as, Lance, began to panic.

"There is no one is the closet, Imani!"

She must've had a gut feeling, because she took off running towards the closet, with Lance, hot on her trail trying to stop her, but it was too late.

She swung the closet door open, we both glared at one another. I had nothing to say, but I did try to take off running, like a fool. She latched onto my hair and drug me across the bedroom, by my poetic justice braids.

I put my hands up to block her punches, because I didn't need a bitch messing up, my pretty face. I yelled, "Stop! Lance, please make her stop!"

He stepped in and yanked her off of me. I was beyond pissed. He told me he loved me, yet he let me get my ass beat, by a woman he claimed he never cared anything about.

"Get off of her, Imani!" He shoved her back, after pulling her off of me.

"You defending this, bitch?" She howled pointing at me.

I was sprawled out on the floor, trying to catch my breath, as Imani stood behind, Lance, trying to catch her breath as well. All of the contents within my purse were scattered on the floor, including the money, he'd given me.

"You taking way too long to get up and get the fuck out!" She yelled as her voice echoed, throughout the room.

I had never been this scared in my life.

Imani briskly walked over to the same closet, she'd just dragged me out of and started going through some boxes. She carelessly threw the boxes to the floor, until she found what she was looking for. I watched in fear as she retrieved a gun and after she took the safety off, she pointed it at my forehead.

I put my hands up quickly, as I said a silent prayer to the man up above.

"God, it's me Nevaeh, please don't let me die today. I promise I'll change my ways."

"I'm only going to say this once. I'm the wrong, bitch to fuck with. Stay away from my husband, stay away from this house, and stay away from our money, bitch."

Imani scooped up the money, that had fallen from my purse and threw it onto the bed. I was pissed and scared, at the same damn time. Shit, I was confused too, because Lance, didn't say anything the whole time. He didn't defend me, it made me feel some type of way.

"Please, just leave." He pleaded with his eyes. I looked away, gathered my things and left. I could not believe what just happened.

Lance

"Where are you going, Lance?" Imani asked, softly as she watched me walk over to our bedside table, to retrieve my keys.

Nevaeh stormed out of here about ten minutes ago, and we had been standing in front of one another, at a loss for words. I didn't know what to say, because a nigga was caught. There wasn't shit I could say to fix this, I hated how she was staring at me. She had a look of disappointment on her face, mixed with a few tears that she wiped away every now and then, with the palm of her left hand, as she still held the gun in her right.

"I just need to clear my head for a bit. I'll be, right back."

I turned to walk away, but she rushed over to me, and started hitting me in my back, with the butt of the gun. I should have known, it wouldn't be that easy to walk away.

I spun around and pushed her back lightly, which made her stumble a bit, as I reached to snatch the gun away from her.

"Let go of the gun, now!" Reluctantly she did, as she was told.

"What the fuck is, yo problem?" When she didn't say anything, I replied. "I don't have time for this."

She scoffed. "Well you better make time. I'm so sick and tired of you embarrassing me, Lance. I'm so—" She sniffled, then placed her face into her hands.

Her body shook uncontrollably, I didn't know what to do, other than place my hand on her back to rub it calmingly.

She moved away from me and turned her back, so I couldn't see her face, as she fought to stop her tears from falling, but that shit wasn't successful at all.

"You got them hoes at my job clowning me, saying they saw you out with some bitch, all boo'd up. That must be her, huh?"

I sucked my teeth. "Fuck them girls at your job."

"Why? It's not like they're wrong."

I just stood there with my hands in my pocket, not knowing what to say, yet again.

"Who's is she?" She had her face all twisted up, with furrowed eyebrows waiting for me to speak. She bit her bottom lip to keep it from quivering.

"I'm not about to do this with you, for real. I'm sorry for my part in all of this. But, you already knew what you were getting yourself into. We weren't even together when you got pregnant, we were just fucking, then came Chyna. I only married you, so she could grow up in a traditional household." I was being honest, whether she wanted to hear this or not. "I wasn't in love with you then, but now I am, and I promise this will never happen again. You have my word."

She knew from jump and she was a groupie hoe, that wouldn't leave me alone, but eventually I gave in. I fucked around and got her pregnant, because we were fucking raw stupidly. The pussy was too good for a rubber.

Imani was and had always been, a beautiful brown skinned woman, with a short, bloody red pixie cut that fit her face perfectly. After having our daughter, she put on a few pounds in all of the right places. She was slim and had very small breasts, but her ass made up for that. Her dark-brown eyes were so chinked; you would've thought she was part

Asian. She had a mole above her lip, an eyebrow piercing, a tongue ring, a nose ring, and a big tattoo on her left shoulder, with my name on it.

When she got knocked up we initially discussed abortion, but she was adamant about keeping the baby. I'm glad that we did, because I love my daughter with everything in me. She was truly a blessing.

We eventually ended up in a relationship because I knew it was the right thing to do. Imani always had suspicions about me fucking other women, because of the late nights I'd spent in the studio, traveling all around the world to find talent, and the women that threw themselves at me, right in front of her face. She knew, there might be a slight possibility of me fucking around, but I always made sure to cover all of my tracks, so she wouldn't find anything. The reason I did all of this was to avoid hurting her feelings. I'll admit, in the beginning, I didn't love her. However, over time she grew on me, and I fell for her, which is why I was adamant about ending things with, Vaeh. Imani didn't deserve that, she was a good woman. When she popped up unexpectedly, I started thinking with the wrong head. Now here I was trying to plead my case, to my wife.

"I—I don't deserve this shit, I swear I don't."

Imani shook her head, and started to walk out of the room, but I grabbed her arm gently.

"Look at me." I demanded.

"No. I don't want to look at you, right now, Lance." She tried to snatch away from me, but I had a firm grip on her wrist.

"For real, look at me." I demanded calmly.

She sighed before looking at me, with a wet face, and red poufy eyes.

"Look baby, you been down for me, for so long, I'm not trying to lose you. It won't happen again. I love you."

She shook her head. "I love you too, Lance with everything in me, but it seems you just can't look past the way that we met. Yes, I was on some hoeing shit back then trying to fuck anyone with money, for a quick come up, but when I met you everything changed despite what you think. I wasn't after your money, I was after your heart. You say you love me, but I know you don't mean it, you never did."

"I do. I care about you, and I love you. You had my first child. I will always have love for you, but if you want to leave I can't stop you for doing so."

She wiped her tears, then turned to walk away again. She grabbed her car keys and purse off the bedside table.

"Really? So, you would just let me leave?"

I shrugged my shoulders. "I don't want you to I promise, I don't, but yes if that's what you wanted to do."

She released a deep sigh. "Fine! I'm done, Lance—for real. I can't do this, right now. I need some space."

She left our bedroom, I followed her to Chyna's room. I stood in the doorway, as she packed a few of our daughter's things into a small duffle bag. Chyna was fast asleep in her frozen themed bed.

"Where you going?" I questioned her, needing to know where she was taking my child and for how long.

"Just please leave me alone, Lance—please." She intensely threw clothes into the bag one by one, with unnecessary force.

"I need to know where you're taking, my baby."

She sighed. "When I'm ready for you to see her, then I'll let you know, but until then you don't need to know where, I'm taking my child."

"Our child." I corrected her, she glared at me with pursed lips, before she countered, "That's is if she is yours." She snickered.

I froze instantly, my eyebrows rose quickly, as I tried to decipher what the fuck she'd just said.

"The fuck you just said?"

I stepped closer to her, until her back was pressed against Chyna's closet door. She tried to pretend, she wasn't afraid of me, but I could read it all over her face. She didn't have that gun in her hand now, so she was cowering under my glare. She looked, as if she wanted to take back what she'd said, but it was way too late for that shit.

"I said, she might not be yours." She affirmed, shamelessly, with a grin and a roll of her eyes.

I turned away for a second and tried to collect my thoughts.

"Yeah—you ain't the only unfaithful one." She sneered.

I didn't know what came over me, but I bum rushed her making her drop her purse, keys, and the baby's duffle bag. Her hands instantly wrapped around mine, as she tried to pry my fingers from her throat. Her eyes bulged, as her mouth hung open. I wanted to kill her ass. She had me fucked up. I instantly started thinking, she may have had other niggas in our home.

A few moments later, when I completely let her go, she fell to the ground with a loud thump. All that could be heard was her gasping for air, while holding her neck.

I bent down, eye level with her. "Now what did you say? Explain that shit to me."

"I'm sorry, Lance. She—" I cut her off midsentence

"She what, huh?" I grabbed her ass by the face, she winced in pain, and began swinging wildly at my face to get me off of her. I let her go when she landed a few punches to my cheek and nose.

"Don't you ever put your hands on me, again!" She countered, as she used her feet to scoot back further away from me.

Her chest heaved up and down, swiftly. "She is yours, okay! I was just trying to get under your skin, because you cheated on me." She looked away from my intense gaze.

I shook my head. "What the fuck! You don't play like that, Imani!" I stood up and towered over her. She fretfully, looked up at me. My jaw compressed tightly, as I gritted my teeth.

"I swear she is yours." She replied, breathlessly. "I promise"

My mind raced a mile a minute, as I watched her try to recuperate and regain her composure. I stormed out of our daughter's room leaving her dumbass sitting there on the floor.

I needed to leave to clear my head, I was on the verge of either saying some shit, I would regret, or doing something I'd regret. Once in the car, I headed to a place I knew, I shouldn't be going, but I needed to see, Nevaeh. I literally only had two options. I could stay in a marriage where I wasn't happy for the sake of my daughter, or I could see where, Vaeh's head was one last time, before I made my decision. I really wanted to be with her, she knew that, but she played a bunch of games. A nigga was real deal confused about this shit.

Heaven

I must've dozed off, I jumped when my phone began to vibrate. I sat up a little and grabbed it from the coffee table. I looked at the number, then instantly rolled my eyes. This fool had finally mustered up enough courage to call me and had been calling for the past three days. Usually, I'd just keep pressing ignore, because I wasn't ready to speak to his no-good ass.

I was confused, upset and practically damaged. I still didn't know what to make of this new life, without him in it. A small piece of me wanted to know, why he did what he did, and a part of me just wanted to get over it.

I stared down at my phone, this time, without a second thought, I answered his call.

The automated voice said, *"This call will be recorded and monitored. You have a collect call from, Naheem Holmes. Do you accept the charges?"*

I replied yes, and my body went completely numb when he spoke into the receiver.

"H—hello, baby?" He questioned hesitantly.

I tried to talk, but nothing came out. I was speechless.

"Heaven, you there?"

Again, I didn't say a word. I heard him sigh deeply, before he continued.

"I know you're mad at me, I don't blame you. I just called to tell you, that, I love you."

I blurted out, "Why Naheem, why would you step out on our marriage?"

This time, it was him that remained silent.

"Cat got your tongue?" I chewed the inside of my lip nervously, as my hands trembled a little. His voice used to always make me want to be in his presence, but at this moment in time, his voice gave me uneasiness.

He paused for a while, I'm sure he was thinking of a lie. "I don't know what made me do it, it was a very stupid decision on my part. I—" He inhaled deeply and exhaled soon after. "—I wish I could take it back, because I don't want you to hurt over me. I swear we can fix our marriage."

I looked at the phone like it had six heads. He must have lost his mind.

"I don't want to fix out marriage, Naheem." I wiped a few unwelcomed tears that fell from my eyes and wet my cheeks, as I waited for his response.

"So, what are you saying?" His voice was filled with concern.

"I'm saying, I want a divorce. I just—I can't be with you. I loved you, and you tore my heart, out of my chest. I just can't stick around."

He gulped. "Wow s—so you want to just up, and be done with, me?" He mumbled, "Just like, Shania?"

My face scrunched up, similar to the face you'd make after eating a lemon. He thought, I didn't hear the last thing, he said, but I did. "Excuse me?"

"Nothing." He murmured. "Why are you doing this, Heaven?"

I chuckled at his idiocy. "So, let me guess—you only started calling me, because she wants nothing to do, with you? Am I, right?" I shook my head.

I couldn't believe, I was ever with someone that could rip my heart out, and stomp on it over a million times.

He raised his voice. "No! I never said that!" He shouted, causing me to move my ear away from the phone for a short-lived moment.

When I didn't say anything, he anxiously countered by saying, "Hello?"

"You didn't have to. I know how to read between the lines." I paused to gather my thoughts. My mouth was slightly parched, as I opened and closed it a few times to speak, but nothing came out "You know what?" I paused to gather the correct wording to say to my no-good, soon to be, ex-husband. "Don't ever call me again, if you do I'll just change my number. My lawyer will be in contact with yours about the divorce."

"No wait. Please don't hang up." He begged, desperately. "I'm sorry, baby."

"I rolled my eyes. "Good bye, Naheem."

I hung up before he could say anything else. I used the back of my hands to wipe the remainder of tears, that still clung to my face. I was sick of crying, but it was like I was cursed with misery with every day, that seemed to pass by.

I got up and headed into the kitchen to grab a napkin, to wipe my eyes and blow my nose. In a way, I felt a weight had been lifted from my shoulders. Although, nothing good came of that phone call, I'd said what I needed to say to, Naheem. He changed somewhere along the line, and was nowhere near the man, I fell in love with. He gave into temptation and committed adultery, because of that, he'd lost his career and his wife. He deserved every bit of whatever was coming his way. I cursed myself, for not telling him to drop the soap before hanging up.

A few moments later, Nevaeh stormed in, like hurricane Irma, with a scowl on her face. I knew, she was mad, so I tossed my issues to the side, for a brief moment. I quickly wiped my eyes once more. I didn't need her worrying about my problems and me. I wasn't over Naheem, but I was definitely over this situation.

She headed straight for the freezer and practically knocked me down when she swung the freezer door open. I could see a bruise forming underneath her right eye.

"Oh my god, what happened to your face, sis?"

I observed her entire appearance and noticed, she had her clothes on inside out, her braids were frizzy, and all over the place, her face was bruised up, and she was barefooted. She looked like she'd gotten into a fight and lost, to be honest. I really needed to know what was going on, because I would help her jump a bitch, if need be.

She scoffed as she grabbed the first thing she could find in the freezer, which was a bag of frozen peas, and placed it to her face. She winced in pain.

"Do I need to fuck a bitch up, today?"

She rolled her eyes. "Nah, I'm good."

"Here let me see it." I tried to get a closer look at her bruise, but she slapped my hand away.

"I said, I'm good, Heaven. Please don't start acting like you're my, damn mama." She joked sarcastically. "Really it's nothing."

I crossed my arms and glared at her. She knew me. I wasn't going to drop this shit, until she told me what was up.

"Where you coming from, Vaeh?"

She rolled the one eye I could see, because those damn frozen peas covered the other eye.

"You are doing too much, right now. I'm 'bout to go lay the fuck down, please don't bother me." She was being a little rude to me, I didn't understand why, she'd never spoke to me this way before. Growing up we'd had arguments about petty things that twins argue about, but today she seemed to be taking her frustrations out on me. I brushed it off, because of my concern for her.

She walked out of the kitchen, with me hot on her trail. I wasn't trying to act like our mom, I was just trying to get to the bottom of the whole ordeal. No one was going to put his or her hands on my sister and get away with it.

We got all the way to her bedroom door, and she turned around looking at me like I was crazy.

"Back up. Why you all up in my space, twin?" She put her hand out to push me back a bit. "Like I said, you doing way, too fucking much. It's my business, I'll handle it. I'm a big girl, you know.

I shook my head. "It's not about being a big girl. I just want to make sure, that you—"

"Look!" She yelled throwing her hands up. "Why don't you go worry about some other shit, okay? Worry about your man and why he's locked up for fucking a—"

I slapped her hard as hell, halting her from saying anything else.

Crash—

She flew back into the wall, I was sure, she'd have a bruise on the other side of her face in no time.

She stared at me, with her mouth hung open, wondering what the hell had just happened. My hand was stinging, and to be quite honest, I wanted to hit her ass again. She had some nerve trying to come at me sideways.

See, Nevaeh didn't know how to fight, she never did. I was the fighter and fought almost all of our battles alone. Bitches were mad and jealous, because we were pretty as fuck, all the niggas at school wanted to talk to the twins. The hate was real. Growing up Vaeh, was more of a girly girl, who wore heels everywhere even to football and basketball games. I was more of a free spirit, I dressed in comfortable clothing, because I loved to dance and knew I wouldn't be able to do so in skintight dresses, and ten-inch heels.

"You know how much that shit hurt me, when my husband did what he did. You brought the shit up like you lost your damn mind!" I shrieked at her.

She straightened herself up, but I could see the panic in her eyes.

"I—I'm sorry, I didn't mean to say that." She countered, as I watched her eyes glaze over. "I was just mad at what happened and shouldn't have taken it out on you."

"Fuck you, Nevaeh. You are so self-centered sometimes, it's not even funny. You're sorry, because I slapped the fuck outta yo ass, but had I not done that you wouldn't be sorry now would you?" I questioned her. She remained silent, just like I knew she would.

I backed away from her silently, with tears streaming down my face, yet again. I turned to leave.

"Heaven wait, I'm sorry."

Her apology fell upon deaf ears, as I grabbed a few of my things. I was so upset, I just needed to leave. I walked out and slammed the door behind me, so hard, I was sure the walls shook.

Nevaeh

I stood there feeling stupid, probably looked even stupider, as my sister stormed out of my house, after slapping me. I deserved it. I was just so caught up in my feelings, I said the first thing that came to mind. I wish, I could take it back, but I already knew the damage had been done.

"Girl you need to apologize to your sister, before it's too late." I thought to myself.

I quickly ran over to my purse, sitting on the counter and dumped everything thing out onto the counter. I retrieved my cellphone, and quickly dialed her number.

"Pick up the phone, Heaven, I'm sorry" I said into the voicemail, because she had sent me directly to it.

I threw my phone on the counter and decided to just go outside to see if she had already pulled off. She couldn't have left that fast, because my place was on the 4th floor, I hoped like hell, she hadn't made it to her car yet.

As soon as I swung the door open, I came face to face with, Lance. His fist was up in the air. It appears that he was just about to knock on the door. I instantly tried to slam the door in his face, but he put his foot in between it.

"I have nothing to say to you, Lance, move your got damn foot, before you end up foot less like, Kunta Kinte."

He didn't budge. "Let me come in."

I stood firm with my hands on my hips. I didn't budge either. "Hell no, go home to your, wife."

He sucked his teeth and forced his way inside of my apartment.

I sighed and shut the door behind him. "Just say what you have to say, so you can leave."

I crossed my arms and waited for a response.

"I'm sorry about what happened, with you and my—"

I cut him off. "No, you're not you stood there and let her drag me across the room, like a ragdoll and put a fucking gun to my face."

He remained silent.

"I'm sorry. She's my wife—what was I supposed to do?"

"You were supposed to have my back, that's what!" I stepped closer to him. I was sure he could see the steam seeping from my head. "You told me, you were going to leave her for me, but then you didn't even have my back, that's backwards as hell."

I snatched away from him, when he tried to grab my hands.

"Don't touch me, Lance, for real. Get to the point of why you're here."

68

He exhaled deeply, prior to responding. "We can't fuck around anymore, I ain't leaving Imani, so this between us is done."

"Wait what?" Yes, I was upset with him, but I didn't want him to end what we had, especially since he paid my bills. "I don't understand."

"It's best for me to leave you alone. I have a wife and child at home, I want to make sure we stay a family, for the sake of the baby."

"When did you decide all of this?" I questioned him.

"That's not important."

I shook my head at what he was saying. I didn't know what had gotten into him. He'd normally get mad at me, but he'd get over it, we'd fuck, and he'd shoot me some more cash. He was really in his feelings.

"I'm not ready for us to be done." I pleaded, when I tried to grab his hand, he slightly pulled away.

"I'm not kidding this time, Vaeh. You been playing stupid ass mind games with a nigga, I'm done trying. You said you ain't wanna be with me, so I'm doing what's best for me and sticking with my family. It's simple."

"But you can't—" I stopped talking to gather my thoughts.

I never thought about the possibility of him actually staying with his wife. I always played games with him, because he was an easy target and always came back, no matter what. I did like him, I just wasn't ready to be committed to him fully. I liked my freedom.

I pointed to the couch. "Can we just sit down and talk about this?"

He shook his head from side to side.

We stared at one another, preclusive of him turning to leave. "I'm sorry."

"Lance, wait!" I yelled, but he slammed the door in my face.

This was officially the worst day of my life, second to the death of my mother.

Chapter 7

Banks

I couldn't stop the smile, that was glued to my face, as my family and I raised our glasses. I had officially signed to TMG records, I was ecstatic as hell. My mom hadn't stopped crying since I told her the news. She invited all of my cousins, uncles, and aunts over to celebrate. We had a packed house. All of the adults bobbed their heads to my music, as my new single blasted from the stereo. I wasn't playing any games.

Rod-C had to damn near tell me to go home and get some rest, some nights, because I was in the studio twenty-four, seven. It had already been a full two weeks since I signed, I was still on my high horse. Nobody could tell me shit, even if they wanted to. I had been so busy and didn't have time for a get together, but my mom insisted on having a congratulatory party in my, honor. She wouldn't take no for an answer.

"Let's toast to my, baby boy." My mom chimed in as everyone raised their wine glasses and some raised shot glasses. "I wish you the best of success in your career, just make sure you don't forget about us little people." She joked, as laughter filled the room. "No, but seriously, though we all love you and wish you well, congratulations again, you deserve it."

"Thank you, mama."

Everyone yelled, in unison. "Congrats!" The sound of glasses clanking together filled the room. I walked around the room thanking everyone for coming, hugging a few people in the process.

My mother's house was so packed, you would've thought, it was a damn holiday. I made my way through the crowd and eventually flopped my tired ass down onto the sofa and propped my feet up on the table.

"Boy, you know better than that." My mama exclaimed. I was just about to get comfortable. "Don't make me pop, you."

I quickly took my feet down, because I knew she was serious, no matter how old I was, she would still pop me.

"Okay, what y'all know about that?" One of my play uncles who was damned near knocking on sixty-five years of age, threw on a throwback Frankly Beverly and Maze joint, and all the old folks got up to dance. "See back in my day, this is what we used to listen to" he said.

I smiled, as I watched the older folks dance around doing old school dances, as the kids ran around the house until they tired themselves out. My pocket vibrated, I pulled my phone out of my pocket, just in time to see that I had a missed call. I almost laughed, when I saw the name run across the top of the screen.

A few moments later a text message came through.

"Look at this shit." I handed my phone to my closest cousin Dino, he shook his head, then handed me my phone back. By now, he was all caught up on all the drama I went through with my ex, here she was hitting a nigga up.

He laughed. "She had the audacity to hit you with a fuck-ing, hey big head, text." He shook his head once more. "She clearly saw you in the blogs over the past few weeks, after TMG released their new artists roster. She ain't slick."

"She gone have to get down on her knees and do a lot of begging, before I pay her ass any mind again, if you catch my drift." Lakenya was trying to get on my good side, but I was not interested.

He just laughed. Hell, I laughed too, that nigga was high as hell, everything seemed funny to him, right about now.

"Come over here and help me with these deviled eggs, Banks." My mama yelled over the music, as she danced around in the kitchen. She knocked me out of my thoughts as I headed into the kitchen.

"Here, tell me how this taste." She practically, shoved a deviled egg into my mouth, which caused both of us to burst out laughing.

"It's good, but I'm a grown man, I don't need you feeding me, ma." I stated with a mouth full.

She glared at me prior to handing me a napkin.

"Well guess what, grown man, you have an even bigger problem on your hands than just these eggs."

I looked at her sideways, after wiping my mouth. "What you mean, mama?"

"Well that lil' fast tailed lil' girl keeps popping up over here, all hours of the day and night, looking for you." she smirked.

I scratched my head, confused at what she was talking about.

"Who?"

Her eyes narrowed. "You know who." she sneered. "That girl you were dating, I can never remember her name, but she keeps stopping by saying, she wants to talk to you. I had to lie and tell the poor girl, you were out of town." she chuckled.

"Don't worry, I'll handle it."

I turned to walk away, but she grabbed my arm.

"Listen to me baby. Things are going to be different now that you're signed to TMG. Please just make sure, that you be careful. I don't need a gold digger like her trying to use up all of your money, or to get a little bit of fame. Watch out for her."

"Okay, ma, I'll handle it."

She gave me a hug and a kiss on the cheek. "Okay, baby, go ahead and enjoy your party. I'm proud of you."

Her words stuck with me for the remainder of the night. All I ever wanted to do was make my mama proud, I did just that.

Nevaeh

"So, what are you, going to do?" Margarita, my best bitch, inquired, as we sat in her living room, scrolling through Instagram. My sister still wasn't speaking to me, and I needed something to do to ease my mind.

I had literally been at, Margarita's place all day moping around, trying to figure out, who I could get some fast cash from. I wasn't in the business of selling pussy, but I might've needed, to go toot this ass up on some nigga tonight, so I could get all up in his pockets. I was trying to secure the bag, by any means necessary. I could go down to the club, that I worked at and bartend for a few hours, but I was tired of working there, and the money was shitty. I was trying to get out of that lifestyle.

Lance cut me all the way off, and my bills were falling behind. I needed to hop on another gravy train, quick. All I wanted, was a nigga with money, to take care of me, because I didn't feel like I should have to work.

I sneered. "I don't know, Rita, but fuck, Lance." I continued, scrolling trying to keep my mind off of him.

I observed Margarita, as she took another swig of Hennessey, straight from the bottle. "You want some?" She quizzed, after she wiped her mouth with the back of her hand.

"Yeah, let me hit that." She passed me the Hennessey bottle, I took about three good swigs, then passed it back to her. After the liquor scorched my chest, I screwed up my face until the piping hot sensation lessened.

"Girl look." Margarita showed me a post on Instagram, about a single release party for some new rapper named, *Banks*. "You might be in luck, finding you a baller tonight, Bitch." She said enthusiastically.

"Who the fuck is, Banks?" Margarita was a stripper at some of the hottest clubs in the city, so she knew more about the niggas, that were balling and the niggas, that weren't.

"You know that song, they're always playing on the radio called, *'Bitch I'm tryna make it'?'*

I thought about it, before it dawned on me. "Oh, shit, that's him?" I looked at the flyer once more, he was fine as hell.

He had waves deeper than the ocean, a smooth dark chocolate complexion with tattoos all over his arms, and a neatly trimmed goatee. In the picture, he was showing off his gold slugs. His eyes were chinked, and his exposed arms were muscular. I was sure, he worked out. He was standing up, grilling at the camera, playfully lifting his shirt halfway up. His glistening six-pack was exposed, making me lick my lips. He just looked like money.

"He's a new rapper, and his song is number one in the whole country. On top of that he's single. I saw an interview, he did last week." She replied stuffing some Doritos in her mouth. She licked her fingers clean, then said, "Plus, the nigga is fine as fuck in person, he came by G-FIVE, a few nights ago. I almost wanted to pounce on his sexy ass." she teased. "He's going to be at the Lexx, tonight."

I glanced at the flyer once more. "Oh shit—he's on TMG Records." I blurted out.

Her eyes widened. "Bitch ain't that the same label, Lance, be working for?"

I shook my head up and down.

"Damn, you are shady as fuck, but so what, fuck him since he wanna try to cut my, girl off." she boasted.

I knew, if I had a chance to get close to him, I could seduce him.

"So, what you wanna do?"

I thought long and hard about what I wanted to do, a few moments of silence was bestowed upon us, as Margarita stared at me with wide eyes.

"Let's go!"

"Ayyy. That's my, bitch!" She yelled, then got up to do a little dance. She bent over and started popping her booty. "Every day we lit, you can't tell me, shit."

She started dancing around in front of me. I playfully swatted her on the butt.

"I can't deal with you." We shared a laugh, then I stood up and stretched a bit. I needed to get home to shave my, under arms and pussy, before going out, tonight. "So, what time do you want to go?"

She looked at the time on her iPhone, then back up at me. "I'll meet you at the club at about eleven-thirty."

I shook my head and agreed. "A'ight, don't be taking all long either."

"Yeah whatever." She playfully waved me off, as I grabbed my belongings, and headed for the door. I was excited, because I had confidence, I was going to snag me a baller, tonight.

****

"It's so damn hot in here!" Margarita yelled, over the music loud enough for me to hear.

I agreed, as I elbowed a few people, who were all up on me. The club was packed, the music was bumping, and my eyes were on one person only. Banks's fine ass was looking so damn good, as he stood up in the VIP section, pouring liquor from way up above onto a few people down below. The crowd was going crazy, and this nigga had just got here.

"Uh, look at that bitch, over there." Rita and I burst into laughter, when we saw some woman, standing underneath the VIP section, with her boobs out. She jumped up and down, trying desperately to get him to notice her, as she jiggled her boobs. She looked pathetic.

"She looks a hot ass mess, with that busted ass weave, Banks don't want her ass." I stated truthfully. I wasn't sure, what his type was, but I was sure, Mrs. Busted weave wasn't it. "We need to find a way to get up in the VIP section."

"Yes, we definitely do." she countered.

See, the thing I loved about, Margarita, was that she was always down for whatever. She was a real ride or die type of, bitch. She was bad as hell. Standing at five-feet and eleven-inches, she was a real Amazon. Men loved how slim, thick she was, and her smooth, long legs were to die for. She had the prettiest dark skin, that looked to be the same shade as a, Snickers chocolate bar. Her eyes were a beautiful shade of hazel, and she always wore her own natural hair, in a cute Afro, with bamboo hoops.

"Look." She pointed, at one of the bouncers who looked to be overweight as hell.

He looked like he was someone, that could be easily bribed with some food or something. I chuckled at the thought.

Rita turned to me and gave me a smirk before she spoke. "I know that nigga, that's my cousin's boy from back in the day. Let me see if he remembers me."

We pushed through a bunch of sweaty ass people and stopped directly in front of the VIP section. I was nervous, because we were only a few steps away from, my new play toy. I pulled my dress up, showing off more of my legs, as the bouncer looked both, Margarita and I, up and down.

"What's up, Teddy?" She said, rubbing on his gigantic belly. "You are looking good, baby." She flirted with his fat ass, and he cracked a smile.

"What's up, Rita?"

She pointed up the stairs, then back at me. "My girl here, is a huge fan, she wanted to know if we could go up and meet, Banks." She continued smiling all up in his face, batting her eyelashes, and rubbing his fat nasty stomach.

"Hold on let me see first."

She turned to me and winked. I was all giddy inside happy, that I was going to snag, Banks's fine ass.

When the bouncer came back, he motioned for the two of us, to head up to his private section.

I walked up there like a super model, on a catwalk putting on my, stank walk.

He was sitting down on the couch, smoking a blunt, and his eyes were low.

"Shout out to the homie, Banks up in VIP. This is his new song '*Shawty Bad*'. Y'all show my nigga some love.

The crowd went wild, when the D.J. dropped Bank's new single. He bobbed his head to the music and mouthed along with the song. God, this man was sexy. Some dusty ass girl, was bent all the way over in front of him, twerking. He leaned forward and slapped her on the ass, she smiled widely, and continued to dance.

The bouncer walked over to, Banks, then he pointed at the two of us. He looked over at the two of us, I felt my panties get moist, when we locked eyes.

Margarita plopped down on the couch on one side of him, and I sat down on his lap. His hands immediately went to my exposed thighs, and he rubbed them softly.

"So, you're my biggest fan, huh?" He questioned, hitting his blunt. Our eyes locked, I bit my lip seductively. I wasn't trying to waste time, I wanted to get right to business.

I leaned in to speak into his ear. "Yeah, you should let me show you how much of a fan, I am."

"Oh yeah? That's how you, rocking?" His eyes widened momentarily.

I shook my head, as I reached down, and placed my hand onto the crotch of his pants.

"Move bitch! He's tired of your whack ass dance moves, now stop dancing in front of, him!" Margarita yelled to the girl, who'd been dancing in front of, Banks for the past ten minutes.

She adjusted her dress and walked off, after she rolled her eyes. I couldn't help, but laugh, my girl was a trip.

He leaned up and whispered into my ear. "You, real pretty ma, but, I already know your type." He said, which instantly made my blood boil.

The fact that, he'd blatantly said, that shit to me, instantly ruined my mood. We weren't even in his section for that long, and I was ready to leave. This nigga was acting like muthafuckin' Steve from Blue's Clues, trying to figure me out, by just looking at me.

"What do you mean?" I needed to know what he meant.

He removed my hand from the crotch of his pants and gently placed my hand back into my lap.

"You see me, and you see dollar signs, but I ain't tryna fuck, or get involved, with you." He hit his blunt again, this time when he blew the smoke out, I quickly waved my hands in front of my face, to fan the smoke away.

"B—but, I can make you feel good, though. Don't you want your dick sucked? I can do that for you." I was desperate.

He had a smug look on his face, as he responded, by saying, "I'm not interested, baby." He stated effortlessly and pushed me gently off his lap, as some groupie bitches surrounded him, practically pushing me out of the way, as they all begged to take pictures with him, and get his autograph.

I sucked my teeth, got up, and pushed through those groupie hoes. I didn't even care, anymore. He probably ain't have any fucking dough anyways.

"Bitch, let's, go!" I yelled at, Margarita, because I was beyond pissed, and quite frankly, embarrassed. This nigga had the nerve to turn me down.

"Call me, boo." She said to the nobody ass nigga, she was sitting with. I practically dragged her out of, Banks's section and out of the club.

As we waited for the valet to bring our cars around, she asked eagerly, "So, did you get his number?"

I lied with a huge smile on my face. "Girl, of course, I did. You know, I wasn't leaving until I got it."

She gave me a high five. "I know that's, right!" She started telling me about, some dude who was trying to hit on her, claiming he was, Bank's cousin, and I began to tune her out.

About ten minutes later, my car finally arrived.

"Thank you." I said to the valet attendant, as he handed me the keys. "I'll call you, later." I bid, Margarita, goodbye, as I hopped into my car, then onto the highway.

I still could not believe, Banks, turned me down. I wasn't going to give up, though, that nigga was going to give up some kind of cash, trust and believe that.

Chapter 8

Heaven

A few nights later

"Hey, what's up bae, how you feeling?" I released a deep sigh.

Although I wasn't in much of a talking mood, I knew, Renaissance wouldn't leave me alone, until I at least confirmed, I was doing okay. She had been blowing me up for the past few weeks, and I managed to get away, with giving her one-word answers, but she was a good friend to me, and I answered, because I felt, she deserved to know, how I was doing. Plus, I wasn't speaking to my twin, since the incident a few days ago, so I needed someone to talk to.

"Well—" I cradled my cell phone between my neck and shoulder, as I continued with my task of sweeping. "I'm in the middle of cleaning and throwing away everything, that reminds me of, Naheem."

"Damn. I know that's got to hurt. You know, I can always come over and help it's no problem." Her voice was always very soothing, although she acted like a crazy fool, half the time, my girl, Renaissance, always had my back. She was a good friend and always made sure, I was good, no matter what. She and I were just as tight as, Nevaeh and me. We met in college, she was my roommate, along with Nevaeh, and a girl named, Margarita. I more so gravitated towards, Renaissance, because we both cared about getting good grades and walking across that big stage in four years, unlike Vaeh and Margarita, who cared about skipping class, staying out late, sleeping with men, partying, and drinking.

"No, it's okay. I really need to be alone, right now. It's like, I know we're over, but the reality, just set in as I started packing up a bunch of old pictures, we took."

"Trust me, girl—" she smacked her lips. "You are going to be, okay. He's going to be dropping the soap in jail and you are going to move on, and find yourself another nigga, that looks better than, Naheem, and dicks you down, way better than that nigga, too." She said, which caused me to laugh.

I really needed to laugh more, because lately, I hadn't been doing that.

"I can't deal with you." I said, which caused her to laugh as well.

She was crazy as hell, but we balanced each other out. At least one of us needed to be sane.

"So, what's been up with you?" I changed the subject, tired of talking about my soon to be, ex-husband. I put the broom down, for a brief moment, and flopped down on my couch, with my feet up.

"Girl." She groaned, and I knew, she was about to tell me a crazy over the top story. "You will not believe what happened. So, I went on a date with this fine chocolate brotha from '*Plenty of Fish*' and I was upset, when I saw this nigga in person. He came to pick me up, looking just as good as his pictures, but this nigga had the nerve, and audacity, to be musky as fuck!" she yelled.

I chuckled, she was too crazy. "Girl, my nose was burning for the entire car ride. I wondered how someone so fine could be so stank." I could just imagine, her face all scrunched up, as she told the story.

I was doubled over laughing so hard, my eyes were watering. I literally had to wipe my eyes with the back of my hand.

"So, how did the date end?"

She gave me a very long, dramatic pause, then replied, "Since he clearly didn't care about my nose, I told his lil' funky ass to pull over, so I could hop out, then I called an Uber."

"Wow." I chuckled. "See that's what you get meeting these men online."

There was a knock at the door, that startled me.

"Oh, hold on real quick girl, somebody is at my door."

I got up to open the door, when I looked out the peephole, I instantly ended the phone call, and swung the door open.

"What are you doing here, Renaissance?"

She sashayed into my place, looking like she was auditioning to be on America's next top model, as she brushed past me.

"I was already on this side of town, I wanted to check on you in person, that's all." She replied nonchalantly, as she made her way into the kitchen, and grabbed room temperature water from the pantry.

She always knew how to make herself right at home. I closed and locked my door, before taking my same-seated position on the couch. I watched, as she looked around, observing her surroundings. My house looked like a tornado had gone through it.

"I'm going to this little get together, tonight, with a friend of mine from work. She told me that on the side, she's a personal assistant for some big rapper, and she's able to bring at least three people." Renaissance replied, as she texted away on her phone. When I didn't respond, she looked up at me, and I watched as her facial features scrunched up.

"Okay, so why are you telling me?" I questioned, with furrowed brows.

"You're coming with me."

I shook my head. "Uh, no the hell, I'm not." I chuckled. "I am not in a partying mood, and I have a lot to do around here. I really want to pack all of these pictures and things, that remind me of him. I don't have the time to party."

"Awe come on, bae. Opportunities like this don't present themselves every day. Skye is a cool girl, you'll like her and she's getting us into an invite only party, with some big named celebrities. We don't have to pay for shit."

"I can't Renaissance, I just—"

"You can, and you will. I know you want to get rid of all his shit, so that it won't remind you of his trifling ass, I get that, but don't let him dictate your happiness. I think, you need to get out, and you probably need a drink."

I gave her the side eye.

"No fuck that, you need like five of them." She burst out laughing at her own joke, I just stared at her stale faced.

"Okay fine, all jokes aside. I'm not taking no for an answer. You're my girl, I hate seeing you like this. Come turn up with me, bitch, you know you're my turn up partner. We can go for like an hour, I promise."

I thought about what she was saying, I did need a drink, to stop me from thinking about, my soon to be ex-husband, my sister, with all of her bullshit, and my mother who had been invading, my thoughts a lot, lately. The anniversary of her death was approaching and had been on my mind daily.

"Okay fine, but only for an hour."

She hopped up from the couch and ran over to me, to engulf me into a hug.

"See that's my, girl." She cheesed widely, after she pulled away from our embrace.

I waved her off. "Yeah, whatever." I replied muttered dryly.

"So, whose party is it, anyways?" I questioned, because I was curious to know.

"That big record label TMG Records just signed three new artists, so they're celebrating and introducing the artists. I don't care much for the two girls they just signed, but you ever heard of a nigga, named, Banks? He's the one that went viral on, Facebook and Instagram, from that song *Bitch I'm tryna make it*. He just got signed to TMG."

I didn't listen to the radio much, I definitely wasn't on social media like that, so I had no idea who she was talking about. I'm sure, she could tell by the perplexed look on my face.

"Well anyways, that nigga is fine as fuck, but I heard he got a girl. Some chick he was with, before he blew up or something like that. He's so cute, I know he isn't your type, he looks a lil' rough around the edges, but I'd take him down any day of the week." She joked. I watched as she pulled out her phone.

"This is the flyer, my girl, Skye, sent me. That's him in the middle."

She pointed to the picture; I almost choked on my spit, as my eyes got wide. He was breathtakingly handsome. He looked, as if he'd just gotten a tape at the barbershop and his waves were definitely on swim. I liked the fact, that his goatee was trimmed nicely, because I hated it, when men let their facial hair grow all over the place. His full crimson stained lips looked so succulent, and he had tattoos all over his arms, with one on the side of his neck. I could tell he worked out, because he was shirtless on the flyer, with his arms crossed. His washboard abs glistened, effortlessly. He was smiling widely, and I could see his dimples. His pants were slightly sagging, showing off his polo boxers.

I normally went for light skinned guys, hence the reason I was with, Naheem, but this Banks character had the darkest, smoothest skin, I'd ever seen. He was a human Hershey's bar.

She snapped her fingers in front of my face to get my attention, then looked at me sideways. "Since when do you like dark chocolate guys, with tattoos, and gold slugs? I thought you liked them light bright, niggas?"

I looked at her sideways. "Chill out. It's not like, I'm trying to date the, nigga, I'm just looking." I fixed my eyes back on his picture after responding to her ridiculous comment.

"Mmm hmm. Well go shower and throw on something sexy."

I lazily stood up and threw the pillow, that was lying in my lap, at her. "Yes master."

I made sure to take my slow precious time, getting ready, because I really didn't want to go. Unfortunately, Renaissance, still made me go, claiming, we could still catch the meet and greet, since I'd made us miss the performances.

****

Once we were backstage, I watched as Renaissance's friend, Skye, walked around, giving a few hugs to people, I'm assuming she knew.

"This is exciting, right?" Renaissance asked me, in the midst of her putting on a fresh coat of lip-gloss.

"Yeah very exciting." I muttered sarcastically, which caused her to shoot daggers in my direction, with her eyes.

"Lighten up. You already made us miss everything, moving as slow as molasses, don't think, I don't know you were doing that to get out of coming."

I sucked my teeth. "I'm ready to go you said, we'd only be out for an hour, we've already been here for one hour and twenty-three minutes, to be exact." I stated matter-of-factly, after checking the time on my phone.

She chuckled. "I'm surprised, you actually believed that lie."

This time I glared at her, if looks could kill, she'd be somewhere swimming with the fishes.

"Okay fine. Right after we do the meet and greet, we can go. I just want to get a few pictures with a few people, and hopefully someone's number, girl I needs me a baller husband." She joked, and I shook my head.

Her friend, Skye, waved us over. I laughed, at the dirty looks we got from all the groupie hoes, that were back there as well, trying to snatch themselves a baller. We pretty much, skipped the line of females waiting to take a picture with and get an autograph from, Banks.

Skye was all smiles as she introduced us. "This is my girl, Renaissance and her friend, Heaven." She pointed to us, as we took turns shaking his hand.

His cologne tickled my nose, although he looked good enough to eat, my mind was on getting out of my heels, and stretching out in my big bed. I was tired as hell, and over this whole day.

"Hey." He pointed at me, as my brows rose immediately. "You look familiar."

"Me?" I looked behind me, trying to see if he was talking to someone else.

"Yeah I met you the other night at the, Lexx."

"The Lexx? I'm sorry, but I don't even know what that is." I laughed nervously. "You sure it was me, you saw?"

"Yeah I'm sure." he smirked. "You still trying to fuck?" His words slurred, so I knew he wasn't in his right mind, but that still didn't excuse what he said.

My eyes widened. "Excuse me?"

I knew for a fact, I always made sure to clean out my ears properly, whenever I took a bath, so I was confused as hell, as to who and what he was talking about. This was only my second time seeing him, the first time being earlier on that flyer. How did he think it was okay, to come at me sideways asking me for sex? He must have fell and bumped his head, because no grown man should try to embarrass a grown woman, in front of his crew whether she was a hoe or not.

He chuckled. "You heard what I said, ma."

"Oh, trust me, I heard exactly what you said, but first of all, I'm not your, mama. So, don't call me, ma. Secondly, I just wanted to know who you were talking to, because it couldn't be me, I don't know you from a can of paint." I said, as I rolled my neck, and pointed all up in his face.

"So, you want to try and act like you weren't trying to fuck me, a few nights ago at the club?"

I looked at him confused, because I hadn't been to any clubs in months.

"A few nights, ago?" I scoffed. "You definitely have me confused with someone else."

He shook his head. "You funny. You was all over me, tryna fuck, rubbing all on my dick, asking me to suck it, but now all of a sudden, you have fucking amnesia." He exclaimed harshly.

Everyone formed a circle around us and looked back and forth, between the two of us, to see where this conversation was headed. I knew, I should have stayed at home. People were pulling out their phones and recording our spat.

I was sure, my blood was most likely boiling on the inside by now. I looked around, it seemed all eyes were on us. When my eyes landed on, Renaissance, she had a scowl on her face similar to mine.

"Uh, hold up, you're not about to talk to, my girl like that she has—"

I cut her off, by holding up my hand. "It's okay, sis, I got this."

I turned back around to face him, so I could address him. "Listen up, Mr. Banks, or whatever the hell you want to call yourself. I don't care who you are, you will not address me this way. Have you lost your got damn mind? I know your mama, taught you better than that."

He opened his mouth to speak, but I cut his ass off.

"I'm not done." I glared at him. "I did not meet you in the club the other night, because if you hadn't fucking noticed, I'm wearing a wedding ring!" I stopped, to point at my ring. I continued with my rant. "My husband and I are divorcing, because he couldn't keep his dick in his pants, so excuse me, but jumping on another man's dick is the furthest thing from my mind, right now. Also, you need to get your facts right before you try to embarrass someone. I have an identical twin sister, who I'm pretty sure you're mistaking me for!"

"It's okay girl, you don't have to explain anything to his ass." Renaissance said, as she tugged at my arm. "Let's just go."

I turned to leave, because I didn't have anything else to say to him.

"I'll call you later, girl." Renaissance said to Skye, as we made our way quickly out of the club. I was beyond pissed. How dare he come at me like that?

"You good." Renaissance asked me, when we finally got back to her car. "I'm sorry, I dragged you out, I just wanted you to have some fun and not to stress over your situation."

I buckled myself in my seatbelt. "It's cool, Renaissance, you don't have to apologize, you didn't know he was going to be a jerk."

She gave me a coy smile, then she cranked up the car and pulled off.

"I have a question, though." she continued.

I looked over at her. "What?"

"Why do you still have on your ring?"

I looked away from her, for a moment, to gather my thoughts. "I really don't know. I guess, I was hoping this was all a bad dream, I was ready to wake up from." I replied.

I twisted the ring off of my finger. "But now that, I know it's not a bad dream, I guess I can remove it."

She shook her head up and down, agreeing with me. "Yes, please remove it! You should pawn that shit!" She yelled, causing me to laugh.

That didn't sound like a bad idea.

Chapter 9

Banks

"Hey, what's up? You wanted to see, me?" My assistant, Skye, stuck her head into my studio session, and because I needed a break, I told everyone to clear out for about twenty minutes.

Once the room was clear, she took a seat on the sofa.

"Am I getting fired or something?" She joked, and when I didn't respond, her facial expression turned quickly, into a worried expression.

I chuckled lightly. "I'm not about to fire you." I paused to gather my thoughts. "I wanted to ask you for a favor."

"Of course, boss anything for you." She pulled a pen and notepad from her bag, something she did often, when she just wanted to jot down something, so she wouldn't forget.

"I want you to invite your girl to the Jet Ski party, tomorrow."

She looked confused. "Who?"

"The one that came backstage with you the other night."

"Renaissance?" she questioned.

"Yeah invite her, I'm pretty sure, she's going to bring her friend."

"Ohhh, I see what this is about." she smiled widely. "You're feeling ole girl, from the other night, and you want to see her again, huh."

"It's not even like that. I just kind of feel bad, for the way things went down in front of everyone. I want to apologize to her. That's not even like me to put a female out like that. You know me, I'm real chill and laid back, but I had too much to drink that night."

She smirked. "I'll see what I can do, but I'm not making any promises." she smiled. "Oh, don't forget about your meeting at three p.m. with the, Nina, sisters. This is probably going to be one of the biggest collaborations in your career, those girls are hot. With your urban feel and their Caribbean tone, I already know this song will climb the charts. I set your alarm for one p.m. The Nina sisters are sending a limo for you at two-thirty p.m. Got it?"

I looked at her, like she had six heads. "I can drive myself." I chuckled. "I'm not handicapped."

"Yes, I know but they want to show you their gratitude, so please just accept it." She pled with her hands clasped together in a praying-like way.

"What would I do without, you?" I joked, and she smirked.

"I don't know, and I'm not trying to find out." She said, then she stood up.

"See you tomorrow at the jet ski party." I placed my attention to my phone, to see if I had any missed calls, or messages.

"Okay see you there, I'll see what I can do about getting your, boo there."

"Oh, you're just full of jokes, huh?"

Instead of answering the question, Skye, left out of the studio laughing the whole way out. I shook my head, but hoped like hell, her friend would show up and bring her friend, too.

Heaven

Renaissance, Skye, and I sat in my living room having a girl's day, binge watching a bunch of horror films and stuffing our faces with ice cream. She was pretty cool. I was giving her a try, because she was a friend of, Renaissance's, but she was very down to earth and goofy, just like me. She told a lot of corny jokes, but she was still cool nonetheless.

"Oh, I almost forgot to tell y'all!" Skye shouted with a mouth full of chocolate ice cream. "TMG is having a party tomorrow, it's going to be so much fun. It's a Jet Ski party, so there will be drinks, music, and food. Y'all should come."

Renaissance chimed in with a huge smile on her face. She was always down for anything. "I'm there, where do I sign up?" she joked.

I shook my head and continued eating my ice cream. "I'm good, I'll just stay home."

Renaissance lightly pushed my shoulder. "Stop being such a Debbie downer, you know you want to come."

"Actually, I don't. I have no desire to be around a bunch of men, who think they're the shit, because they rap into a microphone for a living, or be around a bunch of groupies, that are trying to snatch them up a man." I scoffed.

"Well what if I told you, that someone wanted you to be there?" Skye questioned with a smirk on her face. "He said to make sure, I invited you." she giggled. "Don't shoot the messenger." She threw her hands up in defense.

I squinted my eyes at her, as she tried hard to hide her smile, but failed miserably. "Who wants me to be there?" Although, I had a good idea who she was talking about, I still asked, to make sure.

"If I tell you, will it make a difference, whether you are going or not?"

"Hurry up and tell her!" Renaissance yelled. "Shit I wanna know, too." she laughed.

"Okay fine." Skye said. "My boss, Banks, wants to make sure, you're in the building."

My eyebrows furrowed. "Me?" I pointed at myself. "Why would he want me to be there?"

"Well." she smiled. "Show up and find out, why." She said, trying to be slick.

I shrugged my shoulders. "Maybe I don't wanna know. He was very rude when we first met, I'm not interested in seeing him again. He embarrassed me enough the other night." I replied honestly.

He was a very handsome man, and his music was fire, but if you have a nasty attitude and personality, that makes you the ugliest person in the world to me.

"Oh, come on. Maybe he wants to apologize or something." Skye said, stuffing her face with more ice cream. "He's a good guy, and even if you don't want to see him or speak to him, you should still come.

I gave her the eye, she burst out laughing with ice cream flying from her mouth. "What?"

"Well thanks for giving me a damn ice cream shower." I joked wiping it from my knee. "But, I was looking at you like that, because I hope you're not trying to play matchmaker, with me and this guy, because I'm not interested."

"Me? Play matchmaker?" She shook her head. "Of course not." She gushed sarcastically and ducked, when I threw a pillow at her.

"Okay, so what if you just come with us for a little bit, and if you're not feeling it we can leave?" Renaissance said. Once I didn't reply, she gave me a confused look. I watched, as she ducked, when I threw a pillow at her head as well.

She chuckled. "What did I do?"

"You always say that, and I always fall for it, but not this time. I'm not going, that's that." I crossed my arms to let them know, I meant business. I wasn't interested in seeing him, even if he was fine as hell.

"Okay, babes suit yourself." Skye stood up and gathered her things.

"Uh heffa, where do you think you're going?" Renaissance shouted. "We're having a girl's day, how you just gonna up and leave." she scoffed.

"I know, but, I have to make sure, the guest list for the party is set in stone, by checking all of, Banks's emails to see if I need to add anyone else to the list. I have to call the caterer, to make sure they know to arrive two hours early, to set up, as well as the D.J. I have even more things to do, so I'll try to swing back by." She said, all in one breath.

"I thought it was a TMG party?" I questioned her.

"It is but, it's at Bank's house, he just moved into this big ass mansion and is throwing this party, as kind of like a house warming, to thank the label for signing him." She swung her computer bag over her shoulder, then scooped up her purse and cell phone. "If I can't swing back by, I'll see the both of you, tomorrow."

I looked at her sideways. "I told y'all, I'm not going."

"Yeah, you will see both of us, tomorrow." Renaissance said, emphasizing the both.

Skye bid us good-bye, as soon as she left, I looked over at Renaissance, who was scrolling through Netflix trying to find something else for us to watch.

"I can feel you burning a hole in the side of my head. Why are you looking at me like that?"

We made eye contact, and her mouth slowly curled into a smile.

"Don't act like that, you know you want to go, especially to find out why he wants to see you."

She turned her attention back to the T.V. and I bit my lip, which was a bad habit, I had whenever I was thinking deeply about something.

I guess it wouldn't hurt to stop by the party.

Tamara Butler

Chapter 10

Heaven

The Jet Ski party

"Thank you so much." I grabbed my blue long island iced-tea, from the bartender, and turned around to see, Banks himself, in the flesh looking like a sexy ass Hershey's chocolate bar. He was shirtless, I could tell, he definitely worked out, by the definition in his arms and his six-pack washboard abs. He had a few gold chains hanging around his neck, but nothing too over the top, and a pair of Gucci flip flops to match his Gucci swimming trunks.

I decided at the last minute to go to this stupid party, and was cursing myself out inside of my head. I felt out of place, because the only bathing suit I had, was a bright orange bikini-thong, that I'd worn on my honeymoon with, Naheem. I was looking good as fuck. Luckily, I had a sheer cover-up in the closet to cover my cheeks a little bit.

Skye was busy making sure the party was going accordingly, and Renaissance had run off, by the pool, to talk to some singer named, Zane, that she had the biggest crush on. We had only been at the party for fifteen minutes, and she took off, as soon as she saw him, claiming that she was going to try and get his number, prior to the party ending.

"Excuse me." I tried to walk around, Banks, but he lightly grabbed my arm. I glared at him and he removed his hand from my arm.

"You look good." He stated smoothly, licking his lips.

He was right, though. Not to toot my own horn, but I looked good enough to eat. My stylist hooked me up, so I had a part down the middle, with twenty-four inches of straight, jet-black hair, flowing down my back, and my hazel-green contacts had me looking exotic.

"I know, that." I replied dryly, trying to get him to realize, I wasn't interested in his conversation.

He released a hearty laugh. "No need to be feisty."

I rolled my eyes. "Can I help you?"

"I wanted to talk to you?"

I sipped on my drink, as I leaned my back up against the bar.

"What did you want to discuss? As far as I'm concerned, we don't have shit to talk about."

He stepped closer to me and placed one arm on either side of me. My breathing increased, as I stared into his eyes. His chest was now only a few inches against mine, as he leaned in to speak a little closer to my ear.

"I'm sorry for the things I said, and the way I acted. You are a, beautiful queen. I couldn't go on knowing, I treated you, the way, I did."

I placed my hand on his abs to stop him from getting any closer, because had he moved any closer, his dick would be up against my pussy, and I could tell from his print, that it was big as hell.

When I pushed him backwards a bit, I caught the smirk on his lips. He knew what he was doing.

"You accept, my apology?" He held out his hand, as a truce, and I placed my smaller hand into his bigger one to shake.

"Yes, I accept."

I melted, when he kissed the back of my hand.

"Uh, what's going on over here?" We both turned to see, Renaissance, with a smirk on her face. She too was already sipping on a Long Island.

"Nothing. Just giving your girl, the apology, she deserved." He blurted out and she smiled.

"Okay, good, I thought I was going to have to give you two black eyes." She gave him a demonstration, showing how she was going to beat him up, causing all three of us to laugh. "I don't play about, my girl."

"She's in good hands. Trust me." he countered.

She looked back and forth, between the two of us, with a knowing look on her face. "Mmm, I bet."

"So, what happened between, you and dude?" I asked Renaissance, trying to change the subject, as I continued to sip on my drink.

Banks kept his eyes on me, and I kept my eyes fixated on his lips. They looked so damn kissable.

She scoffed. "He's not trying to give me any play, so it is what it is." She shrugged her shoulders and Banks butted into the conversation.

"Who are ya'll talking about?" He said, being nosey.

She pointed at the guy, she was referring to, which caused, Banks, to start laughing hysterically.

She pushed his shoulder, lightly. "What's so funny? Am I not his type or something?" I could tell, she felt some type of way, about him not giving her any play.   Renaissance was a very gorgeous girl. Her skin complexion was what people referred to as yella, she was about five-feet, seven-inches and she had wide hips to go along with her flat stomach, and fat ass. She normally wore her long, dark brown, curly hair, in a high bun, to show off her facial features and beautiful blue eyes courtesy of her, Caucasian father. She was half white and half black.

"He's playing for the other team." Banks confirmed.

I watched, as her mouth practically dropped to the ground.

"You are lying!" She yelled, being all extra and loud. "I was over there putting my best moves on him."

"Well you did all of that shit for nothing because that nigga is gay. That's my boy, though he's good people." He said, I couldn't help, but burst out laughing.

Banks shook his head and walked away, to sit under an umbrella that had a few couches surrounding it.

"Oh, my God, I am so embarrassed." She said, as she flopped down on the couch across from, Banks, and folded her arms.

I followed suit and sat next to him, since we made eye contact, and he made motions for me to come sit next to him, by patting the seat.

Banks

I watched as, Heaven, fanned herself with her hand. I looked at her, confused. "You okay? If it's too hot out here, we can go inside."

She laughed, nervously. "It's okay, I'm good out here." she confirmed. "Just a little hot, that's all."

She sat next to me, on the couch, but tried to scoot as far away from me, as possible. I snatched her cell phone from her and her eyes grew wide, as her mouth fell agape.

"What are you, doing?" She knew, what I was doing, so I didn't bother answering her. I programmed my number, called my phone from hers, and once it rung, I slipped it back into her hands. She smirked, but she knew she wanted my number, I didn't know why she was fronting.

I flashed her my award-winning smile, I was sure, my gold slugs were shining brightly, with the help of the sun.

"So, tell me about, you." I was eager to find out more about her, for some reason. It was going to be a little hard to focus while she had this little ass bathing suit on, but it was worth a try.

She smiled sweetly, and looked away, momentarily. I looked around scoping out the party, just to be aware of the shit going down at my crib. The music was jumping, niggas were throwing females into the pool, some females were twerking in their little ass bikinis, and we were just getting ready to fire up the jet skis on the lake in the back.

When I looked back at, baby, she was already looking at me. I licked my lips and sat back a little, placing my arm around the back of the chair.

"Relax baby, I'm not going to bite you," I gently sat up and grabbed her by the arm. She had been sitting on the edge of the chair. Once she sat back, I scooted closer to her, and she quickly gave me the eye.

"Chill." She said, trying to remove my arm, but I pulled her even closer. "I think you're a little too close." she scoffed.

"Don't act like you don't want me close to you."

She playfully rolled her eyes. "I don't." She continued to sip on her drink, I reached up to push her hair off of her shoulder a little.

She locked eyes with me and blushed. "Stop playing with me, Heaven, I know Skye ran her mouth to you." I cheesed widely, when her mouth dropped. "You knew whose party, you were coming to, that's why you wore that. You wore that for me."

"Thank you." I said to the waitress that walked up to me and handed me another glass of Hennessy and coke.

"For your information, I wore this, because it's clearly a pool party. I did not wear this for you."

I stared at her momentarily, she looked like, she wanted to protest, but instead she bit her lip and said nothing.

"Yeah a'ight." I shook my head at her lie, but it was okay, because I was going to play along with her game.

"Anyways." She changed the subject. "What do you want to know?"

I shrugged. "I mean whatever you want to tell me."

I watched her facial expression, as she thought long and hard, about what to say. She remained silent, so I assumed, she couldn't figure out what to say. Taking control of the conversation, I took her left hand, and examined it.

"So, you took your ring off, I see."

"Huh?" she retorted.

"The other night, you mentioned something about divorcing your husband."

"Oh." She gave me an uneasy smile. "Yeah, I am." I could feel her soft body tense up underneath me.

"I'm sorry to hear that." I massaged her hand softly. "His loss." I replied simply, she shook her head, signifying that she agreed.

I felt the presence of someone, so we both looked up to see, Kenya, with her lips tooted up. I swore, I saw steam radiating from the top of her head. She crossed her arms.

"I need to talk to, you!" She demanded, and I released a deep sigh.

She was really starting to irk, my fucking nerves, because she wasn't taking no for an answer. When she had me, she ain't want me, now all of a sudden, she shows up to damn near every function, I throw, or I'm at.

"I'm busy." Was all I said, her eyes grew wide. "Was there something you needed?"

"Never mind, don't even worry about it." Kenya was definitely embarrassing herself, but I dismissed her, because of how she played me in the past. When I wanted to talk, she was blocking my number and shit. Plus, this party was not the place to be trying to get my attention.

I chuckled, as Kenya glared at, Heaven, who paid her no attention whatsoever, as she typed away on her phone, and fanned herself, with her other hand. It was hot as fuck outside, felt like got damn three-hundred degrees.

Kenya flipped her hair over her shoulder and stormed off fast as hell. Heaven's home girl, Renaissance, started laughing uncontrollably at Kenya's behavior. "Well damn who got her panties all in a bunch?"

I remained silent and shook my head. Heaven stood up and my eyes roamed all over her body.

"Excuse me, I need to use the restroom." She said, sweet-ly.

"I'll come with you girl." Renaissance stated.

"When you go inside make your first left, then a right." I told them.

She responded by saying, "Okay, I'll be right back."

Something about her intrigued me. Her body language, charisma and vibe, were appealing.

Heaven

"Girl, Banks, was all over you. He wants some of your cookie." Renaissance cracked up at her own joke, as we stepped into his huge guest bathroom and closed the door.

I was barely paying attention to her. I really didn't need her following me to the bathroom, I needed to be alone. My nerves were bad and even the slightest mention of, Naheem, always made me tear up. I wanted to fight him for making me feel this way, my emotions were, all out of whack.

"Girl this bathroom is nice as hell! No as a matter of fact, this whole house is nice as hell. Banks is definitely making good money." She was walking around the bathroom, snapping pictures and videos for Snap chat.

I began to sob rather loudly, causing Renaissance, to rush to my side.

My head was throbbing, I just wanted to go home.

"Heaven, babes, are you alright?" Renaissance questioned. "Is it your period? I have a tampon."

"I feel hot, dizzy, and weak." Just that fast, I was in a sour mood. I blew my nose and wiped my tears. When I turned to Renaissance, I gave her a fake smile, attempting to reassure her, I was fine.

"You don't look, so good." She placed her hand on my forehead, and I sluggishly pushed it away.

"Oh my god." She shouted, as my body fell forward into her. "What's wrong, Heaven?" I could hear the panic in Renaissance's voice.

Once she laid me down onto the carpet, in the restroom, she filled her hands with water, to throw on my face.

I was unable to speak, as I floated in and out of consciousness.

"Stay right here!" she yelled. "I'm going to get some one!" She said, as if I was actually going somewhere.

She ran from the bathroom in search of some help.

Everything went dark. My heart was beating fast, I could barely breathe. Renaissance quickly returned and started fanning me.

A few moments later, I heard a male's voice say, "I think she's dehydrated—back up for a second." I automatically recognized the voice as, Bank's, voice. I felt him lift me up wedding style and my eyes fluttered open. The sounds of people asking, "What happened to her?" and "Is she going to be, okay?" could faintly be heard.

Banks looked down at me, and his face was a blur. "Heaven, everything is going to be, okay. I promise."

"Here's some water, Boss." I heard someone say. Banks laid me down, on what felt like the softest bed ever, then I felt the cool contents against my lips.

"Sip on this for me, baby." His voice was tender and filled with concern.

If I wasn't in the condition, I was in, I may have cracked a smile, because, Banks, was by my side the entire time when he could've been tending to his party guests. That meant a lot to me.

"Bring me some Gatorade out of the cooler, she needs some electrolytes." Banks demanded as my eyes struggled to open. A few moments later, he replaced the water, with Gatorade, and held it to my mouth, with one hand, as the other hand laid behind my head to hold me up. After drinking damned near the whole bottle, my body finally started to cool down.

Banks

2 hours later

"Renaissance I swear to you, on everything I love, nothing is going to happen to your friend." I told her for the millionth time, as she stood outside my guest bedroom, trying to go inside.

She shook her head. "I don't trust that shit. I need to get my friend, so we can go."

She tried to go around me to get into the room, but I blocked her attempts. We stared at each other, silently for about a minute.

She scoffed. "Well can I at least, say goodbye to her?" She questioned, with worried eyes.

"She's sleeping, I really don't want to wake her. She passed out, because of the fact, that it happened at my house I just want her here with me, so I can watch over her."

She pointed at me. "Okay, fine I'll leave her here, but let me find out you tried something, we will be fighting." she joked. "My girl is already going through a very tough time, she doesn't need the extra stress."

Skye, who'd been standing behind, Renaissance, texting on her phone, finally looked up to speak momentarily.

"Girl let's go! My feet are killing me in these heels." She winced in pain, prior to speaking. "My boss isn't that kind of, nigga! Your friend is going to be safe, I can assure you of that."

I thanked Skye for backing me up.

Renaissance released a deep sigh. "Okay, well give me your phone."

I retrieved my phone from my pocket and slid it into her hands after putting in the lock code. I watched, as she programmed her number.

"Please call me if anything happens."

"Okay, no problem." I replied.

Skye gave me a hug and bid me goodbye, so did Renaissance. Once the two of them were gone, I opened up the guest room door, and peeked inside, just to make sure, Heaven, was still sleeping.

I had never been in this situation and I was concerned for her well-being. On top of that, I had a long day of hosting my party and entertaining guests, so I was just about ready to lay my ass down, but I needed to shower first.

Once in the bathroom, I turned the water on high and practically dove in it. I released a satisfying sigh once the hot water hit my back. I had been doing so much lately, I really needed to relax. I was doing shows damn near every night, appearances, and I was in the studio all the time. I was definitely going to enjoy the rest of my weekend, it would be back to business on Monday.

I dried off and wrapped my towel around the lower half of my body when I got out twenty minutes later. When I entered my bedroom to grab a pair of boxers and basketball shorts, I stopped walking when I saw, Heaven, curled up in my bed.

She was so fucking beautiful, even while sleeping with her long jet-black hair sprawled all over the place, her pouty lips looked kissable, even while sleeping and she was laying on her stomach, so her ass was tooted up in the air. She still had on that damn bikini-thong, from earlier. I was literally, two seconds away from grabbing or smacking her fat ass. She must've been hot, because she had the covers down around her ankles.

I walked over to her lightly and pushed her hair out of her face.

"Heaven." I called her name, softly, when she didn't wake up, I shook her lightly and she stirred in her sleep until her eyes fluttered open.

I smiled down at her. "Hey, how you feeling?"

"I'm okay." She said, with her eyes still half closed.

I leaned down and gave her a kiss on the cheek and she smiled sweetly.

"Don't be kissing on me." she joked. "We still not all the way cool."

"Oh yeah?"

I chuckled and made my way over to my dresser to avoid dripping any more water onto the floor.

"I can kiss on you all I want to, you're lying in my bed." I joked, and she playfully rolled her eyes. "What are you doing in my bed anyways?" I was curious to know.

"I woke up with the worst headache ever. Plus, I'm hungry as hell, so I came in here to ask you, if you had anything to eat, but when I heard the shower, I sat down to wait for you. I guess I fell back asleep, I'm sorry." A look of embarrassment washed over her face.

"It's okay. I don't mind."

I grabbed a big t-shirt, and a pair of sweat pants, and handed it to her.

"What's this for?" she questioned.

"If you would like to take a shower, you can do so in the guest bathroom, and here are some clothes for you to put on, afterwards. I'll order some food for us, as well." She smiled and accepted the clothes.

"Thank you." she said, sweetly.

"No problem."

I used one hand to hold up my towel and the other, to help her out of bed. As she walked out of the room, slowly we made eye contact. My eyes traveled down to her ass. It jiggled with every step, she took, it was then, that I realized she had definitely worn that outfit for me today.

I shook my head, to shake off all of the nasty thoughts floating around in my head. Once she was out of the room, I continued my task of getting dressed.

Chapter 11

Heaven

I heard a knock on the guest room door as soon as, I finished getting dressed from my shower. I'd literally, just sat down, because I was feeling a little weak. I was hardly in the mood to be getting up to open the door, but I heard another knock, which prompted me, to try my best to get out of bed. I still couldn't believe, I'd pushed myself so hard, that I passed out. I hadn't been eating much and on top of that, I was dehydrated. I was still embarrassed about passing out in front of everyone, and practically ruining the party.

I opened the door and saw, Banks, standing on the other side. When I swung the door open, the first thing I noticed, was that he'd changed and was in a simple black wife beater, black and blue basketball shorts, black socks and a pair of Gucci slides. What he had on was simple, but he looked good enough to fucking eat, with his fine ass. He smelled so good, too. His cologne tickled my nose, as he licked his lips, and smiled at me. I could tell, he was staring at my body, because his eyes weren't on my eyes.

"You gonna let me in?" He questioned smoothly, as he leaned against the doorframe.

"Oh, yeah, I'm sorry." I was staring at his ass just as hard as he was staring at me, so it slipped my mind to let him in.

I stepped to the side and let him in, he immediately flopped down on the guest bed. He leaned back a little, so he was leaning on his toned arms, as his feet hung off of the bed.

"Thanks for coming to check on me." I took a seat next to him, and he smiled, showing off his deep dimples. This man was literally sent from heaven, with his chocolaty smooth Hershey's colored skin, deep dimples, chiseled abs, full luscious lips, and —

"No problem. I told you, I'd come to check on you beautiful."

I turned my head a little, so that he wouldn't see me blushing. At least some one cared about me.

"So, my phone is completely dead." I changed the subject. "I wanted to contact my friends, to let them know, I'm awake and to come get me."

"Don't sweat it." He said, glancing down at his phone. "I'll text, Renaissance, and tell her you're up, but I really think, you should stay the night."

My eyebrows rose.

"Stay the night?"

"Yeah, it's going on midnight. I can just drop you home in the morning, baby. I don't want her to have to go through the hassle, to come all the way back over here. Plus, I just want to make sure you're okay." He cheesed.

"Well, thank you. I appreciate that."

A few moments passed, as we sat in silence. He seemed occupied with what was going on in his phone, I swore, I saw him screw up his face, in annoyance.

"Everything good?" I said, breaking the silence.

"Yeah, I just have some—"

"Women problems?" I already knew the deal, so he didn't have to explain. Well, I halfway knew the deal, because he definitely, had some girl following him all around the party like a puppy, so I assumed she was his girl.

He lightly chuckled, then looked up at me as he pocketed his phone. "I mean if that's what you want to call it, then sure."

"I call it like I see it. That girl was literally on you, like white on rice."

He sighed. "Yeah, that was, my ex-girlfriend."

The bitch practically, mean mugged every female up in there, including me. She was a gorgeous girl, but she didn't strike me as his type.

"She's trying to get back with me and shit, but I'm not gone let that shit fly."

There was a knock at the door. "Oh, that must be the food. I hope Chinese food is okay, there's a spot down the street, that I ordered from." He left the room momentarily.

I sat on the bed adjusting my hair, hoping I looked good in his presence. He walked back in, with a big brown paper bag.

"I got this for you, I know you're hungry." He had already begun fixing his food.

I was definitely hungry, as hell. I just didn't want to seem greedy. "Yeah, can you fix me a little bit?"

He glanced over his shoulder, at me, and I swear the way he looked at me, made me feel tingly inside. As his tongue snaked slowly out of his mouth, across his lips, I almost wanted to jump on his sexy ass.

"I got you, baby," He responded, casually.

I loved how laid back he was, most rappers were self-centered assholes.

A few moments later, he passed me my plate, and I watched, as he walked across the room, to the mini bar. He grabbed two bottles of water. He handed me one, then sat down in his same-seated position.

He took a bite of food, getting duck sauce on his bottom lip. He even made eating look good, I just wanted to lick the sauce off of his lips.

Being away from, Naheem, seemed to heighten my horniness. We had sex a lot, and I was definitely missing the feel of a real man, on top of me and inside of me. Shit, at this point, I'd take any dick whether it was real or plastic. I just needed a quick fix, from a big, fat, long dick.

"Did you hear me?" He said, causing me to jump. I needed to get my mind out of the gutter.

"What did you say, I'm sorry?"

"This food is good as fuck. You haven't even touched your plate." He stuffed more food into his mouth, all while never breaking eye contact with me.

"Oh, I—"

There was a loud knock, at the front door, causing the both of us to glance in the direction of the door, then back at one another briefly.

"You expecting someone?" I questioned, he shook his head no. I was just as confused as he was.

"Who the fuck is at, my door unannounced? He said, sounding more like he was talking to himself, than to me. He laid his plate down, then stood up.

He walked out of the room, pulling up his pants in the process, I heard him suck his teeth on his way out.

"Why did you show up to, my house uninvited?" I overheard him say.

I wasn'r surprised to see the same chick from earlier, that followed him around the party, barged in and roughly pushed the guest bedroom door open. She didn't look too pleased, quite frankly, I didn't care.

"Yo', you need to get the fuck out, Lakenya! Why you barging in here, like you done lost yo' mind?" Banks roared.

She stared at me, and I glared back at her dumbass.

"What the fuck, you got going on, Banks? Y'all having an after party or something." She was trying to be cynical, but neither of us cared about her sarcasm, at that point.

"What I'm doing is none of your business." I almost wanted to laugh, because he looked overly annoyed, by this girl who I'm guessing was his ex-situation.

She began to pout, like a child, as she latched onto his shirt and put her head on his chest.

"Why are you doing this, baby?" She sobbed, but there weren't any real tears on her face.

He pulled away from her, and when she tried to latch onto him again, he caught her hands into his and shoved her backwards gently.

"Stop fucking touching me, Lakenya!"

Her eyes grew wide as hell, with shock written all over her face.

112

"What we had is done, and it's going to stay that fucking way. You ain't want a nigga, when I had nothing, now all of a sudden I get a lil' money and a lil' fame, now you tryna be all on my dick again." He waved her off. "I ain't tryna go there with you again."

Her mouth dropped open in shock. I couldn't help it, and started laughing.

She rolled her eyes at me, instantly. "Fuck you laughing for, bitch?" She tried to step closer to me, but Banks stepped in between us.

"Don't talk to her like that, she don't have shit to do with our situation."

Lakenya threw her hands up in defeat. "Whatever don't come crawling back to me, when—"

"I won't!" He cut her off midsentence.

"Yeah, because he's going to be too busy, eating this pussy!" I countered, trying to add fuel to the fire.

She gave me a dirty ass look, then she stormed out of the room, so fast you would've thought, her feet were on fire. As soon as the door closed, we both couldn't contain our laughter.

I sat back down on the bed, next to my plate of food and grabbed my bottle of water, to take a few sips as our laughter died down.

Banks walked over to my side of the bed, leaned down, and placed his hands on either side of me. A smug smirk was plastered on his face.

"Oh, I'ma be busy eating that pussy, huh?" We stared into each other's eyes, all I could do was shake my head.

"That's what I said, ain't it?" I replied, bluntly. "I say what I mean—and I mean, what I say." I took another sip all while keeping eye contact with, Banks.

A few moments later, he finally broke eye contact with me.

"You funny." He backed away from me, until his back was against the nearby wall, and he leaned on it casually.

I watched as he pulled his cellphone from his pocket. I assumed he was checking to see, if he had any missed calls or text messages.

"I need to get some sleep, though. You gonna be good in here by yourself?"

"I'm good, go get some rest." I winked at him, causing him to cheese widely.

"Okay, I'll see you tomorrow, and uh I'm sorry again about what just happened with, my ex." I could see the sincerity in his eyes.

I stood up and stretched a little, after I'd placed my water onto the bedside table. I gave him a reassuring smile. I could care less about that damn girl.

"It's okay."

Once we got to the guest room door, he turned to face me. I was surprised to feel his strong arms, as they wrapped around my body. I got up on my tippy toes and wrapped my arms around his neck, as my breathing increased. I didn't want him to leave, because I really wanted some company, but I knew, if he didn't I'd probably do some things, I may or may not regret. He kissed me on the cheek.

"Goodnight." I managed, to say as he gave me the same response.

As soon as the door closed, I released a breath, I didn't know I was holding. I touched my cheek and smiled because, his lips were so soft, I could still feel them on my cheek.

I had been lonely, and was in desperate need of some male companionship. It didn't necessarily have to be a sexual encounter. I just really wanted someone to talk to, cuddle with, go on dates with and just someone, who understood what I was going through. I needed someone to keep my mind off, Naheem.

I didn't know, what the hell Banks and I, had going on, but I was curious to know more about him. He definitely stayed on my mind, as I drifted off to sleep.

She Fell in Love with a Real One

About two hours or so later, I woke up when I heard, commotion coming from the living room. I yawned, stretched, then got out of bed. The music from the living room was pretty loud.

I opened the door and made my way into the living room, only to see Banks sitting on the couch with his head in his hands. I thought about turning around and going back into the guest room, to get back into bed, but he looked like he needed someone to talk to. I put my hand on his shoulder, startling him. He slightly jumped and when he looked back at me, he had a tear stained face. It was then, I realized he had been crying, and the loud music was probably to drown out his cries.

He leaned forward and grabbed the remote to the stereo. Once the music was turned down, he wiped his eyes, previously looking back up at me.

"I'm sorry." I sat down next to him on the couch. "I didn't mean to startle you."

"It's okay." He replied softly. "I didn't mean to wake you."

He took a few sips from the glass sitting on the table, which I assumed was filled with Hennessey, because of the brown contents within the glass.

"Banks it's, okay. I'm more so concerned, with what's going on, with you." I placed my hand on his back, rubbing it up and down a few times.

He released a deep sigh, pausing to collect his thoughts.

He cleared his throat. "My mother was—she was hospitalized, last week due to a car accident. Her face was cut up pretty badly and she's taking it hard. Her car was totaled, but she's doing well. She was released this morning. I was at her house all morning, prior to the party, making sure she was good. I just don't know what to do." He let out another deep sigh, as he sat back, massaging his temples.

"Oh—I'm sorry to hear, about your mother. I had no idea."

He continued, sipping on his Hennessy. His eyes never left mine. "It's not your fault, baby. I've been trying to keep her out of the limelight, as much as possible, because I don't like every fucking body knowing my business."

I didn't know what to say, so I kept quiet. I didn't want to say the wrong thing.

He placed his glass onto the coffee table, then turned his attention back towards me. "My mom is a very strong woman, it kills me to see her like this. To see her all bandaged up, lying lifeless-like in that hospital bed, fucking hurt me. To see my little brother, cry and hear her say, she doesn't think she's beautiful, anymore—" He paused. "I just don't know, what to do. I threw that stupid ass party to get my mind off this shit, but it didn't really help."

I scooted closer to him on the couch, slowly rubbing his back making sure to comfort him.

"All you can do is be there for her in this time of need. Uplift her and comfort her, when she needs it the most. You guys are going to be, okay."

He seemed to be deep in thought. I saw his eyes glaze over and few moments later a tear fell from his eye. I wiped it then grabbed his chin gently.

"Hey look at me." Once I had his attention, I continued. "You're very lucky, to still have your mom on this earth. Do you hear me?"

He shook his head.

"Everything is going to be, okay." I pulled him into a hug, wrapping one arms around his neck, and the other behind his back.

"You lost your mother?" he quizzed.

"Yes. I know she's looking down on, my sister and I. She was truly an, angel." I smiled at the thought of her. "She was an amazing woman."

"What happened to her?" When I remained silent, he reached to grab my hands. "I'm sorry. You don't have to tell me, I apologize."

I gave him a coy smile. "It's okay, I'll tell you."

****

My mother, Vaeh and I, were sitting at the kitchen table scarfing down the dinner she'd made.

"Slow down, child, the food ain't going anywhere." Mom said, as she referred to the meatloaf, mashed potatoes and green peas, Vaeh was eating super-fast.

"Next thing you know, she's going to be complaining about her weight, yet she's always eating. That's like your third plate, right?" I joked.

Nevaeh stuck her middle finger up at me when our mom had her head down.

"Oh, hush up and leave her alone. You want some more mashed potatoes, baby?" Mom said to Vaeh, who was practically licking her plate clean.

"No ma'am" She cut her eyes at me. "I'm finished." I smirked, when she rolled her eyes.

Our mother's smile quickly turned into a frown, when she heard our father come through the door. Instead of him heading in the back, or collapsing on the couch, my dad headed straight for the kitchen. He was stumbling and could barely stand up. My mom shook her head and continued to eat her food.

"Hi daddy." Vaeh and I said, in unison.

He placed a sloppy wet kiss on my forehead and then another on Vaeh's cheek.

He halfway smiled, then said,. "How are my b—beautiful daughters, d—doing tonight?" His words slurred, so we could all tell, he'd had way too many drinks. That didn't stop him from stumbling over to the refrigerator to retrieve a beer.

117

"*Good.*" *We said in union, once more with wide smiles present on our faces. We'd always been daddy's girls.*

"*You know what? Gone on ahead and give ya, daddy and I a second to talk.*"

"*What about the dishes, mama?*" *I always took care of the dishes for her, being that she prepared our meals, but oddly enough, she declined my offer to clear the table.*

"*Okay, goodnight mama.*" *I said, giving her a kiss on the cheek.*

Vaeh had already taken off towards our room, but she managed to say over her shoulder, "*Goodnight.*"

"*Goodnight babies.*" *She said, sweetly.*

Once inside of our room, I sat down on my bed, as Nevaeh plopped down on her bed, across the room and pulled her cellphone from the charger.

She sucked her teeth. "*Marquis's ass still ain't call, me.*" *She said in an irritated tone.*

"*You need to leave his big forehead ass alone.*" *I chuckled.* "*That boy looks like, E.T.*"

I ducked when she threw her pillow at me. It rolled off of my bed and hit the floor.

"*You need to mind your own business.*" *she retorted.*

"*You just mad, because, you know it's true.*"

Our parents began to argue, halting our dispute.

"*You always in the got damn streets acting like you don't have two kids and a wife, at home! I want you to get yo' shit and get the fuck out. I'm done with, your sorry ass!*" *Our mother yelled at the top of her lungs.*

Our parents argued often, but we never paid them any mind, because we just thought that was something married couples did.

A few moments later, laughter poured from within the television. We'd assumed that their arguing was over, but it had only just begun.

"What are you doing?" I questioned, my sister when I saw her nosey ass crack open our room door. She peered at me, with a look of annoyance on her face.

"I wanna see what's going on."

I chuckled. "Girl you to damn nosey. Close the—"

"Keisha! What the fuck you doing?" Our father bellowed, as his deep baritone voice echoed off the walls in our small home. "You better get the fuck on somewhere or I swear to God, I'll kill ya!" The two of us jumped a little, frightened by the tone of voice he'd used and the force behind his words.

She looked back at me, as I sat on the bed with a puzzled look on my face. My hands gripped the edge of, my bed, as we listened to them continue to argue.

"Oh please!" Our mother cackled, sardonically. "Get yo' shit and go Raeshon! You are worthless, I hate you!"

"Yeah well I hate yo' ass too! That ain't nothing new."

"Come over here." Vaeh whispered to me, as she waved me over.

I nervously and reluctantly got off, my bed to peek through our cracked room door, the same way, Vaeh, had been doing. They'd gotten into several arguments in the past and it never bother us, but tonight, this argument seemed different.

Our mother walked over to him and knocked the corona out of his hands. It hit the floor and spilled all over the hard wood floor. "Oh, you think I'm kidding, huh?"

She walked away briskly and headed to their bedroom. She returned with some of his shirts, pants and boxers. She threw them at him with excessive force, showing him just how fed up she was with his mess. He stood up and walked towards her slowly.

"Touch my shit again, watch what the fuck, I do." He gritted his teeth and balled up his fists.

She bent down and grabbed the clothing items on the floor. She threw them at him, yet again.

"I'm touching yo' shit. What are you gone do?"

Our father went into the kitchen, all we heard, was the sound of utensils as they forcefully hit the floor. It sounded like he was digging through the drawers in the kitchen.

I felt an enormous bulge in my throat, as I tried to swallow, and my unsteady hands were clammy.

"What's he doing?" Vaeh quizzed, in an unsteady voice.

"I—I don't know. I'm scared, Nevaeh.

I latched onto her hand, as she tightly gripped, my hand within hers. "Me too." she replied.

From the crack in the door, we could see our father charge at our mother, with a huge butcher knife. She held her hands in an attempt to surrender, but to no avail, he still continued on with his task. They appeared to be wrestling for the knife. Along the way, they knocked over a lamp, our huge DVD collection, and a few glass cups, that had been sitting on the table for the past week, due to our father's newfound alcohol addiction.

We heard our mother scream out in agony, as he stabbed her over and over again.

"Stop! Raeshon please!" She screeched in agony.

By now, both Nevaeh and I, had begun to cry, as we held onto each other for dear life. My heart was beating wildly, and my breathing had increased significantly.

"What are we going do? We have to help, mama?" Vaeh cried out. "He—he's killing her."

My bottom lip quivered, as I opened my mouth to counter. "I—I don't know."

Vaeh ran over to the closet and began throwing things around rapidly, but my feet felt like they were glued to the floor with super glue.

"Look." She said, as she turned around with a bat.

I remembered, we'd had a bat in the closet from the time our parents tried to force us to play baseball. We hated it and got the biggest whooping in the world, after we begged to quit. Our father was so upset, that they'd spent so much money on baseball lessons and he tore our ass up.

"What are you going to do with, that?" I asked because my brain wasn't functioning properly. I was too focused on my mother's screams from the living room.

Instead of answering my question, Vaeh, swung open the door and began to creep slowly in the direction, the commotion was coming from. She held the bat high over her head, as she walked around the corner. I wiped the tears from my damp face, along with the snot, that had somehow dripped from my nose. Hesitantly, I followed her terrified of what was going to happen next.

Our mother's lifeless body was on the floor and our father kneeled next to her holding onto her hand tightly. The bloody knife was lying on the floor, next to her body. Our father, whose vision was most likely blurred, by his tears, didn't see us coming. The hardwood floors made a creaking noise, and once he turned around leisurely he made eye contact with, Vaeh, then he looked over at me.

"I'm so sorry—" He sobbed as his shoulders shook violently, from his intense weeping.

I stood closely behind, Vaeh, so close she could probably feel the hotness of my breath on her neck, as I peered around her shoulder at our father. She lifted her shaky arms and released a loud grunt, once she swung as hard as she could. The bat collided with our father's head. Once he slumped over next to our mother's body, she lifted the bat high into the air once more and hit him two more times.

I quickly shut my eyes tightly, after hearing his bones crack, and seeing blood splatter from his nose.

She threw the bat to the ground and when we were sure, he was unconscious we hurriedly got down onto the floor next to our mother's body.

"What do we do? Is she dead?" Vaeh stuttered a bit confused about the whole thing. I shook his head after lifting it up from our mother's chest.

"She's still breathing. Help me pick her up."

Together the two of us lifted, her up off of the floor. She began to moan and groan in pain, as we tried to get her to walk towards the front door. She was very weak, but her feet moved nonetheless. We managed to carry her across the street to a neighbor's house, after pushing pass the drug dealers, crack heads and prostitutes that hung out in our apartment complex. Everyone stared at us like we had eight heads, but even with seeing the blood all over our mother's body, no one stopped to help.

I couldn't stop crying. Vaeh kept giving me words of encouragement. "Mama is going to be, okay." She stated in a trembling tone of voice.

We used our free hands to bang on Mr. and Mrs. Rodgers front door, until we saw their lights come on. The Rodgers were the only white couple on the block. Whenever our mother worked late, Barbara and Stan Rodgers would watch us, until we were able to watch ourselves. Sometimes our parents barely had enough money to feed us, so they often had left overs, they'd share with our family. They were good people, more like a second family to us.

"Help—help please!" Our banging increased, until the neighbors opened the door.

Sleep was still very present on Mrs. Rodgers face, until she noticed, how distraught we were, as we held our unconscious mother.

"Oh my, God! What happened to, Keisha?" She exclaimed, horrifically with one hand on her chest, the other over her mouth.

"My mama needs help." I exclaimed, as we slowly laid our mother down on the floor. Mr. Rodgers grabbed a pillow from the couch to elevate her head.

He waved his wife over. "Call the ambulance baby— hurry up." She ran as fast as she could over, to the house phone mounted on the wall. Her fingers moved faster, than the speed of lightning as she dialed 911.

"Yes, someone is hurt. Please hurry we're at—" I tuned her out, as the whole room seemed to grow very silent. Vaeh and I caught eye contact, with one another, I'm sure she could see the frantic look on my face. I held onto my mother's right hand, as Vaeh held onto the other.

I sobbed. "Is my mama going to be, okay?"

I felt a hand softly rub my shoulder.

"I sure hope so, suga." Barbara said, after informing us that the ambulance was on the way.

****

Banks wiped away my tears.

"Unfortunately, my mother wasn't okay, she passed away on the way to the hospital. That was the most devastating and traumatic thing that had ever happened to, my sister and I. Our grandmother took us in and raised us through the rest of high school."

"I'm so sorry, that happened to her."

I smiled through my tears. "It's okay. I always try to think of good memories about her, because she truly was an amazing person."

Banks

At this point, I was kind of confused, about what was going on. Here I was sitting on my sofa, with a woman, I barely knew. I had no idea, why I was opening up to her the way, I was. Even my friends didn't even know what was going on, because, I chose to keep it that way.

Her fingertips grazed my back, as she slowly massaged me in slow-moving circles trying to make me feel better, as I did the same. I didn't like to see her hurting. I wasn't able to bring her mother back, but I could be there for her if she ever needed to talk.

I pulled her into a tight hug, allowing her to cry on my shoulder. "I'm here if you ever need to talk, okay?" I felt

123

connected to her, for some reason. I needed her to know, I could be there for here, if ever she needed me.

"Okay." She sniffled.

When we pulled away from our hug, she smiled sweetly at me, pushing her hair behind her ears. I looked at her, taking in her amazingly gorgeous face.

"What's wrong?" She laughed nervously. "Why are you looking at me like that?" She questioned, giving me a puzzled look.

"You're so fucking beautiful, I just can't stop looking at you." I admitted, but it wasn't the liquor talking.

I watched as she blushed, looked down at her hands momentarily, then back up at me.

"Can I ask you something?" she asked. "It's kind of random."

I nodded my head. "Sure."

"I have been racking my brain, trying to come up with a reason why, my soon to be ex-husband cheated on me. I try very hard not to think about it, but I can't stop. Is there something wrong with me?" she asked.

I grabbed her hands, pulling them up to my lips. She was taken aback by my actions, but she still allowed me to move forward. I kissed her hands and massaged them softly.

"Fuck that, nigga. Don't waste your time thinking about someone, who obviously doesn't care about you. He's the one missing out on an amazing woman. You're beautiful, accomplished, and you have a good head on your shoulders. Anyone would be lucky to have you."

"Thank you." she said softly. "You're right."

We stared into each other's eyes and I used my grasp on her hands to pull her closer.

"Come here." I commanded smoothly.

I licked my lips, as she scooted closer to me. She looked nervous, as I latched onto the front of her shirt. As I pulled her closer, I could feel her breath on my lips. Without further ado, I leaned in and kissed her.

Heaven

His tongue glided its way into my mouth, causing my tongue to slow dance with his in a slow rhythm. My hands found their way to the back of his neck to deepen the kiss.

A groan escaped his mouth, as he moved closer to me and closed the space between us, while gripping my hips. There was no hiding the sexual tension floating around the room.

"I want you." He whispered against my lips.

"W—wait." I managed to pull away, we were both breathing intensely.

I had so many things swarming around in my head. I wasn't sure if I wanted to take it there with him, but he was making it hard as hell to say no.

I could see, that his pants were beginning to rise as his dick was becoming hard, it was probably feigning for my throbbing pulsating pussy.

He stared at me as if I was a full course meal. His hands instantly gravitated towards my breasts. We kept eye contact, as he slid his hands up the front of my shirt to fondle my breasts.

"Wait." I said breathlessly, but my plea landed upon deaf ears. His mouth replaced his hands and fully covered my nipples, as he sucked them very delicately.

My hands deceived me and gripped his wife beater to hold him in place, not wanting him to remove his mouth.

"Hold on real, quick." He said, as he quickly got up leaving me baffled.

He went into the kitchen and retrieved a can of whip cream.

"Take this off." He said referring to the shirt he had given me to wear.

I quickly removed my shirt, wanting him to suck on my nipples once more. I watched, as he sprayed whip cream all over my breasts.

"Lay on the floor." he demanded.

Like a child, being punished for some sort of wrongdoing, I obeyed him. "Okay."

Lying on my back, the coldness of the floor, felt good against my exposed back. He smiled at me, causing me to blush. He got in between my legs, and hovered ever me. His tongue glided across my skin, and his lips soon wrapped around my nipples. He equally sucked, licked, and bit each one.

Banks then left butterfly kisses all over my chest leading a trail up to my collarbone. He sucked hungrily on my neck, locating my spot right away. His hands fondled my breasts and tender nipples, while I slipped one hand into his boxers caressing his long, fat, hard dick.

He was harder than a rock and I knew why. This encounter was long overdue. He moved his lower half, thrusting forward, to meet the movements of my hands.

Heading downtown, he began licking his lips hungrily, as he tugged at my sweats. I didn't have on any panties, so once the sweats were fully removed, he had a clear view of my freshly shaved pussy.

Banks dove in headfirst. At the feel of his velvet like lips kissing the inside of my thighs, I arched my back, anticipating the feel of his lips on my glistening pussy.

He took in one deep breath, smelling my clean pussy. The fresh smell made his mouth literally water. He couldn't wait to taste. His lips made an O shape, as he softly blew on my pussy.

The cold air caused me to squirm around. My eyes were shut, so tight, that I hadn't noticed him retrieving an ice cube from the freezer. "I wanna taste that pussy, baby; spread them legs wider." He commanded sucking on a cube, melting it in the process. Banks used his index and pointer finger, to spread my pretty pussy apart, he placed his cold tongue into my slit causing me to gasp. "Don't fucking run, either." he said.

His tongue began to fuck my little pink bud slowly. Taking in a deep breath, I let out a moan, capturing my bottom lip into my mouth. I bit down hard enough to draw blood. With my legs on his shoulder and his hands holding them in place, so I wouldn't even think to run, Banks, now had my whole clit in his mouth, holding it captive, while his snake like tongue flicked across my sensitive clit, driving me completely over the edge.

He reached up, grabbing onto my breasts, giving them a light squeeze, rubbing his thumb over my darkened nipple.

I could feel my toes curling and the sensation building at the pit of my stomach, traveling throughout my entire body. With the way my legs were shaking, I knew I was on the verge of exploding. Digging deeper into my Lotus flower, Banks, awaited the sweet nectar

"Sit on my face, baby." he said.

I did as I was told, as he quickly flipped me over and had me ride his face. He sped up thrusting faster.

"Oh my, God" I moaned. "I—I'm about to cum." Shaking and fighting for air, I rode his face like a horse at the derby. I released my flavoring into his awaiting mouth. Drinking up my juices, like I was a cold glass of water, on a hot summer day, he licked me clean and slowly released my legs, that were still shaking like I was having a seizer.

After removing his head from between my shaky thighs Banks flipped me back onto my back. He slipped his tongue into my awaiting mouth that was still agape; he kissed me passionately and aggressively letting me taste the remains of my nectar of his tongue.

My hands rested behind his head, as he deepened the kiss. Then Banks, hurriedly discarded his boxers and his dick sprung out, like a snake ready to attack its prey. Hovering over me he began to suck lightly on my neck, while stroking his big dick.

"I want it, now." I whispered, more than ready to have him inside of me. As I read the lust in my eyes, Banks, knew what time it was, as he banged my pussy with his dick. He slid inside of me, with no warning leaving me breathless.

My mouth slightly open in an 'O' shape, as a moan slipped out of my attractive flushed lips.

I felt like I was in a daze, while he stroked me hard and deep, causing me to claw at his back, like a cat clawing the bark of a tree.

"Fuck!" he groaned. He looked into my eyes, loving seeing the effect, he had on me.

I moaned loud, hitting a high note, that would put Whitney Houston, to shame. I clinged to him like my life depended on it, holding on tight. With each stroke, our bodies slid across the tiled floor, almost like he was mopping the floor with my sweaty body.

He lifted one of my shaky legs up, so he could get better access to go deeper, then he moved deeper inside my hot pussy, with no mercy.

"Turn around!" Banks demanded, while moving up from on top of me, giving me space to get to the next position. His demands turned me on to the point of no return.

I got on all fours, ass up in the air, with an arch in my back. Banks smacked me hard, on the ass causing it to sting, and make my juices trickle down the inside of my thighs. He entered me from the back fast and hard. I let out a throaty moan.

"Talk nasty to, daddy." He said in between thrusts.

I did as I was told. "Fuck me, daddy." I said.

I squeezed my tight walls around his thick shaft, and twirled my hips around on his dick, throwing my ass back hard as fuck onto his thick long pole. He grabbed ahold of my hair, lightly pulling while, stroking me slow and deep.

"I fucking love it, when you say shit like that, ma."

I could feel his balls slapping against, my pussy, with how deep he was. I could feel him in my stomach. You could hear the banging and smacking of our bodies echoing off of the walls.

She Fell in Love with a Real One

"You feel all of me?" He whispered into my ear.

I nodded my head, answering his question. No words could escape my lips even if I wanted them to.

I was a goner, as tears threatened to fall from my eyes from the amazing feeling he was putting my body through.

I could feel that amazing feeling over coming me once again. I had reached my peak, leaking my sweet nectar all over his dick and the tiled floor, as my body shook violently like a stripper, dancing for single dollar bills.

Banks grunted behind me, and quickly pulled out, spilling his seeds on the arch of my back and ass cheeks. Then he collapsed onto the cold, kitchen tiled floor, right along with me, so drained out, neither of us wanted to move.

Tamara Butler

Chapter 12

Heaven

The next morning

Banks had awakened me to go to breakfast. So, here I was fully dressed in his clothing, looking like a straight up boy. But, the way he looked at me, made me feel like the prettiest girl in the world. I had yet to go home, so his clothes would have to do for now. I was still a little taken aback, after what happened last night. I planned on addressing it over breakfast.

"Thank you." I smiled sweetly, as the waitress at IHOP passed me a tall glass of water. She practically ignored me, and turned all of her attention towards, Banks.

"Here you go. Your food will be out shortly." She said seductively.

I almost wanted to laugh, because he was not paying her ass any mind. He was focused on his phone, as usual.

She leaned forward with her hand on the table, biting her lip. "If there's anything else, you need don't hesitate to call me over."

"Thank you, baby." He said, causing her to squeal.

I shook my head, and when he finally looked up at her, she blushed so damn hard, I thought her cheeks were going to fall off.

It was crazy how women threw themselves at him, but it was quite entertaining at the same damn time. She spun on her heels and turned to walk away.

I smirked, then directed my attention back over to, Banks.

"Uh—excuse me, sir. Am I here to eat breakfast with you, or your phone?" I said sarcastically, which caused him to chuckle.

He locked his phone and placed it in his pocket. I watched, as he intertwined his hands and made eye contact with me.

131

"I apologize, I just had to read a few emails and check with my assistant about my schedule for the week."

"I guess you're a busy man." I said, taking a few sips of my water.

"Not really." he shrugged. "I make time for the people, I wanna make time for, though." His words caught me off guard.

"Look, about last night—" Our waitress came back over with our food, deterring our conversation.

She placed the plates down in front of us and again, she gave, Banks, the googly eyes. He looked at her confused, as she stood by our table for a few extra seconds.

"Call me if you need anything." She tried to be discreet and slip him her phone number, while handing us napkins. As soon as she walked away, I snatched up the napkin and read it out loud.

"I'd love to show you a good time, call me anytime, and I'll keep you satisfied." He tried to snatch the napkin from me, with a smile on his face.

"Oh, so that's how you got it?" I questioned, with furrowed brows.

"I ain't ask her for that shit, and it ain't my fault, I look so fucking good." He popped an imaginary collar, as I threw the napkin at him. It landed on the brim of his fitted cap. He snatched the napkin down and threw it back at me, but I ducked.

"See how you wanna play." He said, but I couldn't stop laughing. "Man, I can't stand yo' ass, Heaven."

"I love you, too, boo." I joked, as I reached to grab the original flavored syrup for my pancakes.

"Let me see, that when you done."

I passed him the syrup, then I started to go to work on my plate. My stomach was growling, I was hungry as hell, and didn't want to wait any further.

"Damn, baby slow down." Banks said, as I glared at him.

"I'm so hungry." I said, with a mouth full of eggs.

"The food ain't going anywhere, baby" I cut my eyes at him, as I watched him cut his pancakes and sausage. He damn near poured the whole bottle of syrup on his food.

I frowned. "Do you really need that much syrup?"

"Mind ya business."

I smirked. "Oh whatever."

The two of us grew silent, as we stuffed our faces with food.

"Girl that is him sitting over there." I overheard, a woman say. WhenI looked over my shoulder, I locked eyes with a dark-skinned woman.

I rolled my eyes and turned back around, to see that Bank's eyes were on her, as well. She walked up to our table and stopped directly in front of it.

"Heyyy." The dark-skinned woman, said eyeing Banks with a big ass cheesy grin on her face.

He gave her a head nod. "How you doing?" He asked smoothly, as he reached for a clean napkin to wipe the syrup from his lips.

"You that nigga, Banks, with TMG Records, right?" She questioned, which caused him to release a small chuckle.

"Yeah that's me."

"I thought, that was you sitting over here. I'm a really big fans of yours. Can you sign my, boobs?" She replied. My eyes grew wide when she tried to really pull her got damn titties out.

I interrupted her. "We're eating breakfast, as you can see." I said, with an attitude.

She rolled her eyes and looked at me. "Good, I hope it tastes real good." She said, sarcastically, then looked back over at, Banks. "Anyways I was thinking, we could get out of here and—"

"Okay, hold up. You're not about to bring yo' ass over here and be disrespectful in front of my face." I interjected.

She crossed her arms with a smug look on her face. I wasn't trying to cause any problems, but I for damn sure wasn't about to sit at this table, while different hoes continued to walk up and shoot their shot.

She scoffed. "No one was talking to you. I did not come over here for you, so you need to mind your damn—"

Banks cuts her off. "Listen, I understand, you're a fan baby, but don't come over here with that. I'm not interested, anyways."

"Why? Is she your girl or something?" She asked, with her hands on her hips. She really wasn't taking no for an answer.

"That's irrelevant, right now. We just wanna finish our breakfast." he countered.

I was ready to shove my foot down her throat, but luckily for her, the manager made his way over to our table in the nick of time.

"Hi, I'm Ricardo, the restaurant manager. Is there a problem?" He asked, as he looked back and forth between the three of us.

I rolled my eyes, "Yes, there is a problem. This woman—"

"Was just leaving." She said, cutting me off. She gave me one last look, then averted her eyes over at, Bank's who'd already went back to eating his food. "Nice meeting you." She said, casually, then walked off trying to strut just like the damn waitress.

"Mr. Banks is there anything you need? It's on the house." He gave the both of us a huge grin.

I could tell, that he probably wasn't used to seeing celebrities up close, with the way, he was nervously fidgeting.

"I'm good. Bring the check, though. I'll pay for it." I was a little impressed, by the fact that he turned down free food.

"Okay, sir, I'm on it." He quickly walked off, as I sat back, and rubbed my full belly. I felt like I was about to burst open from scarfing down all of that food.

"Why'd you do that?"

He looked at me confused.

"What?" He leaned back, as well and gave me his undivided attention.

"The manager said, the food was on the house."

He shrugged nonchalantly. "I know."

This time I gave him a confused look, I felt, I was missing something, especially when he started laughing at my facial expression.

"I never had anything given to me. I had to work for every fucking thing I have now. I did it, without any handouts. I don't need a muthafucka trying to offer me free IHOP, just because of who I am."

I just shook my head.

"Why you over there shaking that big ass head of yours." He joked, which caused me to laugh.

"Hey! It's a bunch of syrup on this table, I'm not sure you really want to go there with me." I teased.

He put his hands up in mock surrender. "I'm sorry, please don't shoot me, with syrup, baby girl." he kidded.

"Here you go, sir." The manager, returned, with the check.

Banks slid him fifty dollars even, though our meal combined was a far less amount, then we dipped.

Once inside of his car, he asked, "So, what do you have planned for today?"

"Nothing much to be honest."

"So, you know, what you should do?" He turned, to look at me, and when we locked eyes he licked his big luscious lips. "You should slide to the studio with me."

My eyes grew wide. "You want me to go to the studio, with you?"

He shook his head. "That's what I said, right?"

I popped him lightly on the shoulder. "Okay—keep getting slick, it'll be your eyes next time."

He tore his eyes away from the road, once more, and glared at me. "I'm up for the challenge."

I was sure, I looked like a straight up fool, cheesing hard as hell, all up in this man's face, but there was just something about him, that made me feel all bubbly on the inside.

"Okay, I'll go."

"A'ight bet."

I was jumping for joy, on the inside, knowing he wanted to spend more time with me. Nowadays, I hated being alone, so, I was definitely down to spend the day with him.

Banks

At the studio

"What the hell are you doing in here, Lakenya? I'm working." Her face softened up a bit.

I wouldn't say, I didn't care about her, because I did, but I wasn't trying to be in a relationship anymore. She left and ignored me, for weeks, so excuse the hell out of me for doing the same shit back to her.

I had been ignoring her calls and text messages, but somehow, she always managed to pop up on me at the wrong moments. I knew, she followed me on social media, that's how she always knew where I was. So, I made a mental note to block her ass.

I shook my head and looked down at my phone to check my emails.

She must've figured, this would be the only place, she could corner me and get me to talk to her, but she was very wrong. I was about to dismiss her ass and get right back in the booth. The only reason security let her back here was because, I allowed it, to see what the hell she could possibly need to speak to me about. She said it was important.

"What's up, Kenya?" I said in an aggravated tone.

She sucked her teeth and pulled me out of my seated position, away from my manager and engineer.

"I'm sorry, for walking out on you, I swear. I should have been more compassionate and stuck by your side. I miss us."

I listened to everything, she said, and wasn't paying her ass any mind, because I remembered, Heaven, had stepped outside to take an important phone call. They'd already got into it and I wasn't trying to have that go down again.

I grabbed her hand and held onto it ever so gently. "Look, I'm not saying, I don't believe what you just told me, but at this point my head is elsewhere. I been focusing on my music, a girlfriend isn't really on my agenda, right now."

In walked, Heaven, she took her same seated position on the couch. Lakenya smirked and placed her hands on her hips. "Who is that? Is she the same girl, from last night?" She whispered, as Heaven glared at the two of us, with an expression, I wasn't able to read.

I sighed knowing, Lakenya wasn't going to drop it.

"That's her isn't it?" Lakenya spoke up again.

She looked so hurt, but it is what it is. I kept it one-hundred and I put it all out on the table. I wasn't interested in pursuing anything with her, at this moment, because when I needed her the most, she bounced on me.

"Does it matter?" I responded, after licking my lips in an unhurried, effortless gesture.

"So that's it?"

I shook my head. "I mean to be honest, I have nothing else to say to you."

She grabbed my hands. "Banks I love you, so much. Please don't do this to us."

I stared at her tear stained face, I felt bad, but I needed to focus on my music instead of getting into a relationship.

I glanced over at, Heaven, who was busy doing something on her phone.

"Lakenya, I'm sorry."

"Okay, fine, but I won't give up on us." She reached up to wipe the tears from her face, to my surprise, Lakenya walked right past, Heaven, and out the door.

I walked across the room and plopped down on the couch next to, Heaven, she gave me a side eye. I already knew what that look was for

"What?" I chuckled.

She shook her head. "Oh nothing." She said sarcastically. "I didn't say anything."

"Yeah well—"

My sentence was cut short, when Lakenya's crazy ass walked back in, with a furious look on her face.

"So, this is the bitch, you left me for, Banks? Is she the reason, we can't get back together?"

We both looked up as Lakenya stood directly over, Heaven, who was in a comfortable position on the couch underneath my arm. Lakenya stood with her hands on her hips, she looked like a complete fool, the way she was behaving.

"Excuse me?" Heaven said.

"I wasn't speaking to you, I was speaking to my man, so mind your own damn business."

I sucked my teeth. "I am not your man, Lakenya." I finally spoke up. "Don't ever call, her out of her name again either. She hasn't done anything to you. She doesn't know you, and she doesn't have anything to do with what the fuck me and you had going on."

"What does she have, that I don't have, Banks? Please just tell me, what I did wrong, I can change."

"Look no need to be rude, but, Banks and I, are just friends and—" She cut, Heaven, off right in the middle of her sentence.

"Is there something going on between the two of you, because I need to know, right now!" Lakenya was acting like a child, in front of all these people.

My manager was laughing, until I cut my eye at him, I didn't find anything humorous about the situation.

"Okay, hold the fuck up." Heaven stood up and threw her things down.

She kicked off her shoes and shoved, Lakenya, hard as fuck. So, hard that she stumbled and almost fell. I hopped up and jumped in the middle of them. Heaven swung at, Lakenya over my shoulder, and got a big chunk of her hair. She began to yank her hair, with one hand and hit her in the face, with her other hand.

My security grabbed, Lakenya, up in one swift motion and carried her out the room, as she yelled obscenities at, Heaven. I couldn't help, but laugh, Heaven, went from zero to one-hundred in less than a second.

"You bum, bitch. Keep talking—"

I tried to calm, Heaven down, but that was no use, because she was tugging to get away from me.

"Hey stop—just chill."

"Let go of me, let me get that, bitch." She struggled, to get away from me, but I had a firm grip around her tiny waist.

"Get off of me." She pushed me hard and walked over to her things.

She put her shoes back on and took a few deep breaths. I assumed she was trying to calm herself down.

"I apologized for getting out of character and ruining your session. That was very un-lady like. I will just get an Uber and leave—"

I cut her off. "No, you don't have to leave."

She shook her head. I knew she was pissed. "No, it's okay. I'm going to go ahead and leave. Enjoy your session." She said, as she left.

Heaven

I finally made my way, outside of the studio. I was just about to call an, Uber and this fool followed me. Banks yanked me up quickly, by my arm and pulled me to him.

"Okay, you need to take your hands, off me." I was pissed and wanted to be alone.

He smirked, but he wasn't giving up that easy.

"No, just talk to me." I rolled my eyes and wiggled my way out of his grasp.

He shoved his hands in his pockets and awaited my response.

"We don't have anything to talk about." I took a few steps away from him and tried to pull up my Uber app, but, Banks, snatched my phone away. "Give me my damn phone back."

"Can you just listen to me for, just a moment?" He asked.

I released a deep sigh, crossed my arms and shifted all of my weight to my left leg. "Fine, go ahead, I guess."

I wasn't necessarily mad at him, I was just pissed off about the situation. I wasn't even his girl, I shouldn't have to fight his ex-girlfriend over him.

"I'm sorry, I didn't invite her. I didn't expect for any of that shit to happen. Don't be mad at me." He stuck his bottom lip out and began to pout.

When I didn't say anything, he cracked a smile trying to lighten the mood.

"I'm not smiling with you." I stated, trying desperately to hold back my smile.

"Listen, for real, though." He stepped closer to me and latched onto my hand. "That shit, that happened between us last night, was real."

I beamed. "Well that's nice to know."

He continued. "I know we just met, but I feel connected to you. I feel like I can talk to you about anything, you're a great listener and to be honest, a nigga just love being around you. I don't know everything about you, but I'm willing to stick around and find out more."

Banks's words were making me blush big time. "I'd like that." I retorted.

He started cheesing, then his silly ass spun me around in a circle and dipped me for a few moments prior to bringing me back up.

She Fell in Love with a Real One

We couldn't do anything, but laugh, as we started making our way back inside. He held the door open for me, so I could step inside.

"I'm about to put your ass on payroll." I looked at him sideways, I wasn't sure what he meant.

"Why?" I interrogated him.

"You got them hands. I know, if I hired you as a bodyguard, you'd protect me."

"Shut up." I pushed him, lightly.

His sense of humor was something I was growing fond of. I must admit, I liked being in his presence, as well, I was all giddy inside thinking about getting to know him more. My depressed days were over, after the amazing dick he gave me last night, Naheem, was the furthest thing from my mind.

Lakenya

"What's wrong, Kenya? You nearly drank this whole bottle of liquor, by yourself. You're not about to get drunk, or liquor poisoning, right in front of me. Give me the bottle." Mena, my cousin, took the bottle of liquor away from me, instantly pissing me off.

I just wanted to drink my whole life away, at this moment. I was still highly upset about what happened earlier. I wasn't upset, because Carter, had a new little girlfriend. I was more so pissed, at the fact, he moved on so quickly.

"What the hell is going on? I came over here, because you seemed a little down and miserable when I spoke to you earlier. Then I get over here and you're drinking your life away. What the hell is up?" Mena questioned me.

"Listen, I'm not up for this conversation, right about now, I just want to go to bed." I lied.

I tried to get up, but she grabbed my arm and pulled me back a bit. "Please tell me, you didn't do anything stupid."

I sighed. "No, I didn't do anything stupid. It's about, Carter."

She sneered. "Carter, didn't you leave him, though? Even after I told you not to?" She said rubbing in the fact, that I made a stupid decision.

"So, whose side are you on?" I asked her.

"I'm not on anybody's side. I just think you can do one-hundred times better. You should probably start thinking about moving on."

I ignored her comment and continued. "I went down to the studio today, to talk to him, because I've been missing him and thinking about him. I just needed to get a few things off of my chest, then in walks some, bitch. I'm guessing she's his new bitch."

"Kenya I can' believe you went down there, after I told you not to. I see, you just don't listen, to me. I told you, I thought you were insane, for wanting to show up unan-nounced, especially after the way you guys ended things. You pretty much left him, when he didn't have shit, now you want to talk." My cousin shook her head.

I rolled my eyes. "Me and his girl, got into a fist fight, I just—I don't know, what to do anymore. This nigga didn't even call me to check up on me."

I foolishly, glanced at my phone, once again only to dis-cover, he still hadn't called or texted me.

Mena grabbed my hands and held them within hers. "Lis-ten little cousin. I love you, so much, I just want you to know, maybe you should leave, Carter alone. You made the choice to leave, he's making the choice to stay gone. After today, I hope you see, that maybe you guys are over, for good. I think you should let go, get some dick, and just live life, without him."

She was wrong. I was sure, Banks needed me, the same way, I needed him, but I wanted her to think, she was right. "I guess you're right."

"Don't cry your eyes out or stress over someone, who isn't doing the same over you, Kenya. Promise me you won't do anything stupid."

"I Promise." I had my fingers crossed, behind my back.

I couldn't guarantee, I wouldn't do something stupid, because I was desperate to either get, Banks, back or to get back at him. Either way, I wasn't giving up without a fight.

Chapter 13

Lance

"Let me get, uh number one with extra mac sauce, hold the pickles." I said once, I pulled up to the microphone at McDonalds.

I got my money ready, after she told me the total. The line was long as hell, so I just sat back in my seat and got comfortable. I was hungry as hell and didn't want to drink liquor, on an empty stomach.

Night had come, and I just wanted to go back home, sip on something strong to put my mind at ease, and try to erase everything that happened, between Imani, Vaeh, and myself.

"Let me get some ketchup, please." As I waited for the chick at the window, my phone vibrated against the console. I quickly picked it up and saw, that Imani, texted me.

Imani: I don't know where you are, but I'll be gone by the time you get back. I'm taking the baby with me.

I pulled out of the drive thru line, fast as hell forgetting all about that damn ketchup. I needed to get home, fast. I knew, she had to have been fed up with me, but I didn't expect her to just up and leave with my baby.

I felt like I'd done the right thing, by cutting Vaeh, off and now this shit. I sucked my teeth, when my bag tipped over, I tried to scoop it up, not wanting the food to hit the floor, but I wasn't quick enough. McDonalds fries covered my passenger seat, but I still kept speeding until I made it to my destination. I ran three red lights, parked crooked as fuck, hopped out and jogged up my driveway.

When I got inside, I saw Imani and Chyna's stuff by the door, so I already knew what time it was.

"Imani!" I yelled, but of course, I didn't get a response.

I watched as her ugly ass cousin, Carlotta, appeared and she stood directly in front of me. I tried to walk around her, but she blocked my way.

"Move, for real, I'm not playing with you." I always thought, she was a man, because the bitch was tall as hell. She had to be at least six-three. She had a mustache, very short coarse hair, she wore in an afro, a strong ass neck, with a uni-brow, an overbite and feet that looked bigger than mine. She smacked on her gum, rolled her eyes, and her neck, before she responded.

"Make me move, nigga!" Carlotta quickly stepped closer to me indicating, that she was more than likely trying to fight.

I don't fight women, but I damn sure fight men, so she had one more, slick thing to say, then it was lights out! "My cousin is leaving and there isn't anything you can do about it, with your cheating ass." she smirked.

I took my hand and placed it on her forehead. I pushed her head backwards, moving her out of the way. Her mouth dropped. Luckily for her, Imani jumped in.

"Okay, Carlotta that's enough! Help me put this shit in the car, instead of entertaining him." She had an attitude, I knew I was in for a rude awakening, but I still needed to shoot my shot.

"Daddy!" My daughter, Chyna, came running up to me, with the biggest smile on her face.

I scooped her up off of the ground and started tickling her. She started laughing uncontrollably, as Imani, stood in front of us tapping her foot with a snare on her face.

"I missed you today, baby girl," I said to her, as I placed a thousand kisses all over her face.

Carlotta scoffed and grabbed, as many bags as she could, and headed for the door. Imani stepped closer to us and tried to reach out for my daughter, but she pulled away.

"We have to go, baby. Come on and go with, mama." Imani said.

My daughter shook head no.

I sighed. "Imani why are you doing all of this?"

Her head jerked backwards, and she looked at me sideways prior to rolling her eyes.

"You need to be asking, your damn self, that question. You know what you did, you know why I'm leaving, so why even ask?"

I placed my daughter down on the floor, and she clung to my leg for dear life. "Baby, I'm sorry. Sorry, for putting my hands on you, and for messing around on you. I need ya'll here with me, I love y'all."

"Listen, don't make this harder, than it has to be." She bent down and tried to grab, Chyna, but grew frustrated when she continued to pull away from her and clung to my leg.

"Forgive me. It will never happen again, I just want you and my baby, fuck everybody else."

Carlotta walked back in and grabbed some more bags. "Too late nigga, my cousin is—"

Imani put her hand up. "It's okay, cousin, I got this."

Carlotta shrugged and continued, her task with a displeased look on her face.

"You put your hands on me, Lance, and because of that I need to leave." I watched as her eyes began to water. "I can forgive you, for what you did, but I will never forget. I was wrong to say, what I said, but you were wrong in doing what you did. Then on top of that, you were cheating on me." She shook her head and wiped her tears.

"I'll buy you something." I offered. "Anything you want. What about a new car or a—"

"Seriously? You know material shit, don't mean anything to me. None of those things can make me happy. I was happy with you, but you went and fucked everything up, by fucking around on me. I'm leaving, I'm taking my baby with me, whether you like it or not."

"Where are to going to live? I am open to giving you some space, until you come around, but I need to know where you're taking, my baby."

"I'll be staying with, Carlotta, you can still see your baby whenever. I wanted to be one of those malicious baby mamas and keep you from your child, but there's no point in doing

147

so. Pick her up whenever you want, but you and I are done."
She picked up Chyna with one arm and used her free hand, to
drag the last and final suitcase outside.

I grabbed her arm and she pulled away gently.

"I'm done for real, Lance. Please let me go. I'm not
changing my mind."

My heart was beating fast and my mind was racing a mile
a minute. This shit was really happening.

I leaned over and placed a kiss on my, baby's forehead,
then I pulled, Imani, to me. I pecked her lips a few times but
eventually she pulled away from me. As Imani turned to walk
away, I grew upset with myself. My actions landed me in this
bullshit.

I flopped down on the couch and placed my head in my
hands, as I heard the front door close completely. I was alone
now, regretting ever meeting Vaeh, in the first place.

"Fuck!" I yelled, as my voice echoed throughout the
house. I wished like hell, I was dreaming, but I knew deep
down this was no dream.

****

I wasn't in the mood, to talk to anyone, hence the reason,
I'd been ignoring everyone's phone calls. I was upset with
myself, about my stupid decisions. Imani had left with my
daughter. It had been four whole hours, since she'd left, I was
still sitting in the same spot.

I sat on the couch, engulfed in my thoughts, as the television watched me, instead of the other way around. I had been
sulking in misery, for the past few hours after she left. I just
didn't know what to do. I initially didn't love, Imani, but I
came to love her over the years. Sleeping around with, Vaeh,
and any girl for that matter, was a mistake on my end. I was
being selfish and look where that got me.

I heard a knock on the door, and I quickly hopped up. I
tripped over my own feet, trying to get to the door. Imani had

given me my key back. I was hoping like hell that, she'd come back, because she had forgotten something, or because she wanted to give us another chance.

I swung open the door, hurriedly, and was surprised at who was on the other side. I should've looked through the peephole for sure, but it was too late.

"What's up, Lakenya?" I was confused, as to why she was at my place and uninvited, at that.

"Hey." She said anxiously, with confusion and regret on her face.

"I know I'm here uninvited, and it's really late, but I just really wanted to talk to you." I watched, as she played with her fingers timidly, and stared at me with puppy dog eyes.

"Sure, I guess, come in."

She gave me a coy smile, as I stepped to the side and let her inside. She'd been to my house a few times in the past, when she was dealing with Banks, but according to him they'd ended things not too long ago, so I was assuming, she was here to talk about him.

"Have a seat." I pointed, to the couch and she gave me another coy smile. She then flopped down onto the couch.

I sat across from her and she looked over at me, with a blank look on her face. I waited a few moments to see what she had to say, but once she didn't say anything I broke the silence.

"I thought you wanted to talk. Isn't that what you said?" She nodded her head. "Okay, so what's going on?" I questioned.

"I was wondering if—" She paused and bit her lip, momentarily. "I don't know if I should ask." she replied.

"Kenya just, ask." I chuckled. She was doing way too much.

"I was wondering if you could talk to, Banks, for me. He's hanging out with this new girl, I don't want him to move on just yet." She said quickly.

149

I was sure my face mirrored a puzzle because I didn't know, why she wanted me to talk to him. She knew me long enough to know, that I never got into anyone's business.

"Why can't you talk to him?" I was curious to know.

"Well, he won't speak to me. I really miss him, so that's why I came to you."

I released a deep sigh. "I don't know about that, Kenya. I don't know what you and bruh, have going on, but I'm not trying to be in the middle of it."

"I'm not asking you to get involved in any drama or anything like that. I just want you to ask him if he could give me another chance."

"How you figure, he'll listen to me, anyways?"

"You guys are very close, so I'm sure, he will."

I sighed heavily. "You do know, what this whole situation looks like, right?"

She looked at me confused. "No, what do you mean?"

"When Banks ain't really have nothing, you left him, now that his songs are climbing the charts, he has three whips, a mansion and more money, than he can even count by himself. He's selling out shows, then here you come trying to get back in good with him." I shook my head. This chick was nuts.

"Wait, are you trying to call me, a gold digger?"

"I'm not calling you anything, I'm just letting you know, what it looks like."

Out of nowhere, this damn girl started fucking crying her eyes out. She was trying to speak, but I didn't understand, what she was saying through all of that damn crying. I sighed and rubbed my hand over my face. I didn't need this shit, right now. I shouldn't have let her ass in.

I got up, moved closer to her, and did the first thing that came to my mind. I rubbed her back.

"I'm sorry, Kenya. I didn't mean it. I'm just going through some shit." I exhaled deeply. "My bad, about what I said."

"It's okay." She sniffled. "I deserved that, but I promise, I'm not after him for his money. I feel bad, that I wasn't there for him. I was being selfish, and just wanted him to at least hear me out."

She wiped her tears and I continued, to rub her back. "You have to keep trying," was all I could think to say.

"Can I ask you something?" She said, as I adjusted myself and sat back on the couch.

"Yeah, what's up?"

I watched, as she wiped the remaining tears from her face. "Can you just keep this between, me and you?"

I chuckled lightly. "No problem, this never happened."

She smiled and leaned closer to me. I was confused about why she was getting closer to me, but I soon got my answer when she placed her lips on mine.

I put a halt to her kissing, by placing my hand firmly on her shoulder. I lightly pushed her away, but she slapped my hand away.

"What the hell, are you, doing?" She was confused, her own damn self. "How can you show up at my crib, unannounced, try to have a conversation about getting my boy back, then kiss me. I'm confused as hell, right now, shawty."

I stood up, abruptly. It was time for her ass to leave. I didn't even allow her to speak. "You got to go, for real."

She stood up as well, and surprisingly pushed me back down on the couch. My eyebrows rose, in amazement. She was being bold as hell.

"I thought you just said, we could keep this between us." She removed her shirt.

"I mean, I did, but I wasn't talking about—"

"Shhh." She placed her finger over her lip and surprised the hell out of me when she straddled me.

"You got a lot on your mind and so do I." She massaged my dick through my pants. "So, fuck me and take your mind off of it." She bit her bottom lip, then leaned in and kissed me again. This time, I kissed her back.

Heaven

When I got to my front door, I didn't say much, as I dug into my purse for my house keys. I was kind of sad, this was coming to an end, because I was enjoying his company more than I should've been. He was a great listener, had a great conversation, and let's not forget about the sex. I was not looking forward to going inside to be alone.

I opened the door and felt his hands wrap around my waist. This instantly brought a big Kool-Aid smile to my face. I spun around to face him, and he pulled me closer.

"So, are you inviting me in or what?" He asked with a smirk on his face.

I knew exactly what he was trying to do and as bad as I wanted to have my legs wrapped around his waist, once again, I declined the offer. I placed my hands on his chest and pushed him backward a little.

"I don't think, that would be a good idea." I lied. Of course, I wanted him to come inside.

I'd already given up the pussy, easily once and I know it sounds kind of backwards, but I wanted him to see me for me and not for what was between my legs. I know, I should've thought about all of this, beforehand, but my hormones were raging and it just happened.

He had a frown on his face. I watched as he took a step backwards and cocked his head to the side a bit.

"Why not? You were with, a nigga, all day. What's the problem, you scared of me or something?" He chuckled, lightly.

I sighed and tried to collect my thoughts. "No, it's not that."

He stepped closer to me and placed his hands around my waist, once more. "Say what you gotta say."

"I just think we're moving to, quickly." I blurted out.

"Why, we ain't doing anything? A nigga like being around you, I want you around more often. I like talking to you, I like kissing you——" His words trailed off, as he leaned in and pecked me on the lips. "I like fucking you, too. So, that's a problem?"

I shook my head. He replied, "Okay, then so, let's go inside. I just want to chill with you a lil' more before I head out that's it. Cool with you?" He looked me in the eyes waiting for me to say something.

It was silent for a moment, but reluctantly I agreed.

Once inside, I led Banks to the living room area. He flopped down onto the couch and made himself at home. I laid my house keys and my purse on the counter, as he leaned back and placed his arms on the head of the couch.

I nervously, stammered. "D—do you mind, if I freshen up?" I don't know why I was acting all nervous, stuttering, for absolutely no reason.

He licked his lips and gave me a small smile.

"Nah, baby gone ahead and do your thing. I'll be right here when you get back." He winked at me, which caused me to cheese widely.

"Okay, I'll be right back." I headed for my bedroom, putting on my, stank walk, hoping he was watching me walk away.

As soon as I was out of his sight, I started running around the room like a chicken with its head cut off. I quickly, stripped out of the clothes, Banks, let me borrow for the day and headed straight for the shower. I needed to make sure this pussy smelled like roses.

I took a quick fifteen-minute shower. After fully drying off, putting on lotion, deodorant and body spray, I slipped into a cute little maxi dress. It hugged my body, in all of the right places and was off the shoulders, showing off my great shape.

I poked my head outside of the bathroom and yelled, "I'm almost done!"

He replied, "Take your time, I'm not in a rush."

I smiled and gave myself, a once over in the mirror. I freshened up my breath, by brushing, flossing, and rinsing my mouth out with mouthwash then I exited the bathroom.

Banks

"Damn." I said out loud, when Heaven entered the living room.

She knew, she was working the fuck out of, that dress and I'm sure, she put it on, just for me. Same shit, she did with that bathing suit. She blushed, as she flopped down on the couch, next to me. I pulled her closer to me and she laid her head on my shoulder.

"You are so beautiful, you know that?" She lifted her head from my shoulder momentarily, to look into my eyes.

I meant what I said. Baby was beautiful, and her body was out of this world. She had perky ass titties, wide hips, a flat stomach, toned calves and a fat ass.

She kissed me on my lips, then she replied, "Thank you."

She blushed again. I observed, as she sat up and grabbed the remote. She flipped on the T.V. and leaned back into my arms.

"What do you want to watch?" She asked, I shrugged.

"I don't wanna watch anything, to be honest. I wanna get to know you."

"I don't have a problem, with that." she replied. "I'll start with the basics. I'm twenty-five, my name is Heaven Holmes, but I'll definitely be going back to my maiden name, Heaven Brookes, after this divorce is finalized. I have an identical twin sister, that you already met——"

She was referring to that night her sister was trying to fuck me in the club. I smirked at her, because she was being petty.

I cut her off mid-sentence. "I don't mean, to cut you off baby, but I want to know more about who you are as a person. I want to know the shit you like and the shit you don't like. Your profession, goals, and shit like that."

She placed her hand over her mouth and giggled.

"Oh, I see." She paused for a moment to gather her thoughts. "I am a dancer."

My eyebrows rose quickly, and she giggled once more. I didn't know she got down like that.

"I'm not the kind of dancer, you're thinking about. I am a dance instructor, I used to teach hip hop classes, until I got fired." She said, dryly.

When I didn't say anything, she continued.

"After that shit, with my soon to be ex-husband, those bastards fired me, because I got into it, with the lil' bitch he was fucking." She shook her head, momentarily, then stared off into space, most likely replaying the events in her head.

"Damn that's crazy." I couldn't think of anything else to say in this situation, so I just said the first thing that came to my mind.

"I know, but hey it is what it is, and everything happens for a reason." Heaven shrugged, then looked over at me.

"So, what do you do now, are you looking for work?"

She shook her head. "Honestly, I've been too embarrassed to look for anything. That scandal, my ex got me involved in, was way too much for me to handle. I feel like everyone knows, I was his wife, and I wasn't good enough, so he had to sleep with a student."

She looked down and began fidgeting with her fingers, nervously. I grabbed ahold of her chin and made her look at me.

"Listen, don't let anyone take away your, God-given talent. If you wake up in the morning and all you can think about is dancing, then you are supposed to be a dancer. Fuck that, nigga, fuck that lil' thot and fuck that school."

She cracked a smiled. "Lil' thot, really?" We both busted out, laughing.

I shrugged. "Hey, I'm just saying."

"I'm really glad, I met you." she admitted.

I grabbed her by the back of her neck, with one hand and pulled her closer. I couldn't stop kissing her. She had the sexiest lips, I had ever seen, and I loved sucking on them and biting them.

I pecked her lips a few times and she surprised me when she started sucking on my bottom lip. She pulled away, with my bottom lip captured between her teeth, then she leaned back in slipping her tongue in my mouth. I was just about ready to get butt naked, and bend her over the couch, but I decided against it. I really did want to get to know her. I pecked her lips once more.

She reached up and wiped the lip-gloss from the corners of my mouth.

"So, uh—back to what we were talking about, before all of that happened." I said playfully, which caused her to blush and hit my chest, lightly. "I think you should get back to what you love."

She sighed. "I will, eventually. Luckily, for me I was smart enough to start my own savings account. I had been saving for years, so I'm good with my bills and everything for a few months. Hopefully, by then, I will be approved for a loan, I applied for."

"What's it for?"

"I want to open up my own dance studio, it's always been my dream to have my own, and not have to answer to anyone."

I made a mental note about everything, she'd said.

"What about, you?" She changed the subject. "What's your real name, for starters?"

"Carter King, but don't ever call me, Carter."

She stared at me with a devious grin. "Not even in the, bedroom?" She teased, my eyebrows rose yet again.

"I can make an exception to that." I joked, which caused both of us to laugh.

"Yeah that's what I thought, sir."

I continued telling her about myself. "I'm twenty-five, a high school dropout, raised by a single mother. I don't know my dad and I have a little brother."

She caught me off guard with her next question. "So, what exactly are you looking for, right now? A friend, fuck buddy, girlfriend, all of the above?" she chuckled.

I shook my head. "I'm just chilling, right now. Whatever happens, happens. I'm not in a rush to hop into another relationship."

"I agree." she replied.

We spent the rest of the night talking about everything under the sun, laughing, making out, and watching movies, until we fell asleep on the couch, around four a.m. wrapped up in each other's arms.

Heaven

I jumped out of my sleep, when I heard a cell phone ringing, quite loudly. Banks, whose chest I was laying on, didn't move an inch. I realized, it was his phone ringing. I sat up and scooped it up from the coffee table, that was near the couch, and silenced it. It was too got damn loud and after looking at the time, it was only nine a.m.

I yawned, stretched, and made my way into the bathroom, to wash my face and brush my teeth. There was no way, I'd be caught dead around this man, with morning dragon breath.

I smiled, after thinking about the amazing night we had. We talked all night, then fell asleep on the couch.

God, I don't know what I did to deserve this wonderful, chocolate man, but good looking out.

Once I was done, I exited the bathroom and headed back into the living room. Only to see that, Banks, had woken up, put his shoes back on and was standing near the door, on his cell phone finishing up a call. He bid the person on the other end goodbye and slid his phone back into his pocket.

157

He waved me over, when I got closer, he wrapped his arms around me giving me a big warm hug. He pulled back a little and let his hands rest on my ass.

"I need to head out, but I'll call you later, a'ight?"

I frowned, I wasn't ready for him to leave, but I nodded in agreement.

He smiled. "Don't make that face."

He kissed me on the cheek and just like that, he was gone. I placed my back against the door and practically stared off into space with a goofy grin on my face. That man was going to be my weakness, I could already tell. He had me on cloud nine, without even trying.

My loud ass stomach brought me back to reality when it began to growl. I walked away from the door and headed straight for the kitchen, to whip up something light. I pulled out some cereal from the pantry and a bowl from the cabinet. Just as I was about to grab the milk, there was a knock at the door.

I started cheesing, hoping like hell, Banks, had left something. When I swung the door open, I came face to face, with my twin. I sighed loudly and walked away from the door.

"Well, hello to you too, sis." I don't even know why she showed up over here, she knew I wasn't fucking with her, right now.

"What do you want, Nevaeh?" I said, dryly.

I headed for the fridge. I fixed my cereal, grabbed a spoon and made my way to the couch. I plopped down and crossed my legs, grabbing the remote, lying next to my knee on the couch.

"I came to see my sis and by the way, you got some ballers living over here, girl. I just seen a nigga pull off in a sexy ass cocaine white Camaro." I almost choked on my cereal. She was referring to, Banks car.

"What?" She asked, and I changed the subject.

"Nothing. Why are you here? You still haven't answered that question."

I looked over at her and she started to pout. "I miss my twin. Why are you still mad at me, Heaven? I told you, I was sorry."

I exhaled deeply. She was blowing my high and I hadn't even smoked. "That shit you said, wasn't cool."

She got down on her knees next to where I was sitting.

"I know, I'm sorry, please forgive me. Pretty please." She clasped her hands together and begged me over and over again, until I gave in.

"Okay fine." I rolled my eyes. I was sure, she could see the look of irritation on my face. "I'll forgive you, if you just shut the hell up."

She giggled. "Okay, I'm done." She got up off of her knees and sat on the sofa next to me.

She wrapped her arms around me and gave me a hug, that ended up being one sided, because I didn't hug her back.

"Hug me back, bitch!" She yelled, but I cocked my head back and gave her a dirty look.

She gave me a dirty look, as well, mocking me. "You ain't the only one that can give dirty looks."

I shook my head and started laughing. I could never stay mad at her for too long. She was my twin, I had to deal with her ass for the rest of my life. I wasn't complaining, though. We argued and disagreed a lot, but we always got out shit together in the end.

"I missed you, Vaeh." I admitted.

"Aww, I missed you more, sissy." she cheesed.

I scooped some cereal into my mouth and responded after swallowing. "What have you been up to?"

She shrugged. "Nothing really, same ole, same ole."

"So, tell me." She sat back on the sofa and looked over at me. "What's this glow, that you have? You look happy. Have you been using, Roscoe?" She was referring to my dildo.

I burst out laughing. "No. I've been getting some real dick fuck Roscoe."

"Real dick?" she questioned. "From who?"

"I ain't telling you."

She started to pout, again, I shook my head. "Nope, that's not going to work this time." I teased.

Banks was my little secret. I didn't want to jinx anything by telling her, just yet.

Eventually, she allowed me to change the subject. I must say, I really enjoyed catching up with my sister, for a few hours. I was still a little tired, so once she left, I drifted off to sleep, with a smile on my face and Banks on my mind.

Chapter 14

Nevaeh

1 week later

"Take your ass home, Vaeh. Do you really want your ass, beat again?" I thought to myself as I sat in Lance's driveway.

Luckily, he was home. With him being so busy, I was never able to catch him. I'd rode past his house quite a few times and he was never home. I realized, after he left my apartment that day, he was dead ass serious about ending things with us. I had to get a stupid, ass part time job at this funky little coffee shop, by my house just to make ends meet, but that money just wasn't enough for me. His money was all, I needed, and I fucked around and lost it all.

He was willing to throw his whole marriage away because he loved me. My foolish decisions made me lose him and his money. Eager for his got damn attention, I hopped up and threw on some clothes. I started driving around the city, wasting a bunch of gas and somehow, ended up at his fucking house.

My palms were sweaty, and my heart was racing fast, as I looked at my surroundings. It was Wednesday and a little after four p.m. His wife would be home soon, so I was going to make this quick.

I got out of my car, slowly and gave myself a pep talk inside of my head.

"Okay, you got this Vaeh. Go in there, get your man back, then you can quit, that dumbass job.

It was easier said than done, but I was hoping for the best outcome, as I approached the front door and knocked on it lightly. I had butterflies in my stomach, I was nervous and didn't know what to expect.

I heard shuffling, momentarily and was surprised, when I came face to face, with a woman who was breathtakingly beautiful. She definitely wasn't his wife, after looking this bitch up and down, my blood began to boil at her attire. This bitch was wearing one of his shirts and some socks. I could tell she didn't have on a bra and her hair was tied up into a messy bun.

She looked at me confused, which caused me to jerk my head to the side and scrunch up my face. I was sure, my expression mirrored some one who'd smelt the world's oldest cheese. I didn't know who she was, but she had better find the right one and quick!

"Where's our food?" She questioned, as she looked at my hands, then back up at my face.

"Excuse me? I did not come here to delivery any got damn food."

Her eyes widened. "Oh, I'm so sorry. I thought you were the Uber eats delivery driver." She stated.

I wanted to knock her ass out, until Lance appeared wearing only boxers as his shirtless chest glistened, with sweat. They must have just gotten done fucking. "You look so familiar, like I've seen you before or something." I ignored her dumbass.

Lance's face practically hit the floor, when he saw me, and I charged at him, hitting and punching him with all of my might. Whoever this chick was, she tried to jump in and pull me off of him.

"Excuse you, get off of, him!" She yelled. Lance used all of his might to push me off of him.

I hit the floor with a loud thud, as both of us struggled to catch our breath.

"What the fuck are you doing here, Nevaeh?" I could hear the frustration in his voice, but I didn't care, because he had some nerve kicking me to the curb, so he could fuck with some new bitch.

I quickly got off of the floor and just glared at him.

"You need to leave." She butted into the conversation once more, then stood in front of Lance. I had no clue, why she did that, because her actions weren't going to stop me from charging at his ass again. She pointed at the door, with a smirk on her face.

"First of all, bitch. I ain't even come here for you, so you need to mind your own business."

"I got this, Kenya, go wait in the back." I watched as he wiped a tiny amount of blood from his lip.

This Kenya chick glared at me once more, then she took her sweet ass time leaving the room.

"Why are you here?" He stepped closer to me, with a stern look on his face. I could see the veins popping out of his neck.

"Who is that? Why is she, here!" I spat.

He gritted his teeth. "None of your business."

"So, this is what we're doing, now? I gave you space to get your mind right, and calm down, because I just knew we weren't over, but you fucking a new bitch already? Wow Lance." I shook my head and crossed my arms. I couldn't control my feet because they had a mind of their own as they paced back and forth. "And where the fuck is, your wife?" I blurted out.

He took a deep breath and exhaled harshly, as I stood in front of him, with my arms crossed. "She left me. After that shit happened, with you, she left."

"So, you playing house with a new, bitch?" I shoved his chest and he grabbed my wrists.

Through gritted teeth he said, "It's not even like that I'm just——"

I shook my arms loose and slapped the taste out of his mouth.

"Fuck you, Lance." I flipped him off and left just as fast as I had come.

I wanted to fight her ass, but that wouldn't solve anything. I just hopped in my car and sped off. I was embarrassed, yet again by this man, and for some reason, I just didn't want to leave him alone.

163

Banks

I was in the middle of preparing for a show tonight when a text message came through from, Heaven. Just seeing her name made me smile. I sat down on my couch for a quick second and propped up my feet. I called her on Facetime, and she instantly giggled, when she saw the funny face I was making.

"Why you sitting over there looking like a blowfish?" She cheesed into the camera, so hard, I thought her cheeks would burst open.

"Oh, you trying to clown me, baby? You know I'm fine as shit." I gloated and watched as she propped the phone up on the kitchen counter across from her.

She playfully rolled her eyes and placed one hand on her hip as she stirred a pot with the other.

She smacked her lips. "You definitely ain't, all that." she teased.

I admired her body, as she swayed her hips from side to side, with some old school Joe, blasting in the background. She was wearing a bra and boy shorts, my favorite attire.

"It's amazing how you knock me off my feet. Every time you come around me, I get weak." She sang into the camera and something just made me feel like she was singing to me. She used the spatula as her microphone, as she continued to sing.

"Oh, shit you singing to a nigga, now?" She nodded her head and continued to dance around the kitchen singing and swaying her hips. She was beautiful, and I was beginning to love everything about her. Our chemistry was A-1, and she always kept me smiling which was a plus. I wasn't an easy nigga to please.

I joined in on signing with her. Completely throwing her off.

"I wish that I could take a journey through your mind, alright. And find emotions that you always try to hide baby."

She chuckled lightly and pointed at me through the camera.

"This song is a solo, Carter, not a duet. No one asked you to join in."

"You know my vocals on point. I'd put Ginuwine, out of the game, if he wasn't already." I joked. "Anyways." I changed the subject. "What you over there cooking, with your hating ass?"

She scoffed. "Oh, I'm the hater when you sound like a dying cat." She continued, to stir whatever it was, she was making on the stove.

"Any who, I'm making spaghetti with meatballs and garlic bread."

"Oh, you like meatballs, huh?" I smirked as a smile tugged at her lips. She gave me her full attention.

"You're so fucking lucky, you're not here. I'd seriously throw one at your forehead."

I chuckled lightly "I'm glad, I'm not there, then."

This time she smirked. "But, aye you miss, a nigga, though?"

"Of course, I do. You miss me?" she questioned.

I could tell by the look on her face, she was hoping to get the same response.

"Who am I on face time with, right now?" I teased, and she rolled her eyes.

"That doesn't mean anything. If you really missed me, you would've came to see me."

"I didn't get an invite, baby."

She frowned. "I'm inviting you, now."

I shook my head. "I got a show, I gotta prepare for tonight, baby, I can't come."

She started to pout, when a brilliant idea popped into my head.

"Fine. Are you going to come see me after?"

I started to get an incoming call. "I gotta go, I have a call coming in."

I watched as her face dropped. I could tell, she didn't want to end the call.

"You free tonight, though, right?" I asked, she nodded.

She looked like she'd just lost her puppy. I knew, she really wanted to see me and I wanted to see her, too so I was going to surprise her.

"A'ight and you're a size four, right? Size six in shoes?"

She looked at me confused. "Yeah why?"

"No reason, but, I'll call you back in a few."

I quickly ended the call and switched over to the other line.

"What's up, ma?"

"Don't what's up, ma me. Did you forget about my book club party, tomorrow? You promised you'd get a caterer, but you ain't said shit about the caterer yet."

I sighed deeply. I definitely forgot. "I'm sorry, mama. I been super busy, but I'll get my assistant to get you the best caterer in the city. How's that sound?"

My mother was hosting a book club at her house and she took her book club seriously. It would be a simple get together nothing major, but I had so much shit on my plate, I forgot all about the caterer for her club.

"Sounds good. Thank you, baby." I shook my head.

My mom was so bipolar at times. One minute she was super nice and the next, she could be the spawn of Satan, but I loved her, though.

I chuckled. "Oh, so you're happy now?"

"I was over here panicking, and your brother wasn't making it any better, by telling me I should have never put you in charge of the food." she laughed. "But anyways, baby, thank you, I love you."

"Love you, too."

I shot my assistant a quick text, after I got off the phone with, my mama. I needed her to set up a caterer for tomorrow and send, Heaven, a little gift.

She quickly texted back, letting me know, she'd handle it. I relaxed, before I had to get ready for my show tonight.

Heaven

"Here you go." I tore my eyes away from the stage for just a moment, to grab the water provided to me, by Skye. She had a huge smile on her face.

"Thank you." I grabbed the water bottle from her and quickly opened it.

I was parched and anxious all that the same time. I knew Banks had something up his sleeve, when he asked me what size I was. He sent me a gorgeous dress, a banging pair of heels and a limo picked me up. He wanted me to be at his show tonight, so here I was.

To be honest, I don't know, why I agreed to go with Banks to his show. I felt all out of place and I was about two seconds away cursing a, bitch, out for mean mugging me. It was so many groupies backstage, all hoping to hook up with, Banks and his crew. I shook my head, at the thought of anyone trying to push up on him. We weren't together, but that shit still pissed me off, to see hoes flock to him. All these girls saw was dollar signs, but I was glad I got to know the real him. Carter definitely had a spell over me.

"Why you cheesing?" I questioned Skye, but she threw her hands up in mock surrender.

"No reason." She crossed her arms with a smirk on her face. "I just think it's cute how you and my boss are all in love and what not."

I scoffed. "I mean we're hardly in love. We just enjoy each other's company." I stated truthfully.

"I bet that's not the only thing you enjoy spending time with." I blushed instantly, thinking about the sex we'd had in

167

the dressing room. Unexpected, nasty, and spontaneous sex is the best. I could feel a smile tugging at my lips and my panties get moist.

I lightly pushed her arm. "Shut up."

"No, but seriously. I can see the way you two look at each other. It looks like he has your head gone. He doesn't even pay these hoes any attention when you're here, or when you're not around. Plus, he bought you that fly ass three-thousand-dollar, *Donatella Versace* dress. If you asked me, you got yourself a keeper girl."

I thought about what she said, she was definitely right. He was all I thought about, from the time I woke up, until I went to sleep. This nigga had my head gone, but I wasn't complaining one bit.

"I'll be right back." She said and rushed off talking into a walkie-talkie.

She disappeared into a sea of people and I focused my attention back on the stage. Banks was walking in my direction, with a microphone in one hand, and a small white towel in his other hand. He lightly wiped the sweat from his face and neck, then shoved the towel into his pocket.

He latched onto my hand and tried to get me to walk with him back on stage, but my body stiffened up. I tried to snatch away from him, but his grip tightened on my hand. He turned around and stared into my eyes noticing my hesitancy.

"What is going on I can't go out there." My heart was beating fast and I needed answers.

"Do you trust me?" He wrapped his arms around my waist.

I shook my head, as he leaned in and kissed my lips.

"Okay, so trust me, right now." Without another word he grabbed my hand once again and led me on the stage where the crowd went wild. There were people everywhere. All I saw was a bunch of people with their phones out recording and snapping pictures of us.

"Can I play a new song for y'all?" He yelled and every-one in the crowd yelled out, "Yeah!"

"Y'all not hype enough." He paused momentarily, I just stood next to him, feeling like a deer caught in the headlights.

"I said can I play a new song for, y'all?" He repeated, and the crowd went wild, again and yelled out, "Yeah!"

"Drop that shit, D.J.!"

A song that I was unfamiliar with began to play as Banks stepped closer to me and grabbed my hand yet again. It was slower than his normal music, but the beat was fire nonethe-less.

As he began to rap he spun me around in a circle, so that my back was up against his chest. I swayed from side to side against him. I tried my hardest to relax and also not fall flat on my face.

"Girl I got a confession, ya body's sent from Heaven."

My mouth practically fell to the floor when I heard him drop subliminal messages about me throughout the song. I quickly turned around to look at him and he winked at me. I was sure I was blushing hard as hell. I wasn't sure if Banks was a magician, but he sure had me under his spell. This had to be some sort of dream, and if it was, I didn't want to wake up any time soon.

Nevaeh

'Bang—bang—bang—'

"I jumped out of my sleep and damned near fell to the floor, when I heard someone banging on my door. I quickly looked around and realized, I must've fallen asleep on the couch, because it was pitch black in my crib. I definitely never made it to my bed. I reached out and felt for my phone, being that I couldn't see anything and eventually I found my phone on the coffee table.

When I finally glanced at the time on my phone, I grew angry at whoever was on the other side of my door. It was super late going on one o'clock in the morning and the person on the other end just kept on knocking.

"I know you hear me knocking on this damn door!" I scoffed, when I heard Margarita's voice.

I groggily got up from the couch, stretch and yawned. She was about to get cursed out that's for sure. I drug my feet across the floor, unlocked the door and when I swung it open she shoved her phone into my face.

"Bitch why didn't you tell me, you and Banks been hooking up? I knew you got his number, but shit. You're all over the blogs girl!" She hollered, with a roll of her neck and I shushed her. "You didn't even invite me to the concert earlier with yo' secretive ass, Nevaeh!"

"Will you keep your voice down, Trey Songz Jr.? I don't need the neighbors knowing my name or calling the police, because yo' black ass is yelling for no reason." I grabbed her by the arm and quickly pulled her inside.

I locked the door and flipped on the lights, which instantly made me squint. I drug my feet across the carpet once more and made my way back over to the couch. I flopped down on it. Margarita stood next to the couch, with one hand on her hip and her lips tooted up.

She pointed at her phone. "I need answers, trick. Why are you withholding information, I thought, I was your girl?"

I glared at her. "Girl I wasn't at no damn concert, I was right here sleeping all this time. What are you even talking about?"

She passed me her phone and my mouth dropped instantly.

"What the fuck!" I was shocked and didn't know what to say. I read the article out loud. "Rapper Banks showed PDA on stage with a mystery woman, who may be his new boo He released a new song and brought her on stage. Sources say that the song is about her."

"Rita." I looked up at her momentarily, then back down at her phone. "This is not me, that's, Heaven."

So many thoughts were floating around in my head. He was supposed to be my man, how dare she be all up on stage hugged up with him? She was being secretive and although she mentioned, she was seeing someone, I didn't think, he was whom, she was seeing. How did they even meet? He's not even her type.

Rita snatched her phone and glared at it hard. Not even a few seconds later, she burst out laughing. "Damn that is, Heaven. Man, I'm high as hell. I really thought that was you for a second."

I should've known, she was high, because her eyes were super low with a hint of red in them.

She flopped down on the couch next to me. "I thought you were fuckin' with him." She kept laughing, but I didn't see anything funny.

"It just didn't work out." I lied.

She shrugged. "Well you win some you lose some, I guess." She paused for a brief moment. "But your sister winning like a muthafucka, right now."

"It's cool. I'ma get my man back." I said more to myself than Rita.

She was occupied with her phone, as she scrolled though Instagram looking at article after article about Banks and Heaven.

"What'd you say?" she asked.

"Nothing." I quickly changed the subject, pretending the situation at hand, didn't faze me, although it really did. "You got some more weed on you?"

She looked at me as if I had eight heads. "Now you know I got that gas in me."

"Roll up, I need to sm—"

She held up a blunt, that was already rolled. "I'm way ahead of you, bae."

I watched as she pulled out a lighter from her pocket, lit the blunt and took two hits prior to passing it to me. That shit in the blogs pissed me off, but I'd handle it sooner than later.

Heaven had asked me earlier today, to go to the nail shop with her tomorrow. I'd definably be bringing this shit to her attention once I saw her.

Chapter 15

Heaven

"Oh, my God look, Vaeh, this color is so pretty. It would look so good on you."

Vaeh had agreed to go to the nail shop with me. I was happy as hell, because we didn't hang out, as much as we used to. I wanted us to get back to how we were. It seemed like she was always bitter about something or annoyed. This wasn't the girl, I'd grown up with and something was clearly bothering her, so I was hoping to get a little insight on what she was going through, so I could help to ease her mind.

I handed my sister bright yellow polish. She scrunched up her face, then handed it, right back to me.

"No sis, you should wear this color. I was thinking of either money green, cocaine white or pussy pink." The made-up colors, she'd mentioned caused me to snicker. She was a trip.

She continued to look through the color selections as I did the same.

"Fine—don't get mad, when you see how pretty it looks on my toes and shit."

Nevaeh scoffed and playfully rolled her eyes. "Trust me, I won't be."

After we picked our colors, we were seated right next to each other, as the employees handed the both of us a flute of champagne.

I decided to go right in for the kill. "Girl, so how's the love life. I know we just saw each other recently, but you haven't mentioned seeing anyone, so I'm just curious." I sipped my champagne and looked over at her, as she pecked away on her phone. Instead of answering my question, she shoved her phone in my face.

I snatched her phone and my heart started to beat fast as hell, when I saw my face plastered all over the blogs. After

Bank's performance last night, people were calling me his new love interest, wife, fiancée, girlfriend and so on. Banks and I were taking it slow, so he and I were none of the above, but I looked up just in time to see, Vaeh cutting her eyes at me.

"I should be asking you about your man, sis. Why didn't you tell me this was your, nigga?" She questioned, with raised brows as I handed her back her cellphone.

"Well, it's complicated, but I wasn't trying to keep him from you. I just didn't want to jinx anything." I admitted.

I hated getting all hyped up over a man, that wasn't about shit. I wanted to make sure he wasn't a reflection of my ex.

"Doesn't look complicated to me sis, he's staring at you like he's trying to put a baby in that thang."

I blushed just thinking about, Banks, being up inside of me. Best dick I'd ever had in my life hands down.

"Whatever." I cheesed, unintentionally.

Right after the show last night, Banks flew to New York to knock out an interview, this morning and should've either been back already or on his way back. I couldn't wait to see him, he said he had a surprise for me.

I felt good about he and I, because for one my sister was right. We could be in a room of a million people and he would still only have eyes for me. He was everything I'd ever wanted in a man. He was handsome, funny, romantic, compassionate, humble and so much more. God took his time when he made Banks.

Nevaeh

Well that confirmed it, my twin was fucking around, with the nigga that turned me down. How does that shit even work? He turned me down and we look exactly the fuck alike. Other than me being a tad bit heavier, than her, we still looked the same. I was annoyed by the whole situation, I felt like he played the fuck out of me and was probably only messing with my sister to prove a point.

Shit, I don't know, but either way he was supposed to be mine. Men don't turn me down, so he shocked the fuck out of me, when he did. He could've been mine by now not hers!

"Why are you sitting over there cheesing?" My sister had gotten a text message and was smiling from ear to ear.

"I'm sorry, apparently I forgot my wallet last night. Banks just texted me saying, he was coming to bring it to me since he's in the area."

I instantly got nervous. I hadn't seen him since that night at the club. I wasn't in any position to see him again looking a hot as mess. I was a little ashy, I didn't have an ounce of make-up on my face, and I needed a touch up on my sew-in. I quickly put on some lip-gloss to at least accentuate my lips.

"I swear, I'm always forgetting something." Heaven said, as she placed her phone back into her purse.

"Like the fact that you're, married?" I blurted out.

I wasn't trying to be harsh, I was just trying to let my sister know about the shit she apparently forgot about.

Her brows rose, instantly, as she stared at me through the slits of her eyes.

"What the fuck is that supposed to mean?" She said, giving me her full attention.

"Nothing. I'm just saying you're running around town, with a man you barely even know, cheesing just at the mention of his name. Seems like that nigga has you dick-matized if you asked me."

She sighed heavily. "That's the thing, Vaeh, I didn't ask you and what's going on with you anyways? You've been acting mad, weird lashing out all the time. This is why I was ignoring you, for the past couple of weeks, you clearly still don't get it."

"Listen sister, I don't mean any harm, by what I said." I threw up my hands. "I'm just saying don't be falling for him and shit, knowing you're still married. Just because you took off the ring, does not mean, you're not married, hun."

"Since when are you all gung-ho for, Naheem. That nigga cheated on me and didn't have a care in the world when he did it. Plus, he was secretly planning on leaving me for her. Fuck him!" She spat. "I sent his ass the dissolution of marriage papers last month and, as soon as they are signed it's a wrap. We been over anyways." She shrugged it off.

"Thank you, so much." Heaven said to the nail tech that'd just finished painting her toes, then she directed her attention back towards me. "Plus, Banks and I aren't together we just have a mutual understanding that's all."

"Oh, so he's still fucking other bitches, then?" She glared at me and before she could follow up with an answer, I heard a bunch of ruckus coming from the front door.

Bitches were breaking their necks, hopping up from their seats, and quickly pulling out their phones when, Banks, walked in with two big ass bodyguards.

"I just wanna have your, baby!" Some big beasty looking bitch, with no teeth in the front yelled out. Her got damned titties were practically sweeping the floor.

I rolled my eyes at her desperation, as if she was trying to get at my man. I quickly straightened my posture and popped in a piece of gum, to make sure my breath was fresh. I watched as he scanned the room, until he spotted us. He walked over with his bodyguards in tow.

I had a huge smile on my face, until he stopped right in front of us, examined the both of us, then made his way over to, Heaven. I guess he was trying to make sure he wasn't all up on the wrong twin, but my blood really began to boil, when she wrapped her arms around his neck, only seconds after he pecked her lips a few times. I was livid.

They were so busy in their own world, they hadn't noticed me mean mugging them. I played it cool, by pretending to scan through my Instagram when it really wasn't shit on there.

I cleared my throat and, Heaven, spoke up. "Babe this is my twin, Nevaeh, Vaeh this is, Banks." She introduced the two of us.

I felt nervous as Banks observed me. I wasn't sure what he was about to say, but I really wanted to touch his fine ass, so I put my hand out for him to shake. He accepted and shook my hand as well.

"Nice meeting you." I cheesed wide, as hell like a fucking fool showing off all of my got damned teeth.

"Nice seeing you, again." He stated being petty as hell. I wasn't sure if, Heaven, knew about our first meet up in the club, but I was going to milk that shit right in front of her.

"Again?" I looked up to the ceiling, pretending to think. "Ohhh—I think I remember meeting you at some point."

He smirked, and Heaven's expression matched his.

"That's irrelevant, right now but again, it was nice meeting you." He directed his attention back to, Heaven, then he handed her what looked like her wallet. "I believe this is yours."

Heaven accepted the wallet, and soon after, he pulled out a couple hundreds and handed them to her.

"I'll pay for you and your sister, baby don't worry 'bout it, it's on me."

"No, it's okay, you don't have to do that."

My naive ass sister tried to hand him the money back. I wanted to snatch it from her hand, but he politely put the money back in her hand, then whispered something into her ear, that made her giggle and shake her head.

"A'ight, I'm out. Catch you later, Nevaeh. I'll see you when you leave here, baby. I'll text you where I want you to meet me at."

"Okay." Heaven said, and just like that he was out the door.

All of his groupies and fans quickly hopped up, not even paying for their nails, to follow him. I wanted to follow his fine ass too, but instead I turned to, Heaven, and tried to see if I could knock her off of her high horse.

"Oh, you know what. I remember him now. He was trying to get with me in the club. He was all up over me and wouldn't take no for an answer." I lied.

Heaven's eyebrows rose. "Oh yeah?"

"Yeah—that's crazy, that he tried to get with me and now he's with you. He probably thought, you were me or something."

Heaven burst out laughing, which caused my head to jerk to the side.

"What's so, funny?"

"You are." She shook her head. "Just be happy for me, Vaeh. Like I said we're not together. Shit is complicated right now, but we're good. I don't need my own sister, lying right to, my face. He told me what happened a long ass time ago."

My mouth dropped, I felt so dumb for lying, but I wasn't giving up on, Banks, anytime soon. All I needed was for him to leave, my sister alone, so I could swoop in and get him. I just needed to figure out how.

Heaven

Later on that night

Banks told me, to meet him at a strip club for whatever reason. I didn't question it, though, I just did as I was told, but now I was a little confused.

"Babe!" I called out to, Banks, as I entered what looked like a very empty strip club. It was huge and quite spacious.

I called out to him, again, but still got no response. We were running late for a dinner, I was just about ready to go.

"I'm coming!" He yelled back to me, as I sighed and sat down on the nearest barstool. I quickly pulled out my cell phone and looked at the time.

She Fell in Love with a Real One

"We're going to be late and——" I stopped mid-sentence when I glanced at his attire.

"Babe, why are you not dressed?"

He came walking out shirtless in a pair of black polo boxers and black socks.

"I am going to kill, you!" He started to laugh, and I hopped up from the barstool.

He leaned in to kiss me, but I moved my head back. He yanked me closer by the collar of my shirt and kissed me on the lips anyway.

"Babe seriously though, you told me you were ready, then I get here to see, you're far from being dressed. The reservation is for eight thirty p.m., it's already five minutes after eight. We're about twenty-five minutes from the restaurant. Are you trying to drop hints that you don't wanna go?"

He shrugged. "I'm just not in the mood, to go out tonight."

I threw my hands in the air, as my eyes grew wide.

"Well damn—when were you going to tell me this? I could have saved an outfit."

I watched as he walked around the bar, towards the liquor. He pulled out a bottle of Hennessy and poured the both of us a glass. I rolled my eyes, because he was being very nonchalant.

"My bad, bae. I just am not really trying to sit next to a bunch of muthafuckas, I don't know. I just wanna be alone with you." He gave me, a big smile showing off his glistening gold teeth.

I rolled my eyes and accepted the glass of liquor when he handed it to me.

He walked back around the bar and stood directly in front of me. We clanked our glasses together, downed the shot, then we both scrunched up our faces after the liquid hit our chests.

"You okay?" Banks laughed.

I cut my eyes at him. "Shut up."

He grabbed me and pulled me closer. "I missed you all day, with yo' fine ass."

I shook my head. "Don't be trying to butter me up." He placed butterfly kisses on my neck. "I wanted to go out."

"Well we can have our own fun here."

"How Banks? There's nothing to do here.

He pulled away from our embrace, he had a look on his face, that I was unable to read. "I'll show you." He was up to something.

He began to walk away, and I was left standing in the same spot, wondering what the hell was going on. Banks turned off the bright lights in the strip club and dimmed the lights. The lights begin to flash blue, green and red. All of a sudden, R-Kelly's voice filled the club. Seems like you you're ready blasted through the speakers as, Banks, reappeared with a grin on his face.

"I don't like that look. What do you have up your sleeve?" I pointed at him and he started cheesing.

"Dance for me." I burst out laughing, only to see that he wasn't laughing, this fool was dead ass serious.

"Banks—seriously? Do I look like Diamond from the Players Club?"

He just looked at me.

"You're really serious." I replied again, as he walked over to me and grabbed my hand.

He led me to the stage and helped me up the stairs. "There's no one in here baby, do something spontaneous for once. Dance for ya, man."

My hands began to get a little clammy. I knew how to dance of course, but not on a pole. Had I known ahead of time, I would've watched a YouTube video or something.

He pulled up a chair in front of the stage and sat down. I walked slowly over to the pole and wiped my sweaty hands on my skirt. I didn't want him to think I was boring, so I decided to do it.

"You got this, baby." he reassured.

I nervously stood in front of the pole and swayed my hips slowly, from left to right, making sure I was at least dancing on beat. Banks sat back in the chair and his eyes were directly on me. I continued to sway from left to right. I slid down the pole, with my back against it. Once I was in a squatting position, I started to act as if I were riding a dick, by bouncing up and down on my imaginary partner. My skirt was hiked up around my hips giving him a clear view of my non-existing panties.

I leaned forward onto my hands and I was now on my hands and knees in the doggy style position. I faced the pole, so that my ass was facing Banks. My ass was jiggling in every type of direction, as I put an arch in my back and threw it back, like I had his dick inside of me. Banks started to throw fifties and one-hundreds at me.

I looked over my shoulder, he was eyeing me with lust in his eyes.

I used the pole to get back onto my feet and seductively stood up. I was now facing, Banks. I removed my skirt and shirt and threw them to the ground next to me.

At this point, I must've lost my mind, because I decided to do one of those moves I'd seen in movies. I walked briskly around the pole, and when I gained enough momentum, I jumped up and wrap my legs tightly around it. As I was spinning on the pole, I leaned backwards and tried to hang upside down, but ruined the whole mood, when   I fell on my head.

'Crash!'

"Ahhh!" I yelped in pain, as my head instantly started to hurt.

The music was loud, but I could still hear Banks's laugher over the music. He quickly got up and jogged to the back, to turn the lights on and turn the music off.

181

He could barely hold his laughter, as he climbed on top of the stage to help me up. I was so embarrassed, I couldn't look him in the eyes.

I moaned and groaned in pain as, Banks, scooped me up into his arms like a baby. He took me to the back and sat me down on a couch, in what appeared to be an office. He disappeared, momentarily.

"I can't believe I fell." I exclaimed.

The worst part about the whole thing is that I fell in front of my bae. Had it been my friends, I wouldn't have cared, but I was definitely mortified.

"Here babe." He handed me a bag of ice.

I gave him a weak smile, as he stared at me lovingly. He sat down on the couch, next to me and I immediately put my hand up.

"I don't even wanna hear it, Banks."

He tried to hold his laughter in. "What? I was just going to say, you did a good job before you—well you know."

"See this is why I wanted to go out. Now, I'm sitting here holding ice to my head when we could have just gone out like normal people."

We stared at one another and he burst out laughing again.

"Oh my God, I'm leaving." I got up to leave, but he grabbed me and pulled, my bare ass down onto his lap.

I had a permanent mug on my face, but he was able to ease my mind, with his gentle touch and coy smile.

"I'm sorry for laughing, I truly didn't bring you here for all of this." He reached into his pocket and pulled out a set of keys. "In fact, I wanna give you these."

Once the keys were in my hand, I looked at them with a perplexed look on my face.

"Okay, so these are the keys to what exactly?"

"I bought this place for you." He stated which confused me even more.

"You brought a strip club for me?"

He chuckled. "Yes, the owner was shutting down soon, so I bought the space from him, so that you can have your own dance studio."

My heart started to race a thousand miles per second.

"We have a lot of work to do, but once we remodel it, you'll have your dream studio. You deserve it." He was cheesing, by now my mouth was agape, wide enough to catch flies in. I was stunned. I brought my hand up to cover my mouth, as I looked back and forth between Banks and the keys in my hand.

My emotions were running amuck. I tried not to cry, but it didn't work the waterworks couldn't be stopped. "Oh my God."

He reached up and wiped the tears streaming down my face, then took my hands into his and kissed the back of them tenderly.

"All I want is to see you succeed, to do what you were destined to do. You have been through a lot. I just want to help steer you in the right direction. You don't ever have to answer to anyone ever again because this here—" He pointed to the walls and ceiling. "This here is all yours, baby. I believe in you, and I'm falling for you more and more each day. You're special to me."

I leaned forward and pecked his lips a few times. He stood up and lifted me in the air, so I wrapped my legs around his waist. I nuzzled my face in between his neck as he rubbed my back.

"I'm so grateful for what you've done, you made me the happiest girl alive."

"Good." I lifted my head, just in time to see him smirking. "Now come give daddy some of that ill nana."

I silently stared at him, with a blank face, but burst into laughter a few seconds later. I shook my head and tapped his arm, indicating, that I wanted to be placed to my feet. "My head hurts and I'm not in the mood for that, but good try."

He sucked his teeth and shrugged his shoulders. "Shit it was worth a try.

I got up on my tiptoes and kissed him. "I don't know how, but you made me fall for you. Literally." I admitted.

We shared a laugh together, then I retrieved my clothes and got dressed. We headed back to his place and spent to the rest of the night, talking. We fell asleep in each other's arms.

Naheem

"Don't look so sad, baby. I promise all of this will be over soon." My mind was elsewhere, but I instantly looked up when I felt my mom's hand on mine. She gave me a reassuring smile, when our eyes locked.

My mother sat across from me every, Thursday faithfully, with no excuses. I commended her for that, because she was my biggest support system. No one else really gave a damn about me. As soon as I got locked up, everyone turned his or her backs on me, including my wife. Yes, I fucked up and got another girl pregnant, but I didn't expect her to give up on us so soon. I love, Heaven, with everything in me, but I messed up bad and if I could take it back, I would.

I didn't respond to my mother, I just remained quiet. I knew, she could sense, that I wasn't really in the mood to be bothered. I just wanted to go back to my cell and sulk in the fact, that my life was going down the drain.

I looked around and watched, as other inmates were all smiles as they were visited by their girlfriends and wives. Here I was being visited by my mother, and only my mother, for the umpteenth time.

"Look at me," She demanded, once again my thoughts were interrupted, so I did as I was told and looked at my mother. "Are you thinking about that, bitch?" She said, only low enough for me to hear.

"Ma, for real. Don't call her that. She didn't do anything to you, she didn't do anything wrong, to me. I'm the one that cheated on her, remember."

She sneered and pursed up her lips. "Listen, she sent you over those fucking dissolution papers and you're seriously defending her? She doesn't give a damn about you, to the point where she's trying to divorce you. I know you saw her parading around town with that rapper boy. I forget his name, but she don't care about you and—"

My eyebrows rose, at the mention of, Heaven, being with another man. "Wait what?"

She shook her head. "Yeah, it's such a shame, she has practically moved on to this famous rapper. She's all over the blogs, cheesing and smiling all up in his damn face without a care in the world, acting like her husband isn't behind bars." she scoffed. "Don't even get me started on that supposed, baby mama of, yours. I talked to her dumbass daddy. He wasn't trying to give me any info, but I told him straight up, that I deserve to know about my grandbaby. He said that there wasn't going to be a baby, because she got rid of it. The nerve of that little bitch."

I felt a sharp pain in my chest, I was sure, it was my heart, which felt like it was being ripped apart. Another man was with my woman and I couldn't do a got damned thing about it, because I was locked up. On top of that, this was all news to me about, my baby. Shania could not contact me and vice versa due to the predicament, we were in, with her being only seventeen. So, my mom had been having conversations with, Shania's family. They'd given her a hard time, initially, but once she finally convinced them, she didn't want to miss out on her grandchild's life, they'd told her something, I didn't want to hear. She aborted my fucking baby. I was pissed as fuck, but again, I couldn't do anything because I was behind bars.

"Listen to me, son. I promise, I will do any and every-thing, I can to fix this mess you're in. You just have to trust me."

At this point everything, my mom was saying went into one ear and out of the other. I always thought, marriage would last through thick and thin, but it was evident to me that after six months. I was the last person on, Heaven's mind, especially after she blocked me from calling. It took everything in me, not to break down when I got those dumb ass dissolution of marriage papers.

"You hear me?" My mother chimed in.

"Yes ma'am." I replied, to get her off of my back.

"I'm telling you, I got you son, just trust me." She gave me a reassuring smile.

"Okay ma, I trust you." I didn't know what my future would look like, but I was praying like hell, I wouldn't spend the rest of my life rotting in a cell.

Chapter 16

Heaven

"Stop splashing that water over here!" Margarita yelled. I slightly rolled my eyes. She and I were always cordial, because she was Vaeh's girl, but I really didn't fuck with her like that. Vaeh invited her to the family BBQ, that Banks was throwing at his house, and all she was doing was yelling and complaining about his little cousins splashing in the pool.

Renaissance wasn't too fond of her either, but I put my big girl pantries on and tolerated her for a few hours. The four of us sat in a circle, in some lawn chairs near the pool, grubbing on some of the best macaroni, collard greens, cornbread, corn on the cob and BBQ ribs, I'd ever tasted. Banks said he could cook, but we normally went out. I didn't know he could throw down like this. We were all smacking our lips and licking our fingers clean. Then out of nowhere, Margarita, just had to be the one to break the ice.

"Girl, does your man have any single homies? I mean, you're really out here living your best life." she joked.

I gave her a fake smile. "I have no idea girl, sorry."

"Aww come on. I know he has to have a single cousin or something." She was adamant, but even if I did know I wouldn't tell her.

She had a bad rep for smashing pretty much anybody. I didn't need anyone thinking, she and I were the same way, because I was associated with her.

"Damn, Margarita, you want something to drink?" Renaissance said causing me to damn near choke on my food. Margarita had a confused look on her face, so she obviously didn't get the joke.

She popped her lips. "No why?"

Renaissance chuckled. "You acting a lil' thirsty, baby."

Margarita rolled her eyes and shot, Renaissance, the bird as we all began to laugh at her expense.

My attention was taken away from the girls momentarily, when Skye walked over to us. She was helping out with the party, so she didn't have much time to chill.

"Hey, my beautiful black, queens." She said then flopped down into an empty lawn chair near us. She reached over and grabbed a spare rib from my plate. "Girl, ya man threw down, I can't stop eating." she joked.

"I wonder, if that's the only thing he's throwing down." Vaeh said, which instantly annoyed me, because she was always trying to start shit, nowadays when it came to Banks.

I glared at her, giving her a perplexed look. "What the hell, is that supposed to mean"?

She pointed across the pool where, Banks, was laughing and talking to a few girls that were dressed rather provocatively. One girl was laughing so hard, her boobs were jumping up and down. The other kept hitting his chest every time she laughed. I noticed him take a step back, putting a bit of space between him and those nameless females.

"He's looking a little too cozy over there. You know these rap niggas ain't shit, they fuck and any everyone." She chuckled, like something was actually funny.

I didn't know what to say, so I kept quiet to keep myself from cursing her out.

"Get your man, sis." she continued.

Sister or not, she was really doing the most.

Skye scoffed and put her hand up. "Hold up, I know you're not insinuating, that my boss is a hoe, or even that he's fucking around on, my girl. I'm always around him, I'm the one that sets his schedule. I know more about his whereabouts probably, more than anyone. He's not messing around on, my girl." Skye was pissed. I could see the veins in her neck popping out.

Vaeh cocked her head to the side and her jaw tightened, as she pursed up her lips. "Oh, so you're taking up for him? Shit if you asked me, you probably fucked him too, since you're supposedly always around him."

I looked at Skye, she looked like she was about to body slam my sister. I definitely wouldn't allow that, but it was funny to think about since, Vaeh, was talking a lot of shit at the moment.

"Okay, you're doing way too fucking much, right now, you need to chill out." Renaissance countered, and Margarita co-signed.

"Yeah, just chill he's just over there talking we have no idea what the conversation is, it's wrong to assume." Margarita said.

The fact that Margarita was siding with us was crazy to me, because her and my sister were like two peas in a pod. I always knew she had good sense, she just fucked too many niggas for my liking.

"You just gonna let them talk to me like that, Heaven?" Vaeh tried to flip the script and play victim, as she always did, but this time it wasn't going to fly.

"Listen." I sighed. "You're my sister, and I love you, but you are way out of pocket, right now. Even if he was a hoe and fucked around, which he's not, it's my concern, not yours."

Skye hopped up and stepped closer, which caused me to stand up too and step in front of her.

"I'm not going to hit her, I have way too much respect for you, Heaven, to fight your sister." Skye directed her attention back to Vaeh. "I'm not fucking, Banks, nor have I ever. You need to stop being such a jealous, bitch!"

She stormed off just as, Banks, walked over asking everyone if they were okay. Rita shook her head and walked off with Renaissance in tow. Nevaeh had her face all screwed up, like she was sucking on a lemon. She too hopped up and stormed off.

"What's going on?" Banks flopped down into one of the now empty lawn chairs.

I shrugged. "It's nothing, babe."

"Okay. Well I was just checking on you, making sure you were okay and having a good time."

I smiled sweetly. "Thank you, baby."

He leaned over and pecked my lips a few times, then stared into my eyes.

"I have something on my face?" I questioned, because he was looking at me funny.

"No, you're just, beautiful." I loved his compliments. He always made me feel special, even at the worst times. He lightly massaged my shoulders.

"You're tense babe, are you sure that ——"

"Aye! Get over here and tend to this meat!" One of his homeboys yelled out.

He chuckled. "Aye, chill on that gay shit." He yelled back, then he kissed my neck and stood up to finish cooking on the grill.

I sighed heavily, and got up as well, in search of my sister. When I found her, she was in the foyer pecking away on her phone.

She looked up and rolled her eyes once she saw me coming. "Don't worry, sis, I'm leaving. Y'all bitches wanna gang up on me so I'ma do y'all a favor and catch an Uber." She was pissed, and I didn't understand why.

I wasn't angry though, only hurt, she was acting this way

"You don't have to leave, Vaeh, you just need to chill out on the shit you're saying. You and I both know, you can get a little carried away at times with your mouth, but I know you don't mean any harm by it."

"Heaven you are my sister, we shared the same womb together. I'm not trying to hurt your feelings. I was only trying to give you a reality check. Banks may not be the nigga you think he is. He has money and groupies on his dick. I just don't want you to be naive." She shifted all of her weight to one leg and crossed her arms. "I don't mean any harm in my words, but just be careful."

"I will, I promise. He's a good man. I know the two of you don't really mesh well, but trust me, he's good to me. That's all that matters, right now." I smiled at my own words.

I pulled her into a hug. "You're my sister, I love you to pieces, but if you get out of line again. I'm gonna have to put them paws on you." I was halfway joking. I didn't know why, Nevaeh, had been acting funny these past couple of weeks, but I would definitely be keeping an eye on her.

The two of us, laughed, and decided to go back outside to enjoy the BBQ along with, Skye, Renaissance and Margarita.

I enjoyed the rest of my day and ended my night in, Banks, arms as usual.

***

"You ready for round three baby?" Banks had the audacity to ask, when he knew how tired I was. Hell, I was surprised, he wasn't tired. He had definitely, blown my back out. I needed to recover, but he wasn't trying to hear that with his nasty ass.

I looked over my shoulder, since my back was facing him, then glared at him through the slits of my eyes. I made sure he knew, I wasn't up for anything any time soon, just by the expression on my face.

"Let's go to sleep, babe. I'm sleepy." I whined, causing him to chuckle. "It's been a long day.

Banks attempted to lift my leg, so he could slide inside of me in the spooning position.

"You don't even have to do anything, just let me do all of the work." His tone was laced with lust.

"Babe stop it." I giggled, when he kissed me on the back of my neck several times.

"Your pussy is lethal, it should be against the law to be this fine, with pussy this good." Banks sat up momentarily.

I giggled. "Nice try, babe." I got out of the bed, when I got to the doorway of the bedroom, I turned to say, "I'm a little thirsty, I'm going to get something to drink.

Banks

I got up five minutes later, and followed Heaven into the kitchen, anxious to get in another round. She stood in the doorway, of the fridge stuffing her mouth with strawberries.

"Get out of my damn strawberries!" I yelled, causing her to yelp and place her left hand on her bare chest. Her breasts were jiggling, when she began to laugh. She reached over and slapped me on the arm when I closed the space in between us.

"Why are you eating my fruit, with yo' greedy ass?"

She cut her eyes at me, then playfully shoved my chest pushing me backwards.

"It was calling my name." she joked. "Why are you, sneaking up behind me, anyways?"

"You were taking too long, and I missed you."

She smirked. "I bet."

She continued, to stuff her mouth with strawberries, so I reached into the container and grabbed one. I was sure, she knew what was about to go down, by the sinister look on my face.

I trailed the strawberry down her chest slowly, swirling it around her nipples. Her eyes grew wide, when I bent down and started licking on the strawberry and her nipple at the same time. I was already hard as fuck.

"Let me eat in peace, babe."

I grabbed the entire container from her hand and placed it back in the fridge, closing it right after.

"What are you ——." I grabbed her by the neck and slammed her into the closest wall. I just couldn't help myself, I attacked her lips and she let out the sexiest moan ever.

I removed my hands from her neck and brought them down to her ass. I cupped both cheeks in my hands, as she brought her arms up to lock tightly around my neck.

"Fuck me." She blurted out, no longer able to deny my advances.

I used one hand to jack my dick and the other to finger her. She was wetter, than a fat bitch in a sauna. I couldn't wait any longer. I picked her up and her legs automatically wrapped around my waist. She instantly, began to leave a trail of small kisses on my neck. I sat her on top of the counter, sliding inside of her, without warning. She gasped for air, like a fish out of water, then quickly latched onto my shoulders, as I pumped in and out of her.

"S…slow down." she stuttered.

"Why? Don't it feel good?"

She shook her head, frantically. "Oh fuck! I'm about to cum already."

"Nah, don't cum, yet." I slowed down a bit, pulling out real slow, then slamming back into her repeatedly. She hissed each time I did.

She leaned up, pulling my head lower to steal a kiss, as I continued to fuck her roughly, showing her pussy no mercy.

"Hold on real tight to my neck."

"Okay" she said, breathlessly.

When her grip on my neck tightened, I lifted her up into the air. Taking a couple steps backwards, making sure I had enough space. I placed my hands on the palm of her ass, with her legs dangling over my forearms. I started to bounce her up and down on my dick. Her head fell back in ecstasy, as we moved in unison. As her body began to shutter, I could feel my nut coming. After six or seven strokes, I bust all inside of her. We came together. Her hair was wet and stuck to her face. Her eyes flutter open, and her grip on my neck loosened, as her body went limp. Once her feet were back on the ground, her legs appeared to be a little wobbly, as she leaned on me for support.

"That was amazing." She said, still trying to catch her breath.

"No, you're amazing." I moved the hair from her face and kissed her forehead. "Lets go to bed now."

She latched onto my hands, that were delicately holding onto her cheeks, with the biggest smile in the world on her face, "Oh now we can go to bed, huh?"

"Shut up." I joked, causing her to shriek when I unexpectedly scooped her up wedding style. "Let me help you to the bed. I know daddy dick got you paralyzed."

"I hate you, so much." She stated, as we made our way to the bedroom.

Once in bed, it was only a matter of minutes, before the two of us were knocked out.

Chapter 17

Banks

I was tired as hell, after my show last night, waking up early for some business meetings, catching a flight back home to Fort Lauderdale from Texas, and then listening to a few beats Rod-C wanted me to listen to.

I had been gone for almost three weeks performing, attending awards shows, and doing interviews all over the got damn world.

At this point, all I wanted to do was go home so I could lay the fuck down in my bed. I wasn't feeling good so definitely I didn't want to be bothered. It was nothing personal towards anyone, that's just how I got when I was sick. The only person, I wanted to see was, Heaven. I made a mental note to slide by her place, right after my nap.

When I pulled into my driveway, I saw a car, I didn't expect to see. I sucked my teeth, then got out.

"What are you doing here, just sitting in my damn driveway?" I was beyond annoyed. She couldn't get her words out fast enough, so I decided to voice my opinion.

"You can't just be showing up to my house, unannounced, Lakenya. Why are you here?"

I stood next to her car, with my hands in my pocket, after sliding my keys inside, waiting for her to give me a legitimate reason.

She looked distraught. "I miss you, Banks, I miss us."

She stood in front of me looking as beautiful as the day, I met her, which made it hard for me to stay mad. Her beauty was mind-blowing, and she appeared to get prettier every time I saw her. She had on a simple pair of stone washed jean shorts, a white spaghetti strapped shirt, that barely held up her big ass titties, and a pair of all black Huarache's.

I could see in her eyes, that she really missed me, but I wasn't over the way she left me. She wasn't even trying to see my vision. I told her, I was going to make it, but she thought it was just a pipe dream. Now she's all on a nigga, trying to get back with me.

"Can we go inside to talk?" She pointed towards the door, but I shook my head.

"We don't even have anything to ta—"

"Please talk to me." She stepped closer to me, invading my personal space. "Or at least hear me out." She pleaded with her eyes, as I swore, I saw them bitches get all glazed up, as if she was about to cry.

I released a sigh. "A'ight man you can come in."

She gave me a small smile. Once we got inside, she sat down on the couch. I decided to sit across from her on another sofa.

"Why do you have to sit all the way over there?"

I Looked at her, like she was crazy, because we had been sitting here for five minutes, silent as hell, and the only thing she wanted to know, was why I wasn't sitting by her ass?

I slouched down on the couch, laying my head back. I knew, I should have left her outside. My head was killing me, all I wanted to do was take some meds and be out like a light, right after.

"What's wrong, baby? Are you okay?"

I let her slide calling me baby, only because I wasn't in the mood to argue. I closed my eyes momentarily.

"I'm good. What did you want to talk about?"

It was silent, and I exhaled deeply when I felt her hand on my forehead.

"Oh my God, baby, you're burning up." I opened my eyes for a moment, to see a look of concern on her face as she also placed her hand on my neck.

I grabbed her hand gently, removing it from my neck, as she looked at me confused.

"What?" I asked. "I just want to be there for you. Like I used to be. I still love you. I just hate being away from you."

She Fell in Love with a Real One

"Here comes the water works Banks." I said to myself.

She started crying, just like I knew she would. My whole demeanor changed a little.

"Don't cry, Kenya."

"Why shouldn't't, I?" She sobbed, with her face now in her hands. "You hate me, and I don't blame you."

"Look at me." I grabbed her chin, making her look me in the eyes. "I don't hate you, I just hate what you did."

I watched as her lips began to quiver, and her chest heaved up and down at a fast pace. "I know baby, and I'm sorry. Please forgive me and take me back."

I just stared at her. Even while crying, she was still beautiful, as hell.

"I don't know, about that right now, Kenya."

She shifted around on the couch, so that she was now on her knees, as she reached to caress me through my basketball shorts. She tooted her ass up in the air in those little ass shorts.

"Let me make you feel good, baby", was all she said, as she pulled my dick out. My shit had already bricked up. Even though, I wasn't trying to go there with her again, I didn't see any harm in getting my dick sucked.

She stuck her tongue out, swirling it over the tip of my dick. She made sure to keep eye contact, with me the whole time. She spit on it, slurped it back up, then spit on it again. She was definitely giving me that, sloppy toppy.

As she moved her head up and down, sucking my shit like a vacuum cleaner, I put my hand on her head, so I could hold her hair up. I needed a full view of the peepshow.

"You gonna be mine again, baby?" She asked, before deep throating my dick, making it hard for me to talk.

I stayed silent, because she thought she was slick asking me things, while giving me some good ass head.

"Suck that dick." I bit my lip, as I felt my nut coming.

"Wait, baby let me get on top."

Lakenya quickly stood up, I glared at her, as she seductively took off her shorts and panties. I jacked my dick, as she removed her shirt, leaving her only in her bra. After she straddled me on the couch I tried to put my dick inside of her but she moved my hand.

"Let me put it in." She always wanted to be in charge during sex. I never really seemed to care, as long as I was getting my dick wet it didn't matter.

"As a matter of a fact hold up." I tapped her thigh, so she could get up. I reached down into my pants pocket to retrieve a condom.

She scoffed. "What's that for? We never used those."

I ignored her, rolling the condom on.

"You want this dick or not?"

She nodded, like an obedient child. I spit into my hand, then rubbed it on her pussy. Soon after she got back on top of me, grabbed my pipe and slid down on it slowly. She winced in pain, as she tried to adjust to my size.

I put my hands on her waist, pulling her down harder, until I was sure she felt me in her stomach. Her mouth hung open, as she instantly put her hands on my shoulders.

"Mmm, you like it, when I ride it like this, baby?" She rode me, like she was trying to win a got damn horse-riding contest. "This dick feels so good." She moaned, as I met her downward thrusts with upward thrusts.

My breathing increased, as I could already feel my nut coming. I almost forgot how good her pussy was.

She leaned down and kissed me. I hadn't kissed her in so long. I swear, all of my feelings for her came rushing back, as we sat on the couch fucking like jack rabbits and kissing, like it would be our last time. I didn't realize how much, I missed her, until this moment.

"I love you, baby." She said as we came together, trembling and shuddering.

Her hair was now wet with sweat. It was plastered all over her face. The only thing I could do, was sit back and try to regain my normal breathing speed. She stayed on top of me, just staring at a nigga.

"What?" I questioned.

"I said, I love you, Banks, don't you love me back?"

I stood up with her, still in my lap. I dropped her gently onto the couch, put my dick back in my boxers and pulled my pants up. She was legit waiting for a response.

"Kenya." I paused. "I ain't in the mood for this conversation, right now."

She rolled her eyes, getting up quickly to throw on her clothes.

"Oh, but you were in the mood for some dome, though, right? You had no problem, with me doing that or with fucking me."

She stepped into her shorts quickly. She threw her shirt on, so damn fast that she put it on inside out.

"I didn't ask you for head, Kenya or sex."

"Whatever." I could tell, she was upset, and I wasn't really trying to argue with her, or make her feel like I was using her. "Let me go!" She yelled, when she tried to brush past me hurriedly.

"No, hold up a sec."

She avoided eye contact with me, as her jaw clenched.

"Why you acting like this?" She remained silent. "Huh?"

"Because, Banks, you won't even give us a second chance. You act like I mean nothing to you!"

"First of all, lower your voice when you're talking to me, because I'm not yelling at you."

She pursed up her lips and crossed her arms. I watched as she rolled her neck, doing all that extra shit. "Fuck you, okay."

My eyes widened as I pointed to myself. "Oh, so it's fuck me now?"

"Yeah, because you are being difficult for no reason. You got me out here looking stupid, begging you to be with me. Just forget it." She pushed past me and as she walked away. I thought about the whole situation at hand. She was right in a way. She was un-happy in a relationship, because I was not financially stable to be a real man and provide for her. It wasn't, that she didn't love me, she just got fed up with struggling. Maybe I needed to see it from her point of view.

I followed her outside, to see that she hadn't even pulled off, because she was sitting in her car crying. I knocked on the window, and she reluctantly rolled it down.

"What?" She sniffed, wiping her nose with a tissue. I assumed she got out of her glove compartment or something.

"I'm willing to work on us, but, we gotta take it slow."

"Really?" She smiled halfheartedly. I opened her car door and held out my hand.

She gawked at it for a moment, then she placed her soft, gentle hand into mine. I pulled her from the car, and she stood directly in front of me.

"Yes really." To seal the deal, I leaned down and wrapped my arms around her, as she wrapped her arms around my neck. I just hoped this worked out well, in my favor and I wasn't getting myself into some shit, I wouldn't be able to get out of.

Nevaeh

"Girl is that, Lance? Heaven pointed across the room at, Lance, and some white bitch.

Heaven dragged me to some party for TMG and I came knowing, I'd see him, but didn't expect to see him with another girl.

"Yeah, that's his dumbass."

The bitch looked basic as fuck rocking apple bottom jeans and some got damn boots with the fur. Maybe she was trying to fit in, being that we were at a predominately black club. My blood instantly started to boil, because I took Lance to this same club plenty of times. It was a spot we visited often, because they played amazing dancehall music, and served the best jerk chicken in town. I knew that he was obviously trying to make me mad, by showing up to our spot with another bitch.

I glared at them waiting for him to look up, so I could flick him off or something. I was so mad, flames were probably visible on the top of my head.

"What's the problem?" My sister didn't know what was going on between, Lance and I, and I wasn't trying to get into all of that shit, right now, anyway.

"Nothing, I'm cool."

She laughed a bit, then she took a sip of her rum and coke. "Well you don't look cool. What y'all, beefing?"

"Nope. He called his self, cutting me off, because I don't wanna be in a relationship."

She looked at me confused. "Uh, and why don't you? That is one fine ass, white boy."

I couldn't help, but roll my eyes. "He wants too much, and I just want to fuck, that's it. I mean I enjoy his company, but why ruin a good thing. All he needs to do, is keep giving me dick and money."

"Well clearly you like him more than, you're willing to admit. You look like you're ready to go over there and fight that, bitch." My sister was completely right. I didn't care who she was, ole girl was about to catch these got damned hands for being all over my man.

"I really wanna clock her ass."

"But why? You don't want him, remember." Heaven said sarcastically.

I'll admit in my head, she was right, but I'd never say that shit out loud.

I sucked my teeth at her revelation. "Shut up! I'm going to the bathroom."

"A'ight you want me to come with?" She tried to get up, but I put my hand up to halt her motions.

"Nah, I'll be right back."

"Okay."

I made my way over to the bathroom and pushed past a bunch of sweaty ass men and women, who were grinding to some Jamaican song. I tried to keep myself together, because I was a complete wreck after seeing, Lance, partying with another bitch. I wasn't trying to lose the only finances, I had coming in.

I reapplied my lip-gloss, pushed my boobs up, and fixed a few stray hairs. I was going to rain on his fucking parade. He hadn't been answering my phone calls, as usual and he'd been ignoring my text messages. Then I come here, and see him here with another bitch, other than the one I caught him with.

I left the bathroom hoping, they were still here.

"Excuse me!" I pushed through the crowd, heading towards Lance and this mystery, bitch.

"Dance with me, shawty." Some dude with hot ass stale breath, said damn near burning my got damn nose off.

"You need to get yo' hands off of me and go find some damn gum!" I shouted, dude rolled his eyes and eventually he danced away.

Once I was close enough, I tapped, Lance, on the shoulder and he turned around with wide eyes.

"Oh—hey, Vaeh."

My head jerked back a little, was this nigga being nonchalant, with me?

"Hey, I guess your phone is broken, huh?"

He looked back and forth, between me and whoever home girl was. The girl looked over at the two of us. She smiled, but I gave a stank look.

"Can I have another beer?" I looked around trying to figure out, who in the hell she was talking to.

"Bitch, do I look like, I fucking work here?" I countered, causing, Lance, to immediately intervene.

"I'm sorry, I just thought—"

I cut her off. "Well you thought wrong, bitch!"

"She doesn't work here, Jennifer." Lance said standing in between us, with Jennifer in front of him and me behind him.

Then the bitch tried to be slick by saying, "Well she looks like she should work here."

She ain't know who she was messing with. "You better get this hoe! I will drag her ass, all across this damn bar!"

Jennifer looked at, Lance, with fear present on her face.

"Who is she? What's going on?"

"I'm his girlfriend, who the fuck, are you?"

Lance swiftly eyed me and shook his head.

Jennifer laughed nervously. "I'm only a friend, but that's funny, he never mentioned you." I wanted to slap her ugly ass. She looked so damn dirty, like she needed a bath and.

"She's not, my girlfriend." He said, which pissed me off even more. I mushed his head.

"Just the other night, when you were begging to be with me, after you ate this pussy!" I lied.

"Okay, Vaeh you really need to leave. I'm here with, Jennifer, she's a new artist, I'm working with and I'm not inter—"

I felt someone tugging on my arm and looked back briefly, to see twin standing next to me, with a concerned look on her face.

She pursed up her lips, as if she already had an idea what happened, but she still asked for clarification. "What's going on?"

"Nothing I had to check a bitch, real quick, but I'm good now." I mugged that, Jennifer, bitch and pushed past Lance's ass.

"Girl let's just go." Heaven grabbed me by the arm.

I looked back and locked eyes with him, as she was being pulled away. I wasn't worried, he'd be hitting me up probably as soon as he dropped chick home.

I snatched away from my sister and took off towards the exit of the club. I needed to get out and fast. I wasn't in the mood for this shit, I needed to get high.

"Wait, where are you going?" I heard her yell, but I kept walking, until I was no longer around her.

I needed to get the fuck away from everyone. I was two seconds away from losing my cool.

Heaven

The Deejay was spinning some of, Banks's music, it immediately made me smile, because that meant, he was in the building. It was all love, as every man and woman in the building recited his words with ease.

I couldn't believe, I let, Nevaeh talk me into going out to the club, bar, or whatever you want to call it. She knew this wasn't my kind of thing, but she insisted on me going out with her. We were having a good ass time and then all of a sudden, she popped off on some chick.

Unfortunately, Vaeh, ditched me and I hadn't seen her in almost an hour. I finally gave up looking for her, because she wasn't responding to any of my texts. Since I was already out, I wanted to enjoy myself. Luckily, Banks had an appearance tonight, at the same club for his album release party. So, I figured, I'd just meet up with him. My sister was probably somewhere getting some dick or trying to knowing her.

I pulled my phone out to shoot him a text versus calling him. I already knew, he wouldn't be able to hear me over the music, so that option was out of the question.

Me: Wya?

It took him about five minutes to respond.

Banks: Just got to the VIP section. You here?

Me: Yeah and my damn sister ditched me.

Banks: Lol. A'ight well come up here baby.

A huge smile spread across my face, as I made my way through the crowd and made, my way over to his VIP section. As I got closer, all I saw were groupies surrounding the VIP section, snapping pictures, trying to get into the section. I laughed at their facial expressions, when I walked up and was let into the section immediately, by the bouncer. I was getting mean mugged, and a few of them rolled their eyes, but I didn't care.

Banks was busy texting and didn't notice me, until I was standing directly in front of him. His cologne immediately, hit my nose and he was looking sexy as fuck. I gently grabbed his chin to make him look at me and once our eyes locked, he smiled, and leaned in to give me quick, kiss on the lips.

All of a sudden, I felt someone yank me away from, Banks, roughly by my arm. My eyes widened, when I turned to see, Lance, with a mug on his face.

"What the hell is going on?" He said to me, his words slurred. He was pissy drunk, and I had no idea what his problem was.

His grip on my arm got tighter, as I tried to push him off of me. "Stop, you're hurting me!" I tried to pry his hands from my arm.

I looked over at, Banks, who had a confused look on his face. He shoved, Lance, making him stumble, as he released his hold on my arm. He tripped over his own damn feet and fell back on a near-by couch. He looked stunned that Banks, had even pushed him.

"Bruh, what the fuck are you doing, grabbing on her like that?" Banks pointed at me to get his point across.

They were having a staring match, Lance definitely lost, because he tore his eyes away from, Banks, to look at me.

"Why you kissing on, her? Th—this is my—my girl."

If looks could kill, I'd be six feet under. Banks looked like he was about to murder, my ass. His fists were now balled up and his jaw tightened. Shit, Lance, had the same look on his face.

"The fuck is he talking about, Heaven?"

"I—I don't know." This nigga had me stuttering, from his piercing glare.

I quickly turned to, Lance, when it dawned on me. I'd only met, Lance, about three times. He hadn't been around me long enough to be able to tell my sister and I apart.

"I'm Heaven not, Nevaeh." I said to him, as his facial features started to soften.

Banks jumped into the conversation eager to find out what was going on.

Banks thought long and hard, about what I'd just said. "Nevaeh, your identical twin sister?"

I shook my head in agreement. "He must've mistaken me for her." The two of us looked at, Lance, waiting for him to say something.

His ass was out of it, you could tell, as he failed to get up on his feet.

"I got it muthafucka, don't touch me!" He said to the same white woman, I'd seen Vaeh, get into it with.

The woman threw her hands up and stormed out of the section. I guess she was tired of his shit, for the night.

Finally, he managed to stand up on his legs, that resembled noodles, and stepped closer to me. I felt Banks's hand on my stomach, as he pushed me back gently, so that he could step in front of me.

"Now wh—what did you s—say?"

I peeked around Banks's shoulder, so I could repeat myself. "I said, I'm not Nevaeh—I'm Heaven."

For a moment, none of us said anything. Lance looked like he was in deep thought.

"Oh, shit, my bad." he chuckled.

I didn't find anything funny about the situation. My arm was still hurting, and I wanted to yank on his arm, to see how he'd like it.

"I'm sorry, bruh, I didn't know."

Banks stepped closer to, Lance, and said something in his ear, so I wasn't able to hear what was going on. Once he stepped back, he gave his bodyguard a head nod. I watched as the body guard, escorted Lance out of the VIP section.

"What happened?" I asked him, being nosey as hell.

"I told him to take his drunk ass home. I had my bodyguard escort him, outside to make sure he's good, and to have my driver take him home. But, you good, though? I apologize, I've never seen my boy, this drunk."

I lightly rubbed my arm but gave him a coy smile and shook my head.

"Good."

He leaned down and pecked my lips a few times. "You want something to drink?" He asked, pointing to all the different bottles on the table, in front of him. He had Ace of Spades, Hennessey, Ciroc, Remy and Bacardi.

I shook my head, as someone tapped him on the shoulder, diverting his attention away from me. I did however, help myself to an empty spot on the couch. My damn feet were killing me.

We made eye contact for a few moments then he looked away. He was the finest man up in the club. I wasn't just saying that, because he dicked me down on a regular basis. He licked his juicy succulent lips then took a sip from his glass. From the looks of things, it looked like he was drinking Hennessey straight. I smirked, because I knew first hand, that he performed exceptionally well in bed with the Hennessey in his system. I was horny and needed him inside of me, tonight.

The song smoothly switched over to, Drake's *Nice for what*. My feet were just going to have to deal with me, for a few more moments, this was my favorite song. I stood my ass right back up and allowed my body to move seductively, to the beat of the song. I pushed my way through his little friends and a few groupie hoes. I made sure to stop directly in front of him. I grabbed his hand, as he watched me inquisitively. I pulled him off to the side in the corner, where there weren't many people.

I pushed him against the wall and he sneered. "I have been missing you, for the past few weeks." I admitted, and it was the honest truth. He was on my mind a majority of the day.

I leaned in and pecked his lips a few times before he slid his tongue inside my mouth. His hands slowly slid down my backside, landing directly on my ass.

"Oh yeah?" He questioned, in between kisses.

I pulled away and pecked his lips a few more times. "Did you miss me?"

He took my hand and placed it on his hard dick. "What you think?"

I didn't answer his question. Instead, I turned around and placed my ass right up against his dick. Once I was able to catch onto the beat, I began to give him a show. I bent all the way over, so he could see, that I didn't have any panties on. He slapped my ass turning me on.

When I looked at him over my shoulder, he was biting his bottom lip. I began to grind on his dick, as his hands rubbed all over my body. My nipples got hard, as his hands softly rubbed them, through the thin material of my dress.

His hand landed on my neck, as he gripped it roughly. He turned my head to the side, so he could speak into my ear, as I kept grinding up against him, slowly and seductively.

"Why you fucking with me in this club? Bend over again." He said into my ear, as I bent over, once again. Banks slipped a finger into my exposed pussy. He began to slowly finger fuck me, and it felt so good, I started to moan. Luckily, the music was loud, so no one heard me. We were in the cut and it was dim in the corner, so I was sure that no one was watching. He added a second finger and I started throwing it back on his finger.

He stopped abruptly when one of his boys approached him.

"Yo, Mike is fucked up, we taking his drunk ass home." I overheard the guy say. Mike was Banks's manager.

He discreetly pulled his fingers out of me. "A'ight."

His friends motioned towards the exit, by pointing in that direction. "You leaving with us?"

"Nah, bruh, I got a ride." He pointed at me, which caused me to smile so damn wide. I was ready to hop on that dick, a.s.a.p.

They spoke for a brief moment, and then shared a friendly handshake. Banks bent down, biting on my booty cheeks through my dress, which caused me to swat him away playfully.

"Stop silly, we're in public." I looked around making sure that no one saw that, when I spun around, he was giving me bedroom eyes.

He grabbed my hand and kissed it. "So, what's your name?" I realized what he was doing, and decided to play along, with his little game.

"Heaven and you?"

"Banks."

"I like that. So, how old are you?" I countered.

He grinned. He started this game, so I was going to finish it. "I'm old enough, baby."

I bit my lip, leaning in closer to him. "Old enough to fuck me, tonight?"

"If that's what you want to do."

I smiled and latched onto his hand. "C'mon, lets go." My pussy continued to throb, as I led the way.

We made our way past a bunch of groupie bitches and a few paparazzi that were waiting outside.

Once we made our way to my car, I said, "You know how to drive, right?"

"Yeah, why, what's up?" He questioned, as I walked around to the passenger side of the car.

"I want you to drive."

"Why?"

"You'll see." I winked at him and got inside.

He followed my lead and got into the car on the driver's side.

"I don't live too far from here. We can go to my place." He said, and I agreed.

"What's the freakiest shit you've ever done?" I asked, as his eyebrows rose in amazement.

"Nothing really." He shrugged his shoulders. "I'm a little shy." He lied. It was all a part of this little game.

I made myself a little bit more comfortable. I leaned back and propped my legs open.

"Give me your hand." I grabbed his free hand and placed it on my bare pussy.

"You see how wet I am? It's all for you, baby."

He tried to keep his eyes on the road. I took my top off and let my titties free. I propped myself up on my knees. Then leaned over into the driver's seat. My hands latched onto his neck. I pulled him in for a kiss at the stop light and stared seductively in his eyes. Our lips touched, immediately.

"I'm going to have fun with you, tonight." Our lips connected, and I began to suck on his bottom lip hungrily as his free hand fondled my breasts. Our kiss became more intense. Our hard breathing could be heard throughout the car, as our tongues massaged one another. Car horns blared letting us know, the light had turned green. I readjusted myself in my seat, so that I was now in the face down, ass up position. I began to unzip Banks's pants, then pulled out his long, throbbing dick.

"You like yo' dick sucked, baby?" I said, as I watched his dick jump in anticipation.

"I mean, you can do it if you want. I've never done this kind of thing before." He answered, timidly.

I spit on the head and leaned back a bit, so he could watch the spit fall from my mouth, slowly onto his dick. My tongue swirled around on the head, slowly taking him into my mouth. His right hand instantly found the back of my head, as he pushed my mouth down further on his shaft.

I gagged a bit, but continued my task, moving my head up and down, down and up. He released the sexiest moan, I'd ever heard, as I looked up at him. His eyes were on the road, but I could see him biting his lip. He glanced down at me and I winked at him.

"Ohhh fuck, Heaven!"

I began to move faster and faster, picking up speed as his shaky hands pushed my hair back, at a stop light. I guess he wanted to get a full view of the show.

"You about to make me cum."

His breathing increased, as I continued to suck and play with his balls.

His body stiffened, as he released his seeds into my mouth. I continued to suck, until I slurped up all of his nut. I wiped my mouth, with the back of my hand, then adjusted myself back in the seat.

He looked over at me, shaking his head.

I giggled. "What?"

"I can't fuck with you anymore, you got to go." He joked. The game we were playing must've ended when, I started giving him the best head of his life.

I smirked. "Why?"

"You kept sucking while I was catching my nut. Shit, you sucked the soul, out of a nigga." We both laughed at his silliness. We finally pulled up to his crib and got out of the car. I adjusted my clothing, making sure not to expose my goodies to the neighbors in case they were outside. He'd recently purchased another home. I'd never been to this crib because we always went to his other spot.

"Heaven." He broke my concentration.

I was so fascinated by his home, I hadn't noticed, I stopped right in the middle of the living room to admire the décor and paintings on the wall.

"Come on." He led me upstairs to his bedroom.

I couldn't get a good look at his room because he instantly grabbed me and threw me to the bed.

"Take this shit off."

I slipped out of my clothes slowly, as he did the same. I was standing fully nude in front of him. His eyes immediately went to my pussy. I leaned back on the bed and lifted my legs into the air.

I bit my lip as I watched him jerk his dick for a moment.

"Come here." Banks got on the bed and climbed on top of me.

He leaned down to bite and suck on my neck. I was sure, it was going to leave a few passion marks as he rubbed the head of the dick back and forth on my wet pussy.

I could feel his dick threatening to push into my opening. My hands danced across the top of his waves as, he made a trail of kisses down my neck, until he stopped at my titties.

He began to slowly flick his tongue back and forth on my nipples. We made eye contact for a brief moment. He unexpectedly slid inside me. I gasped as my hands instantly clung to his back. He smirked, leaning down to place small kisses on the corner of my mouth. He pulled all the way out, then slammed back into me.

Fuck." he muttered, lowly.

He continued fucking me at a slow pace, moving in and out of me. I latched onto his shirt and pulled him even closer to me.

Our lips connected, and I opened my mouth slightly to invite his tongue inside. Our breathing became erratic, as he picked up speed.

"Harder!" I managed to say, between kisses.

"What you want me to do?"

"Fuck—me—harder."

Banks sat up to pull off his wife beater. I watched as he grabbed my legs and pushed them, as far back as they'd go. I was flexible, so it didn't hurt to have my legs pushed back near my head. He began to speed up pumping in and out of me harder and harder, with each stroke.

"Keep fucking this pussy, just like that." I said through clenched teeth, as my sweaty hands gripped the sheets with every stroke.

"You feel all this dick in yo' stomach?"

I shook my head hurriedly. "I feel it."

In between strokes he said, "Shit, you feel so damn good."

I couldn't control my body from having its second orgasm, as my body stiffened up.

"Oh, my God, baby, I'm about to cum."

He murmured. "Cum on this dick."

We both rode the wave of ecstasy together, as he let out a very loud growl. If I weren't in the middle of catching my nut, I probably would have laughed, he sounded like a damn lion. He collapsed on the bed next to me, as I glanced over at him watching his chest heave up and down rapidly.

I placed my head on his chest and he wrapped his arm around me.

"You falling asleep already?" His eyes were fully closed, and he wasn't saying anything, so I already knew the deal. I just thought it was funny and decided to ask.

"That pussy done put a spell on, a nigga." He said, still a little out of breath.

I slapped him on the chest. "Oh, shut up."

"I'm about to go take a shower." His eyes were still closed, so I leaned over to kiss him on the lips. I couldn't help the huge smile on my face, as I got my naked ass up to shower.

I grabbed a fresh towel and rag from the linen closet and just as I turned on the shower, my damn phone started to ring.

I wrapped the towel around my waist and jogged back into the bedroom, because I didn't want to wake Banks up.

When I snatched the phone up from the bed I realized, it wasn't my phone, it was Banks's phone. We both had the same case. My eyebrows furrowed, when I realized who'd called him. My mind was racing a mile a minute and my eyebrows rose quickly, when he received a text message from the same person.

Lakenya: Hey, baby, I just called to say goodnight. I'm so glad we're working on us, I love you, baby. I promise, we're going to get back to how we used to be
.

'What the fuck, working on us?' I thought to myself. I gently laid his phone back down on the bed.

I shook my head, as I walked back into the bathroom. Banks and I weren't together, but the actual thought of him hugging and kissing other girls sickened me. I wanted all of his time, attention and most importantly his dick. I made a mental note to bring it up to him, whenever I got the courage, to do so. We'd been messing around for a while, maybe it was time to put a title on us. He was a good man and had been there for me, through so much already. I just hoped, when I did decide to have a talk with him, he felt the same for me, as I did for him.

"Ahh!" I screamed, when I felt someone wrap his or her arms around me.

I quickly turned around to see, Banks, who was fully naked with a very hard dick. I was almost done washing up and hadn't heard him come in. I hit him in the chest, a few times and he tried his best to block my hits.

"The fuck is you doing, Heaven?" He said, with a hint of laughter present in his voice.

"Why would you sneak up on me? You almost gave me a heart attack." I had my hand over my chest, as I tried to catch my breath.

"Calm down, baby, I'm sorry. I rolled over and you weren't next to me." He began to pout like a child. "You know, I had to come find, my baby."

His words made me smile. He knew how to be sweet even in the shower.

I wrapped my arms around his neck, when he pulled me closer to kiss my lips.

I stared into his eyes and although, I wanted to discuss us possibly being a couple, now just wasn't the right time.

"Uh—what are you doing?" I looked down, after he grabbed my leg and lifted it up.

"What you think?" He said, then he fully lifted me up into the air.

My legs wrapped around his waist, as he positioned his dick at my opening.

I gasped. "Oh, fuck, baby." He slid me down slowly, right onto his dick. My eyes closed instantly, I could feel him placing kisses on my neck and chest, as he lifted me up and down onto his dick.

Yeah, this definitely, wasn't the right time to have this talk.

Chapter 18

Lance

After I heard a knock at the door, I hopped up to answer it, already knowing who it was. Banks wanted to talk to me after, last night and I didn't blame him. He felt like a nigga was acting distant, he wanted to chop it up with me. Plus, I already knew, he wanted to talk about the shit that happened with, Heaven, so I was already prepared for that.

I had my baby for the weekend, she followed right behind me, as she always did, whenever I got up. She was always hot on my trail.

When I opened the door, he instantly started cheesing and scooped, Chyna, up into his arms. She giggled, as he showered her with kisses all over her cheeks. Banks flopped down on the sofa and I did the same thing.

"I feel like I haven't seen, my god baby in, forever. You need to bring her to see me more often." He wasn't lying about that, but she hadn't been around him, because I hadn't been around him. I was going through shit with, Imani, Vaeh, and now his ex-girlfriend, Kenya, so I was just trying to clear my head.

I watched as he kissed her one more time then placed her feet on the floor. She instantly took off running towards her toys.

"Yeah, my bad in that, bruh. I been real distant lately, because I got a lot of shit on my mind." I admitted.

No one really knew about my separation from my wife because everyone didn't need to know my business. Since he was my boy, I wanted to fill him in.

"I didn't come to sugarcoat nothing with you, my, nigga." Banks spoke up. "What the fuck was that shit at the club, last night? You were all over my girl, on top of that, you were drunk and falling all over the place."

I sighed. "Yeah, my bad, my mind wasn't in the right place."

"Okay, so what happened?"

"Man, I just don't even know where to start. Imani left me, ever since then, I just been keeping to myself."

Banks squinted his eyes at me. "She left you, as in she gave you some space or she moved out for good?"

I nodded. "You hit the nail right on the head. She left me, took my baby and everything. All because of, Nevaeh."

"Wait? The Vaeh, you were talking about all this time, was Nevaeh, Heaven's twin?" he chuckled. "This is a small ass world."

"Yeah, I know." I wiped my hand down my face slowly and took a deep breath. "Imani came home, caught, Nevaeh in the closet and pulled the strap out on her."

His eyes widened. "The strap? What the hell was she trying to do pistol whip, her?"

I shook my head and shrugged my shoulders. "Shit, I don't know, but I didn't let that shit go down, which is why, I'm in this predicament now. Imani felt like I shouldn't have taken up for, Vaeh, but I wasn't about to let her shoot the girl up in our crib.

"I mean—you can't really blame, Nevaeh, for this shit, though. You said this all happened, because of her, but I been telling you for the longest to give all that shit up and just work things out with your wife."

"I know, I wish, I would have listened to you, now my wife is gone. Vaeh had me under some type of spell." I laughed just thinking about it. "The pussy was amazing, and she had me ready to risk it all, but she was playing so many games with a nigga." I paused, to gather my thoughts. "Now Imani's gone and I'm sitting here pissed, at myself for even letting any of this shit go down."

"Damn, that's tough. But you know I got yo' back, whenever you need to talk just come to me. I don't need you causing anymore scenes in the club or pulling in my girl ever again. I'm liable to fuck you up next time."

We shared a laugh and a brotherly handshake.

"You won't have to worry about me, bruh." I threw my hands up in defense.

"Good." He stated. He then stood up, which prompted me to stand as well. "I'ma head out okay, I promised, Heaven, I'd take her out for ice cream."

"Ice cream? Nigga you getting soft on me? You damn near bodied me in the club over her, so, y'all must have something serious going on."

He looked as if he was smiling at the thought of her.

"She's pretty special, but at the end of the day, I'm just taking shit slow. Nothing major."

"What about, Kenya?"

"See that's the thing—she showed up to my crib the other day, crying her eyes out, dropped down and gave a nigga head too. I wasn't trying to fuck her, but the shit happened. We're working on us, thinking about possibly getting back together."

I can't lie, there was a tiny part of me, that wanted to tell him, I was now fucking her, but I felt like it wasn't the right time.

"Wait hold up. After she chased you for the past couple of months. You finally gave in and you're actually thinking about messing with her over, Heaven?" I questioned him.

I was confused as hell, she made it seem like she was over him, every time she came over here to hop on this dick.

"I know it sounds crazy, but we never really had any closure. A nigga feeling like giving her a second chance, to see if that love is still there." he said.

Kenya as I only fucked, and we had some conversation here and there, but it was kept to a minimum. With all the shit going on between me and Imani, I was getting consistent pussy from Kenya and it just dawned on me, the bitch was probably using me to make, Banks, angry.

"I'll figure it out, though—I'm out, I'll holla at you later on, bruh."

"A'ight." We dapped each other up and just like that he was gone.

Just talking about this whole ordeal, pissed me the fuck off, because, Imani, was gone, Nevaeh was about games and it seemed, Kenya, was on the same shit as, Vaeh. I pulled out my phone and texted Imani.

Lance: Imani baby, please just come home, let's work on us.

She knew just how to get under my skin, because she read my message and didn't reply. I guess she had to think of something to say, because about an hour passed since I'd messaged her.

Imani: If it's not about, Chyna—don't text me

I sucked my teeth, and threw my phone across the room. It hit the wall and shattered. I couldn't be mad at anyone, but myself. Although I was successful as hell, my love life was in shambles. It seemed like, I needed to just focus on myself, my baby and my career, because these women were driving me crazy.

Banks

Heaven and I decided to go out for ice cream, because she was craving some of that birthday cake ice cream. She put me on, that flavor was actually good as hell. She was still on her first cone, I was practically devouring my second cone. We parked at a nearby park and after walking and talking for a few minutes, we got cozy on an unoccupied bench.

"Did you hear me?" She said, bringing me away from my thoughts and my ice cream, momentarily.

I looked down at her, she had a puzzled look on her face.

"No, I'm sorry baby, repeat the question." I said, as I pulled her up from her seated position, next to me and pulled her onto my lap.

She sighed heavily. "So, I hate to ask this question?" She nervously bit her bottom lip.

I lazily looked over at her and released a yawn. A nigga was beyond tired and worn out.

"What's wrong, baby?" I was sure her puzzled expression, had jumped onto my face, I could sense something was wrong.

"Well, we've been spending a lot of time with one another. I really enjoy your company, but—" She looked away for a moment, trying to gather her thoughts.

"But what?"

"I just want to know how you feel about me." I knew something was up, because she was stammering over her words. We locked eyes and she looked away once again.

She chewed on her bottom lip nervously once more.

"I may be in way over my head with this one, but I want to be with you." She took her free hand, the one not holding her ice cream, and wrapped it around my neck.

I smiled. "Me? You wanna be with me?"

She shook her head yes.

"Why?"

Her face dropped instantly, and I felt her body tense up. "Do you not feel the same?"

It was my turn to release a hearty sigh. "I haven't been in a relationship in a while, baby. I might be a little rusty."

She gave me a coy smile and linked her fingers with mine. "I mean that's, okay. I'm willing to try with us. I wanna give us a try."

"So, you really tryna be with, a nigga?"

Her eyebrows furrowed together. "Yes, is that a bad thing?"

"Look, I just feel like—"

She cut me off and stood up abruptly. "What Banks, you don't feel the same?"

When I got quiet, she sucked her teeth and said, "Never mind just forget I said anything." She turned to walk away, but I rose to my feet and quickly latched onto her arms. "What Carter?" She snatched away from me roughly. "Don't touch me, I understand. You don't want to be in a relationship with me."

I rubbed my hand down my face slowly. "I didn't say that." I retorted.

"You didn't have to. "Actions speak louder than words."

"Look." I grabbed her arm, to get her to look at me. "Just chill."

"No, I'm not going to chill. I just told you how I feel and that I want to be, with you. You didn't even say anything, you just sat there looking dumb. You know what—I'm just going to leave."

She grabbed her cellphone and purse from the bench

Heaven

I tried to get out of his grasp. "Move!" I yelled. I was beyond livid, and quite embarrassed. I just wanted to leave.

"No, let me talk." He paused for a moment, then released a deep sigh. "I do feel the same about you, I swear I do, but—"

I cut him off, I already knew the deal. I already saw the text messages from his ex and he was obviously getting back with her.   "But what?

Unfortunately for me, I wore my heart on my sleeve, so controlling my emotions was never my strong suit. Tears fell from my eyes and I felt like a fool, for investing so much of my time with him, sleeping with him, and worst of all falling in love with him.

"Are you and your ex working things out?" I questioned.

His face scrunched up, as his head jerked backwards. "Hold up, why you ask me, that, Heaven?"

"Yes or no?" I said, with a shaky voice just above a whisper.

He looked away, diverting his eyes elsewhere, that pretty much answered my question. "We decided to—"

"No!" I yelled. "Look at me and say that shit. I want you to look at me." By now, I was sure, I looked like a fool, with my mascara running, but I needed to know the truth.

He looked me directly in the eyes, then I watched as his lips parted several times, but he obviously couldn't find the words to say, because nothing came out.

"Are you getting back with her?"

He nodded. "But, I would still like to be friends with you."

I sobbed. "Friends, wow Banks—friends huh?"

"Look I never meant to hurt you, I'm sorry for that. We just thought, it would be best to work things out and see where things go from here."

I threw my hands up in mock surrender. "No problem. You want to know what I think about this, friendship?"

I stepped closer to him and smeared my ice cream cone all over his shirt, then threw the cone on the ground.

He had the nerve to say, "That was uncalled for."

"Fuck you and this friendship, I'm done!"

I ignored him and continued to walk away. I just couldn't look at him, anymore.

This was a horrible end to my night.

Tamara Butler

Chapter 19

Heaven

3 weeks later

It was mid-afternoon on a Saturday, I headed to the mall to buy a few things. I was going out later on tonight and was also in desperate need of buying some new bras and panties. I was just about ready to go because people kept staring at me and asking if I was, Bank's Ex-girlfriend. Although he and I were never together, the paparazzi always caught pictures of us, when we were out and about, holding hands. Or when I was sitting on his lap or something. People automatically assumed, we were together and because of that men and women, had been following me around the whole damn mall, trying to ask me questions or to take pictures with me.

Although this was something I was used to, it made me sick to my stomach, to know they were asking me questions about a man, I'd never speak to again, despite the love I had for him. I felt played, so I definitely wasn't looking to talk about him in any way shape or form. He told me from the jump, he wasn't looking for a relationship, yet, he ended up in one with his Ex. I guess he was just trying to say, he didn't want one with me.

I was so engulfed in my thoughts, until someone walked past and bumped the hell out of me.

"Uh, excuse you!" I looked up and instantly my blood began to boil, Lakenya's annoying ass was standing in front of me, with a smirk on her face. I was tired of seeing this girl's face and for some reason, she had the nerve to be all up in mine. My eyebrows rose in astonishment. We had nothing to discuss, so I was not really interested in finding out what she had to say.

I stretched my arm to put a space between us, lightly pushing her backwards. She pushed my arm, and I gave her the side eye, I was two seconds away from knocking her lights all the way out.

"Move back, don't get all up in my space like that. I don't know you like that, nor do I care to."

She chuckled and clapped her hands. "Wow, what an award-winning performance, you just did. Please, can I get an encore?"

I hung the clothes in my hand, back on the rack. At this moment, I was no longer interested in shopping. Had I kept the clothes in my hand, I would've clawed her face with them. I didn't need to be getting kicked out of any stores.

"Lakenya what the fuck, do you want? Every time I look up, I see you, are you fucking following me or something?"

"Don't worry about, what the fuck I'm doing, worry about staying away from, my man. How about you do that?"

I mean mugged her ass, I felt that was the only thing I could do, at the moment. It's not in my character to cause scenes in a department store.

"Who is your, man?" Yeah, I was being sarcastic, but so the fuck what.

This chick obviously, didn't know her place, and she had better learn it quick and fast. I wasn't even checking for, Banks. So, if that's who she was talking about, which I'm pretty sure she was. I wasn't interested in arguing over him.

"Let's not play dumb. You know exactly, who my man is. When you see him, just know, that's me."

"Okay, great you came over here, just to say that bull-shit?" I shook my head. "News flash, I'm done with Banks, and if that's your man, tell him to stop calling my phone, boo."

She looked surprised, by what I had said. I was very bothered, by the fact that she had the man I wanted, but if that's where he wanted to be. I wasn't going to beg him, to be with me. I wasn't lying when I told her, he had been blowing up my phone. I could have easily kept that information to myself, but since she wanted to play, I decided to be petty right along with her ass.

She Fell in Love with a Real One

"You might want to pick your mouth up off the floor, it's dirty down there. Oh, wait you're probably used to being on the floor. Never mind."

She scoffed, as I lightly chuckled. I was on a roll.

"You ain't funny, bitch." She pointed her finger in my face.

I shoved her ass backwards, which caused her to stumble and slip, on a pair of pants. She hit the floor and I stood over her.

"Put your finger in my face again, I swear, I'll beat yo' ass the same way I did, in the past. I was trying to spare you."

She stood up and looked around embarrassed, to see if anyone had seen her fall.

"Stay away from him, like I said."

"Bitch you—"

My sentence was cut short, when her scary ass quickly walked away. I didn't know, who the hell she thought she was, coming here trying to check me. I did what I wanted when, I wanted and if I wanted to still fuck with, Banks, I would.

I mean, I did want to, but my pride just wouldn't allow it. He fucked my head all up, by saying he didn't want a relationship, yet he got back with his ex. I saw them together all over the blogs and social media, so I knew what she was saying was true. He was her man. I wanted to jump up and down and scream, at the top of my lungs, but instead I hurried out of the store, so that no one would see me cry.

I cried my eyes out like a big baby, once I got to my car. I was tired of crying and just hoped, that one day the Lord would send me a man, who was all about me. A man who truly deserved me. I was tired of falling in love, with assholes. I needed my prince charming, fast because I was losing hope on my love life.

****

I didn't want to go out, tonight. What I genuinely wanted to do was stay at home, with my head gorged to the point of no return, underneath my pillow, but Renaissance wouldn't permit it. She felt, I needed to live my life, instead of moping around, being all sad and shit over, Banks. Plus, I was on edge after, seeing his *girlfriend* in the mall. That bitch had one more time to try me. I was going to knock her lights the fuck   out.

"Heaven, that man over there, is giving you the eye. If you know what I mean." Renaissance elbowed, me in order to try, and avert my attention, away from my rum and coke, but it didn't work. I already had a splitting headache, and my feet were hurting so bad, I couldn't even think straight.

I sucked my teeth incoherently, and looked over to see, he was in fact giving me the eye. Yes, he was handsome, dressed nice, and had the most beautiful complexion and enthralling grayish eyes, but I didn't come to the club to find a man. I came to have a good time. To be honest, I wasn't even really doing that either.

"What's your point?" I asked, as if she was going to give me some kind of reasonable answer.

"My point, is that he's not just looking over here for his health. He obviously, sees something he likes."

"Okay and?" I was beyond irritated and hoped that Reba would just drop it.

Banks was on my mind anyway, I wanted to think about him in peace.

"Get your ass up and go over there." There was a hint of annoyance in her voice, but I didn't care. I should've been the one, annoyed not her. She basically, kidnapped me and brought me here, against my will.

"I'm not going over there. I don't know that, man!" I exclaimed, she'd see my point and drop it.

"I know. That's why you should get up and walk your ass over there, to get to know him." She had a smirk on her face. I was sure my face, was all twisted up, like I'd just eaten a lemon.

"What part of, I don't know, that man don't you understand, Renaissance?"

"What part of, go over there and get to know him, don't you understand, Heaven?" She rolled her neck.

I prayed, she'd go dance with some random nigga and leave me alone. "I just want to sit here and enjoy my drink."

"Well, it doesn't even matter, now." She pursed her lips together.

"Why not?" I questioned.

"Because, he's coming over here. "Don't look."

"I should kick your ass, for bringing me here. I really don't feel like being bothered."

I sighed heavily, as he got closer.

"Well you can kick my ass later, but, right now. I'm going to go mingle and leave you two love birds alone." She insignificantly, chuckled prior to vanishing into the crowd.

The random, handsome, cutie smiled and I gave his ass the fakest smile back. I bobbed my head to the music and continued to sip on my drink, pretending he wasn't even standing right next, to me. He extended his hand, obviously expecting me to shake it. He laughed and put his hand down when I didn't attempt to shake it.

I really don't know, why he was laughing. I didn't see anything funny. But, I guess it was one of those nervous laughs, or one of those embarrassed laughs.

I gave him a funny look, when he pulled up the seat that, Renaissance, was previously sitting in and decided to take it upon himself to have a seat. He scooted his chair a little bit too close to me, but I didn't say anything about it, I just continued to sip on my drink.

He was beginning to irritate me and get on my nerves, because of the fact, he pulled up a seat next to me and still hadn't uttered one word. Since Mr. Silent Bob over here, decided not to say anything, I broke the silence.

"My friend is coming back, that's her seat. She had to take a shit, but she'll be back in no time." I lied, but he didn't care.

"No worries, I'll get up when she comes back. But, in the meantime, I wanted to get to know you, a little bit better. My name is, Chance, and yours?"

I had to think fast on my feet, I wasn't about to give this brotha, my real government name, so I made up something stupid and ghetto, so that maybe he would not want to talk to me.

"Jawackamatima." I tried to keep my composure, because I was about to burst of laughing sooner than later.

He stroked his goatee. "That's different."

"Yeah, I know I've been told that, all my life."

I glanced over his body and attire, he wasn't a bad looking guy. He smelled good, his facial hair was lined up neatly, he had perfect teeth, and I could see his muscles practically bursting out of his shirt.

He knocked me out of my thoughts when he spoke. "Are you enjoying, yourself?"

"Look, Mister Chance, I'm not trying to be rude. I am not interested. In fact, I eat pussy all day I'm a lesbian."

I shut his ass down real quick, and barely gave him a chance to say anything else. I got up from my seat and walked right over to Renaissance. She was on the dance floor bumping and grinding to some throwback, R-Kelly, with a man who looked old enough to be her, daddy. I guess she was trying to find herself, a sugar daddy. Shit, I don't know, but either way, I was ready to go.

She gave me the keys to her car and told me she'd catch up with me later. I guess she was trying to get her freak on, with her new, sugar daddy. I gladly grabbed the keys and dipped. I was not feeling it tonight.

Once I made it outside, I practically ran to her car.

"Excuse me, wait!" I heard someone yell out.

I rolled my eyes when I saw that Chance had followed me. "Yes?" I leaned against, Renaissance's, car momentarily.

"Listen, I think you're very beautiful. I honestly want to get to know you better, that's it. I want to get to know the real you and—"

"I can't, I just got out of a situation. I really need to get my mind right before I start dating again."

"You can talk to me, I'm a great listener. I promise you, I'm a real good guy. I have a PhD, no kids or baby mama drama, I own two houses and two cars. I'm just looking for a friend. My now ex-wife passed away, and uh—sometimes I just wished, I had a female friend to talk to, hang out with and just have fun."

My eyes widened. "Oh, my God, I'm so sorry to hear that." I felt like a complete asshole.

"It's okay." He smiled, sweetly. "I'm just taking things one day at a time."

"Okay, well I guess it would be okay, to call me sometimes."

He pulled a business card out of his pocket and handed it to me. "I'll let you be in charge of that, I hope to hear from you soon."

He flashed me a smile and turned to walk away.

"Wait—my name is, Heaven, by the way." I decided to give him, my real name this time.

He reached for my hand and kissed the back of it, with a sweet delicate kiss. "Nice meeting you, Miss Heaven."

I didn't see the harm in getting to know him. I'd definitely be hitting him as soon as I was ready. My mind was in a thousand places, but the moment I got myself together, Chance would be only one call away.

Banks

I was lying on the couch half way asleep, when Lakenya came home and flew past me, so damn fast, you would've thought she was a hurricane. I heard her throw her purse down onto the counter in the kitchen then she started to open and slam my damn cabinets.

I knew she was pissed about something, but I was too damn tired, to try and find out what the hell was going on. I had just gotten back from, Honolulu doing a show there. After being gone for three days, I just wanted to come home to my girl, lay-up, fuck and go the to sleep. When I pulled up, my baby wasn't even here, now she was storming in here, slamming my shit, like she lost her mind.

I sighed deeply, then I placed my feet to the floor and stood up. I released a loud groan, as I stretched, trying to relieve some of the tension in my sore body.

When I got into the kitchen she had her back turned, as she bent over and looked in the fridge.

"What's yo' fucking problem, Kenya?"

She jumped at the sound of my voice, but nonetheless she continued her task. She searched through the fridge until she found what she was looking for. She retrieved a pitcher of Kool-Aid, slammed my fridge and poured some into a cup she'd already placed on the counter.

She was doing too much, and I was about two seconds away from walking out of the kitchen. A nigga was tired as hell, I hadn't been to sleep in forty-eight hours, so she had better get to talking.

"I don't have a problem." She said, with an attitude as I watched her sip from her cup.

I shook my head and turned to leave. "A'ight then."

"I saw yo' little, bitch, today." She yelled, when I was halfway out of the kitchen. I looked over my shoulder and she had a smirk on her face.

She put her cup down and walked over to me.

"Who?" I was sure, she could see the annoyance on my face, the way that I had it all twisted up.

"Yo' lil girlfriend."

"I don't know, who you're talking about, nor do I care, you're really about to piss me off, you trippin'."

She put her hand on her chest and her mouth was slightly agape. "Oh, I'm trippin'?"

"Baby, you really doing the most, right now. My head is killing me and—"

"I saw, Heaven."

My eyes widened, at the mention of her name. She'd been ignoring my calls and texts messages for about a month now.

She crossed her arms, with her lips all bunched together.

"Why are you bringing her up?" I seriously wanted to know, where she was going with this conversation.

Heaven wasn't fucking with me. I didn't really need, Lakenya, to be bringing her up, reminding me.

"Do you mess around with her, behind my back?"

I sucked my teeth. "I never cheated on you, you know that."

"I don't know anything!" She shouted, which caught me off guard.

"Why are you trying to start an argument over nothing?"

She stepped closer to me, and I stepped back a little, not because I was scared or anything, but I knew, what I was capable of and I didn't need to be going to jail for choking her ass.

"I'm not starting an argument. I just wanted to know, if my man was fucking around on me."

I shook my head, and she rolled her eyes. "See that's the insecure shit, I be talking about. Yeah, I'm always on the road, doing shows practically every night, but that don't mean, I fuck around. I used to deal with, Heaven, but I don't anymore, so end of discussion."

"No, it's not the end of discussion. Yo' little bitch put her hands on me, so what are you going to do about it? She questioned, I almost wanted to laugh. She was obviously testing me. I didn't have the patience, to be taking any got damn tests right now.

"Why you out here getting into a fight, with her anyways?"

"Oh—so you care about this, bitch?" She squinted her eyes as the corners of her eyes crinkled. She looked up to the ceiling, released a deep breath, then looked back at me. "You want her back in your life or something?"

When I didn't respond, Lakenya, had the nerve to lift her hand and push my head back. "I know, you hear me talking to you." she said.

My facial muscles tightened as I clenched my jaw forcefully. I was just about ready to break every finger on her damn hand. My forehead creased as I thought of the right words to say. I acted on instinct and shoved her ass backwards, until her back was pressed firmly up against the counter.

Her bottom lip trembled, as terror overtook her face. I grabbed the same hand, she'd pushed my head back with and bent it behind her back, until I heard her whimper.

"You're hurting me, Banks." She tried to get out of my grasp, which made things worse on her end, when I intensified my grip.

"Don't you ever, put yo' hands on me again, do you understand?"

"Y—yes, I understand." she stuttered.

I let her ass go. She quickly massaged her arm and stared at me, with a very unreadable look.

We stood there in silence, glaring at one another, as both of our chests heaved up and down rapidly.

I closed my eyes and raked my hands slowly down my face, trying to figure out how to break the silence.

"You know what, you begged to be back in this relationship, but you ain't been doing shit, but complaining, nagging, accusing me of dumb shit and spending up all of, my damn money. I'm all the way fucking done with you and this relationship." I turned to walk away.

She latched onto the back of my shirt. "Wait."

I snatched away from her and gave her a dirty look.

"I'm sorry, I promise, I'll do better." she pleaded.

"I'm sorry, Lakenya, but I'm done. You need to be out of my place by tomorrow. I'll let you stay here, tonight, but tomorrow it's a wrap." I said, this time I quickly walked out of the kitchen and back towards the living room ignoring her sobs coming from the kitchen.

I was tired and didn't need the extra stress, so I stretched out on the couch in front of my eighty-five-inch flat screen T.V., kicked up my feet, and a few moments later, I was knocked out.

****

I had been sleeping for no more than two hours. I jerked out of my sleep, when I felt a hand on my crotch. I was just about ready to fight, as my eyes struggled to open. I saw, Lakenya, standing in front of me fully naked.

"Kenya what the hell are you doing?"

She put her index finger up against her lips. "Shhh." She silenced me and continued her task.

I wasn't sure, if a nigga was dreaming or not, until I felt her pull my semi hard dick from my boxers. She dropped down to her knees on the side of the couch. I watched her through the slits of my eyes, as she spit on the head of my dick. I watched, as it slowly dripped down my dick. She stuck her tongue out and flicked it back and forth on the tip. Her tongue movements were similar to a snake's tongue. She gazed up at me, with a seductive glare.

She smiled prior to wrapping her lips fully around my manhood. She began to suck my shit, like she was Supahead's lil' sister and when she removed her mouth my dick was fully hard. She had me standing at attention.

Kenya stood up and climbed on top of me. She positioned my dick at her pussy entrance and rubbed it back on forth on her clit, making sure it was extra wet. She slowly, slid down and released a gasp once I was fully inside of her.

"You like it when I slide down on that big, fat, dick?" She knew I loved that nasty shit. I watched, as she closed her eyes and threw her head back.

She started to bounce up and down on my dick. I instantly wrapped my hands firmly around her waist. She opened her eyes and looked down at me. My eyes were now on her, as my grip got tighter, when she sped up the pace.

"Fuck!" I yelled out and began to meet, Kenya's downward thrusts with upward thrusts. "Yeah, ride that dick."

"I'm riding it, daddy." She said seductively, as I reached up and grabbed her by her hair, so that I could pull her closer. Her perky titties bounced up and down and I slowed down, so I could suck on them. She moaned when I flickered my tongue back and forth on her nipples, giving them both equal attention.

"Damn—you're so fuckin wet."

"All for you, baby." She retorted, as my body stiffened up.

"Don't cum yet, daddy. I wanna cum with you."

I didn't say anything. As my breathing increased, so did my grip on her waist. She bounced faster and tilted her head back, feeling her own body stiffen up.

"Cum on this dick."

She gripped onto my shirt tightly, as we came together. I made sure to pull out and released my seeds on her thigh. We both tried to catch our breath, but her bliss was soon cut short when I tapped her on the ass and told her to get up.

"Get up, Kenya."

She looked confused, but did as she was told. Once she got up off of me, I stood up, stretched and put my limp dick back into my pants. I headed into the kitchen, without saying a word. I had worked up an appetite, and hadn't eaten anything since my flight landed, earlier that afternoon at four p.m. I glanced at the clock plastered on the wall in the kitchen. The time was now ten p.m., although I hated to eat late. I needed to snack on something. Unfortunately, Kenya was hot on my trail.

She stood in the doorway of the kitchen and watched, as I proceeded to pull out some bread, ham, cheese and mayo. I looked up at her for a brief moment, but I still didn't say a word. I eventually, tore my eyes away from her and continued with my task. She sucked her teeth, loud enough for me to hear, so I chuckled.

"You still mad at me, babe?" I still didn't respond. "Hello!" When I didn't respond the second time, that made her angrier.

"I'm not about to start, this arguing shit again. I was never mad, I'm just done with you. I hope you didn't think, fucking me was going to change my mind. It's over."

Kenya walked over to me and tried to grab my hand.

"Don't touch me, Heaven."

Her head jerked backwards, I could've sworn, I'd seen it spin into a full circle. Her eyes grew bigger than flying saucers. I cursed myself silently, for calling her the wrong name.

"You can't be serious! I can't believe, you just called me another girls name, especially after we just made love!"

I didn't know what to say, so I just kept quiet and continued making my sandwich.

She sighed and looked down at her feet. I wasn't trying to get into another argument with her, especially while she was standing in front of me naked. I really just wanted her ass out of my crib, right now, but at least I was being nice, giving her until tomorrow to move out.

"Listen." she exhaled. "Can we talk? I'm sorry, about what happened a few hours ago. I was just all in my feelings because—" She nervously bit her lip.

"What?" I cut her off.

"I didn't know how to tell you this, but, I'm pregnant."
I dropped the knife, I'd been using to make my sandwich and gave her my undivided attention.
"Hold on, what?"
She released a nervous laugh. "Uh—surprise."

Chapter 20

Banks

I must've pulled up to my mama's house just in time, she'd just finished cooking. I'd told her, all about the bullshit with, Lakenya, over the phone. She already knew what was up, but I still decided to come over to get some advice.

"It's okay, baby you win some, you lose some." My mama said, as she sat a plate down in front of me, filled with macaroni and cheese, collard greens, neck bones and potatoes.

I'd come over to her house to talk about all the women problems in my life, mainly, Lakenya. She just so happened to be finishing Sunday dinner, so she fixed me a plate.

"Thanks mama." I replied, referring to the plate, she sat in front of me. "But, I just don't know what to do at this point. I fucked up, now Heaven isn't trying to fuck with me."

"You know what I think?" She asked, then she sat down next to my brother and I, at the dinner table.

"What?" I said, with a mouth full of food. I was hungry as hell and hadn't eaten much due to stress and all this damn touring my label had me doing.

"Cover your ears, Camden." My little brother gave her a look, but nonetheless, he did as he was told.

"I done told you 'bout fucking these girls raw. You not a regular nigga, bitches see you, and see dollar signs. You got so caught up with the pussy, now you have a fucking baby on the way. Wrap ya dick up, next time. I don't need these girls tryna use you."

"Ewe!" Camden blurted out, which caused the two of us to look over at him. She slapped him in the back of the head

"See that's why you should've covered your ears and since you were listening, you better wrap yours up too, when you get to that stage in life. I don't need you bringing home, any babies you understand?"

He nodded and replied, "Yes ma'am." He slightly rubbed the spot she'd hit then he stuffed his mouth with food.

My mom turned her attention back to me. "Are you in love with, Heaven?"

I shrugged my shoulders. "I don't know to be honest."

"Well, I think you got caught up with that girl. You were thinking y'all would only be fuck buddies, but it turned into something more. You love this girl, I can tell."

My mama was, right. I did have very strong feelings for her, but, love never crossed my mind.

"When it hurts to know, that you may never talk to her again, kiss her, hold her, touch her, or fuck her, then you're in love. When all you can think about is her smile, the way she laughs or gets mad, when you do stupid shit, the way she sleeps, eats or talks then you're in love. If you're out with another girl and she keep popping into your mind, you're in love." She said, as she sipped on her glass of red wine.

"I mean, yeah I guess I do love her, but I messed up. She told me how she felt, I stupidly got back with, Kenya instead of trying to make it work with her."

"Listen to me, baby. Kenya was a convenient relation-ship. Y'all had history together, it's not wrong that you wanted to see if the spark was still there, but you and I both know, you belong with, Heaven. I definitely want to meet her one day, so you need to make things right."

"So, what should I do? She won't answer the phone."

"Shoot, I'd pop up over there. If she loves you like you and I both know, she does, then she hasn't moved on yet, so it's not like she's going to have another nigga over there."

My mom always gave the best advice, she never sugar-coated shit. I kicked my chair back and hopped up.

She chuckled, knowing what was on my mind. "Sit down and eat your food, baby you can't win her back on an empty stomach."

"I just really wanna head over there now. I'm not trying to waste any more time."

My mom stood up as well. "Okay, baby I'll make you a To-Go plate."

I watched, as she grabbed my food and made her way over to the cabinet to retrieve the aluminum foil. Once my food was covered up. I kissed her on the cheek, bid my brother good-bye and rushed out of her house. I sped all the way to, Heavens house.

I parked crooked as fuck, but didn't care, as I hopped out and jogged up her driveway. My hands were all sweaty. I was nervous as fuck, I missed her like crazy. I didn't want her to continue ignoring me. I wanted to tell her, how I felt, I just didn't know how.

Heaven

I'd heard a knock at my front door and assumed it was Chance, my date for the night. I smiled, thinking about how much of a gentleman he was. In twenty-eighteen, niggas liked to honk the horn and wait for you to come outside.

I gave myself a once over in the mirror and checked to make sure, I didn't have any food in my teeth. I wasn't trying to embarrass myself in front of the man.

He knocked again, so I headed to answer the door.

I swung the door open, with a wide smile on my face, but it instantly dropped when I saw, Banks's stupid fucking ass on the other side. I tried to slam the door in his face, but he'd placed his foot in the doorway.

"Move your got damn foot." I stated, with a slight attitude. After what had happened, I wasn't interested in being in his presence.

He sucked his teeth. "Why haven't you been answering my calls and text messages for the past week.

"I've been busy." I said sardonically. I was lying, but he didn't need to know that.

He pushed past me and made his way inside. He flopped down onto my couch and propped his feet up on my coffee table.

I dramatically, slammed the front door walked over to where he was sitting. I pushed his feet off the coffee table and he smirked.

"Answer the question." I looked at him, as he as laid back.

"I don't have to answer shit!" I shrieked.

Ignoring him, I went into my room to finish getting ready for my date. I wasn't going to allow Banks to ruin my mood, more than he already had. I sat down on my bed after grabbing my lotion from my nightstand. I swiftly rubbed the lotion on the areas that looked a little ashy. I looked up to see, Banks, leaning in my doorway with a grin on his face.

He stood with his hands in his pockets. I gazed back at him, wondering why he was still here. I didn't know, why he felt the need to stop by. I had already made up my mind, to leave him alone, hence the reason I'd ignored all of his calls up until this point.

"I'm sorry." He blurted out.

I rolled my eyes at the mention of the word sorry.

"Okay." I stated, sarcastically. "What's your point?"

He sighed and walked closer to me. He kneeled down in front of me, next to my bed and looked up at me. I tried to move, but he quickly grabbed my hands.

"Move Banks for real for real."

"Why won't you look at me?" he quizzed.

I looked at him, for a millisecond then looked away. He had a concerned look on his face, but I didn't understand why. He wasn't concerned, when he was working things out with his Ex. I was probably the last person on his mind, at the time.

"I just—I can't do this with you, right now." I got up quickly and practically knocked him over. "I told you, I have some where to be, you need to leave." I stood in the mirror

242

and spun around in a circle, giving myself a once over once more. I grabbed my lip-gloss and applied a small amount, as he stood behind me watching my every move. I rolled my eyes again.

"I'm not leaving until you talk to me." He stated, matter-of-factly.

I turned around to face him, when I did he closed the gap between us, by stepping closer to me. He wrapped an arm around my waist and attempted to lean closer, to kiss me. I put my hand up just in time to block his kiss. I really didn't need to be this close to him. Unfortunately, I knew I'd give in to him sooner than later.

"Stop acting like that, Heaven." He had the nerve to say, I could tell, that he was annoyed by my behavior, but I didn't care.

I should be the one upset. "I'm not doing anything." I removed his arm from around my waist, so I could turn around and continue fixing myself up for my date. "You really need to back up. We're cool right? Like homies and what not." Sarcasm dripped from every word, I said, and I watched in the mirror, as his brows rose from my choice of words.

He lightly, chuckled. "So, you're really tripping off of what I said huh?"

"I'm not tripping off of anything. I'm all good, baby."

"Look." he exhaled. "Kenya and I are over."

"I don't care, Banks." I cut him off. "Do what you want. Now are you done, I need to finish—"

He grabbed me by the arm and spun me around, to look at him. I looked at him, like he'd lost his mind. When he lifted me up and sat me on top of my dresser, I was at a loss for words. I swallowed the huge lump in my throat. I could already feel myself melting underneath his touch.

He leaned forward and my body shuddered, at the feel of his lips on mine. My breathing increased, as my hands betrayed me. They immediately went up around his shoulders. I attempted to push him back, but he snatched my hands away and held them down onto the dresser. He sucked hungrily, on my bottom lip. Although, I didn't want to give in, I kissed him back.

"I'm sorry." He said, in between kisses.

He slipped his tongue, in my mouth and wrapped his arms around my waist, to pull me closer to the edge of the dresser. "She doesn't mean anything to me."

My eyes fluttered open, having being closed for the past few minutes. I watched, as he pulled away and bit his lip. My lips longed to have his on top of mine again, but I knew deep down inside, that what we were doing wouldn't last. He obviously, didn't feel the same about me. I didn't want to play myself, by continuing to deal with a man, that didn't have any intentions on ever being with me.

I watched, as he stepped back and stepped out of his pants. His dick was hard as a rock and although I would've normally spread my legs to receive his package, I just couldn't

He had a jumbled look on his face when I pushed him back and hopped down off of the dresser and pulled my dress down.

"What are you doing, Heaven?" I brushed past him and into the bathroom to retrieve my cell phone, I'd left on the bathroom counter. I scooped it up to see, that I'd missed a call and text message.

Chance: I'm on the way beautiful. See you soon.

I shook my head, when I realized that Chance had texted me fifteen minutes prior. I wasn't in the mood to go on any dates with anyone, right about now. Banks had ruined my mood. He thought, he could just show up to my place and sleep with me to make everything okay.

244

"For real, Banks, you really need to—" My words trailed off, when I noticed him standing butt ass naked, with his hands directly on his dick.

He was stroking it slowly. I watched, as his tongue snaked sexily across his lips. I couldn't help, but admire how fine, my man was. His chocolate ass had me hypnotized.

My mouth was now wide open, I wasn't expecting him to be standing in front of me in his birthday suit. "W—what are you doing?" I stammered.

He released a small grunt, as he continued to stroke his dick. "I'm about to fuck you."

"Oh yeah?" I bit my bottom lip, I could feel my pussy as it started to get moist. "That's what you think?"

"That's a fact, baby." Banks walked closer to me and grabbed my hand.

He sat down on the toilet seat and pulled me in front of him. He slowly slid his hands up and down, my smooth thighs until they landed under my dress. He used one of his hands to rub my pussy through the material of my panties.

My breathing increased immediately. I missed his touch so much.

I whined. "No, I can't do this with you."

He ignored me and pulled my panties down without breaking eye contact with me. My breathing increased. I was so fucking horny, my body betrayed me. I willingly stepped out of my panties although, my mind kept telling me not to. He pulled me forward and placed my legs on either side of him. I sat down onto his lap and he instantly attacked my lips, while taking his dick, rubbing it against my opening.

I stood up slightly and slid down slowly onto his very hard dick. My head slowly fell back in ecstasy, as he grabbed onto my waist instantly. He started to thrust his hips upwards before I could really allow my pussy to adjust to his length. My shaky hands instantly grabbed onto the back of his neck. I missed him so much, I just knew, I wouldn't be able to push him away any longer.

Tamara Butler

"Fuck!" He said underneath me, as he continued to thrust himself upwards into me.

"You know what?" He said against my lips.

"What?"

"I love you. Tell me you love me." Banks demanded.

"I—"

"Speak up." he grunted. "I can't hear you."

I remained quiet as my mouth hung open. I couldn't make a sound, it just felt so damn good, as I grinded on his dick and he thrust upwards into me.

"I missed this pussy." He sucked on my neck turning me on even more. I could feel my body shuddering against his touch.

My phone began to ring breaking me out of my trance. I tried to push away from him, but he held me tighter.

I removed his arms from around my waist as whoever was calling hung up and started to call once more. "Stop!"

Although my body wanted me to continue, my mind knew that this shouldn't be happening.

I stood up off of his lap quickly and grabbed my phone from the bathroom counter. I walked off into my room with him hot on my trail, dick flopping all over the place.

Chance has sent me a text stating that he stopped for gas but was about two minutes away.

"Banks I just can't—" He cut me off midsentence.

"Can't what?"

"Do this with you anymore. You made it perfectly clear, we will never be anything. I don't like feeling the way I do. I told you how I felt, you pretty much friend zoned me. I'm a friend that you like to fuck. That's it."

He sucked his teeth.

"What?"

"That's not true."

"How is it not true, Banks?"

246

"I'm sorry about that. I wasn't thinking, my mind was somewhere else. I guess, I just didn't know how the fuck to express the shit, I really feel for you."

"Well, it's a little too late for that. We are not together, and I have things to do, so can you please leave. I have a date with someone, who's actually interested in getting to know me, not just my body."

"Man, Heaven, the fuck is you talking about? We are friends, you knew up front, I was not looking for a relationship. So, stop acting like you didn't know that up front."

I laughed. "Wow, that's how you feel about the situation?" I shook my head, he could not be serious, right now. At this point, I was upset at myself for sleeping with him.

He reached for me, but I pulled away and he sighed. "I'm sorry that didn't come out right. We both weren't looking for a relationship, but we fell for each other. I love being around you. I love spending time with you. I feel like, I love you, Heaven."

I tried to gather my thoughts. "Like I said, Banks, it's too late for all of that. I told you how I felt, you pretty much chose another woman over me. Now all of a sudden, y'all ain't work, so you come crawling back, like I'm fucking second place. You should have chosen me first."

"I think you should get your things and go." I stated, as I threw my perfume, keys and phone into my purse. I then sat down onto my bed and put on my heels.

We glared at one another silently, for a few moments, his gaze was so intense, I looked away. I was on the verge of crying and putting up a front for him wasn't working, too well for me. On the inside, I was longing for him to leave, so I could release the tears that so badly wanted to fall. I refused to cry in front of him again.

I heard him mumble under his breath, as he put his clothes back on.

A knock on the door, caused the two of us to look on the direction of the door.

"So that's it? You ain't fuckin with me, anymore?"

"I am beyond done with this conversation. I already made myself crystal clear."

I stood up and turned off my room light, letting him know, I was heading out, so he needed to follow. I had everything I needed. I was looking bad as fuck, so I knew he was pissed on the inside.

My heels click clacked against the floor, as I swiftly made my way to the front door, not wanting to keep milky waiting any longer.

"Hey." I greeted, as he leaned in the hug and kiss me on the cheek.

"Hey beautiful you ready to—" His words trailed off, as he looked over my shoulder and saw, Banks, headed our way with a scowl on his face.

I smirked, I knew what he was thinking. Banks had to be fuming on the inside, however I didn't care. No one told him to pop up over here anyways.

Chance had a confused expression on his face, but to alleviate some of the tension, I changed the subject.

"You look nice." I complimented him.

He smiled, shyly. "Thanks."

"Oh—this is my, friend, Banks. He was just leaving." I made sure to put emphasis on the word friend.

"What's up?" Chance said to, Banks as they exchanged a friendly handshake.

"Nothing much, I was just leaving. Nice meeting you, you two lovebirds have fun tonight." He said sarcastically.

I shook my head, at his antics and tried to put the whole thing in the back of my mind. We were officially done, I didn't need to be breaking down in front of Banks or Chance. I watched as he jogged down the driveway, hopped into his car and pulled off.

"Oh, this is for you." He said pulling me away from my thoughts.

I diverted my attention back to him, to see that he'd been holding a single red rose.

I gave him a coy smile. "Oh my God, that was so sweet of you." I reached to give him another hug. "Thank you."

He bashfully flashed his million-dollar smile and placed the flower in my hand. His gesture was cute, it was the thought that counted the most.

He led the way to his car, of course he held the car door open for me. I sunk into the seat, once inside and released a very deep breath.

Heaven just breathe and get it together. I thought.

I hoped to have a good date, to put me back in a good mental space.

****

I played around with the food on my plate, simply because I didn't have an appetite.

"Is something wrong?" Chance questioned, bringing me back to reality.

I gave him a fake smile, as he leaned over to place his hand on top of mine. "Who me?" I answered, stupidly. "I'm good."

"You barely touched your food" Chance said, as I looked up into his worried eyes. "I thought you were hungry."

"I am—well I was hungry, but I lost my appetite." I tried to avert my eyes away from his by looking around the restaurant, but he grabbed my chin and made me look at him.

"What's wrong?"

I shrugged my shoulders. "Nothing."

"For real, just be honest with me. I mean if you're not feeling a nigga, just let me know." He joked, which caused me to crack a smile.

No, it's not that." I gently moved his hand from my chin. "I just got out of a bad situation. I think, I just need a little time to myself." I said honestly, without saying too much.

"Okay, I understand."

I was glad, he was so understanding, but I could definitely see the hurt on his face, I immediately felt bad.

"I hope this doesn't change anything between us." I did want him to kick me to the curb, because my feelings were all out of whack. I really did want to get to know him.

He flashed me a reassuring smile, then responded, "Not at all. You are very, beautiful, Heaven. I'd love to get to know you more, but only when the time is right."

I released a sigh of relief. "Thanks for being so understanding."

He waved the waitress over once he was able to get her attention. She walked over with a smile on her face.

"Can you bring the bill and some to-go boxes please?"

"Sure thing, I'll be right back." The waitress disappeared, that left the two of us alone to sulk in silence.

I felt bad, because my mind was on, Banks. I just didn't understand, what this man was doing to me. In such a small amount of time, he showed me what it was like to feel love again, then he ripped my heart out, the same way, Naheem, had. He treated me with respect, made me laugh, showered me with gifts and made me feel things, I had never felt before. He made my body shudder, with the simplest touch. He captivated my mind, body and soul. I thought I'd found the one, in such a short period of time. It hurt to know, he didn't feel the same.

I hadn't realized, I'd finally broken down and released a tear, until Chance reached over and wiped that same tear.

"Come here." He said and pulled me in closer.

I needed the comfort, so I leaned in and hugged him tightly, as he rubbed my back. "Everything is going to be okay." He said, as I cried on his shoulder.

He was a good guy from what I could see. I felt so bad for crying on his shoulder, over another man.

"I'm so sorry, to burden you with, my problems."

"It's okay. I'm here if you ever need to talk."

"Thank you." I said, after I pulled away from his warm embrace. I grabbed a nearby napkin and dabbed my eyes.

"Here's your check and to-go boxes." The waitress had reappeared, with our things.

Once Chance paid for our meal, we hopped into his car. Although the ride was silent, I needed that silence to get my mind together. I was heartbroken, again and it hurt like hell.

Tamara Butler

Chapter 21

Heaven

A few nights later

"Okay, so all of the mirrors will go along this wall, and each wall should have a different design. I love color, so I was thinking, that one wall could be pink, the others blue, orange, and so forth with polka dots, zigzags and striped patterns."

Today, just like any other day. I was putting in work for my dance studio. After a month and a half, the crew had done everything, I asked and everything was coming together nicely. I could barely contain my excitement. We predicted, that my studio should be done, within the next two months.

Although, Banks and I, weren't on speaking terms. I was still very grateful, he got me this place. The strip club didn't need much remodeling and was in great condition. The only thing I needed, was for them to build three dance rooms in total, replace the carpet on the floor, with hardwood and turn the bar area into a smoothie station. My customers would be able to get a healthy smoothie, water and any other refreshments, along with healthy treats from this station, before or after class.

My lobby area looked amazing, I could already envision how everything would look, once I had all of my furniture, and once all of the walls were painted. There'd be couches with tables covered in magazines, flat screen T.V.'s on the walls and an area to sign up for classes.

"Okay, ma'am, no problem."

Skye came through for me, by hooking me up with her cousin, Justice, who was looking for work as an assistant. I watched as she scribbled some things down on a notepad, to give to the painters first thing in the morning.

She was super cool, professional and did everything I asked with no problems. She was my new assistant, and I was appreciative for her. Lord knows, I wouldn't have been able to put all of this together alone. She assisted with ideas, over seeing that the contractors were doing everything I asked, based upon the blueprint I had drawn up, and pretty much anything else in between. She was a lifesaver.

"Oh and Mr. Chance, called about thirty minutes ago. He said call him back when you get some free time."

"Thank you, Justice." I headed towards my office, to grab my keys and purse, because after a long day at the studio, I was beat.

Justice and I spent, the entire day surfing through catalogs online, then purchasing furniture and decorations for the studio. Plus, we'd finally put the finishing touches on my website. Customers would be able to book one-on-one sessions, sign up for classes and rent out the space for music videos or photo-shoots as well.

A yawn escaped my lips, as I looked over my shoulder to see, that Justice was hot on my trail.

"I almost forgot. I know you don't want to speak to him, but, Mr. Carter called. He said, to tell your stubborn ass to call him, because he misses you and wants to see you badly." Justice passed me the message, she'd written down on a piece of paper.

I almost wanted to laugh, she read it in the most professional way she possibly could.

"Thanks, hun." I took the paper from her, quickly balled it up and threw it in the trashcan.

Justice's facial expression indicated, there may have been something on her mind. As she stood in my doorway, silently, she bit her bottom lip prior to responding, "Hey, I don't want to intrude on your business, but he calls you at least five times a day, sends you lunch, chocolates and flowers. He seems like he's really sorry for whatever he did. I'm not taking up for him in any way, but just remember, everyone deserves a second chance. If he messes up again, at least you tried."

"I don't know about that. In this case, he may have just lost me forever."

Justice gave me a coy smile. "Just think about it."

I rolled my eyes playfully. "Okay, fine, I'll think about it. But in the meantime, get some rest. I'll see you, tomorrow."

"Thank you, Ms. Heaven, I'll see you bright and early in the morning."

We bid each other goodbye, then I pulled out my phone and called Chance. The phone rang for a few moments, then I smiled when his deep baritone voice filled the line.

"What's up, beautiful?"

It was something about his voice, that always made me smile. "I don't know, you tell me. I got the message you left with my assistant."

"Yeah—I was hoping to see you, tonight. A few friends of mine are having a get together. There will be food, liquor, games and a little music, but nothing major."

Another yawn escaped my lips. "I might have to take a rain check, I am beat."

He chuckled. "Awe come on, just come out for about an hour or two. You deserve to have some fun and a drink to unwind."

I glanced at my watch seeing, that it was a quarter to eight p.m. It wasn't that late.

"So, I'll see you around nine-thirty, nine forty-five, or so?" He questioned, still trying to get me to agree.

I sighed. "Okay fine, text me the address. I'll swing by."

I could tell, he was cheesing through the phone. "Okay, cool, see you soon, beautiful."

I locked up the studio and headed to my car. Luckily, I was already dressed in casual attire, so I popped the trunk, pulled out some heels and threw my hair up into a high bun. A few minutes later, a text massage came through from Chance.

Chance: 6568 NW 89th Street

Once I applied a pop of color to my lips and replaced my studs with hoops. I was ready for this party, so I plugged the address in my GPS and hopped on I-95.

****

'Girl, why in the hell, didn't you just go home, now look at what you got yourself into.' I thought to myself, after walking into a party full of people.

I saw a familiar face and instantly rolled my eyes. I didn't know, if the fool was following me, or if him and Chance had the same group of friends. But, here, Banks was front and center playing Dominoes with a few of the party guests. They were all laughing and having a good time. As soon as I walked in, I saw him and made a beeline straight to the bathroom.

'Girl, just pinch yourself, you are definitely dreaming.' My thoughts were running amuck, I was sure, I probably either saw a, Banks look-a-like, or I was in fact dreaming. I was in the bathroom, breathing in and out, over and over again, like my name was Fat man Scoop. The only thing missing was the music.

Anyway, I exited the bathroom a few moments later, and his eyes caught mine. I wasn't dreaming, but I gave him a fake smile prior to making my way over to hug Chance.

"You look good as hell, Heaven." He said into my ear. He kissed me on the cheek soon after,

Banks was staring us down and it made me feel uncomfortable, so I turned away.

"Thank you."

Chance wrapped his hands around my waist and pulled me in closer.

"You're welcomed, beautiful. I'm glad you came. Let me introduce you, to my friends."

I was happy, he pulled me away from the area, Banks, was sitting in, and walked me around the house, introducing me to a few of his college friends and colleagues. I tried my hardest to engage in conversation with, Chance, and his friends, but my eyes kept wandering. Luckily, he didn't pick up on it.

"You want anything to drink, Heaven?" Chance's friend, Aaron, asked me and stood up to assist. "Mi casa es su casa." He said in a very bad Spanish accent.

"No, it's okay, I'll get it."

He pointed towards the kitchen, and I quickly walked off, thinking of some sort of way to get the fuck out of this house, without causing a scene. I didn't want, Chance, to feel any kind of way about the fact, that I was dipping out early. I hurriedly opened the fridge and searched for something to quench my thirst. I settled upon a bottle of water and practically pee'd in my pants, when I turned around to see, Banks, standing directly behind me. He scared the shit out of me.

"What do you want?" I inquired, lowly making sure, no one was able to hear us.

"I want to know, what the fuck you got going on with dude, and why you showed up here for him?"

I raised my eyebrows in amusement, how dare he come up here questioning me, about what I'm doing when he stopped fucking with me to get back with his ex.

I could see the veins in his neck, every time he got upset. "You fuckin that, nigga?"

I sucked my teeth and released a deep sigh. "No! Even, if I was, why do you care?"

He ignored my question, and continued to question me about, Chance.

"Oh, so you're not fucking the nigga, but you partying with him and shit, like everything is all cool."

Again, I did not understand, why he cared. I shrugged my shoulders.

"Everything is cool. I'm not understanding, what you're getting at." He stepped closer to me, to reach behind my back and grab a beef from the counter.

"Uh, excuse you." I said, when I noticed, he was too close for comfort.

This time he sucked his teeth. "Man, why you playing with me, for real for real?"

"No one is playing with you, Banks. Why don't you go mingle with the other party guests, or with your girlfriend? You do remember your girlfriend, right?"

"So, that's what this is about? I got back with her, so you decided to go out with this clown." He was being irrational. "Me and her not even together no more."

"I am a grown ass woman, I can do whatever the hell, I want to do. You and I are not in a relationship, you made that perfectly clear to me." He was tripping for real.

He licked his lips and just stared at me silently, for a few moments, latching onto my arm and yanking me into him.

"That nigga, know how good, I was fucking you, huh? Does he know, that I used to eat that pussy, until you cried, huh?"

"You know what, I'm not going to stand here any longer, to have this conversation, with you. Clearly, you're drunk and obviously jealous of what I have going on with, Chance. We are not fucking, we are just friends, but like I said that's none of your damn business."

"I told you we broke up!"

I was confused. "Huh?"

"Me and Lakenya."

I smirked at him. "Okay, so now I really get it. You broke up with her, then you were trying to come crawling back to me, after you practically kicked me to the curb. It didn't work out, so you're trying make things right, with me."

He ignored my question and changed the subject. "So, you don't miss me?"

"That's irrelevant and besides, the point."

Chance entered the kitchen, and I awkwardly pushed past Banks. Chance had a confused look on his face.

"I thought you had gotten lost." He said looking into my eyes, as I gave him a fake smile.

I didn't bother to respond, I just simply grabbed his hand and led him back out to the party. I don't know, what the hell was going on with, Banks, but he was really tripping. He didn't want me, so why was he wondering who I was sleeping with? I shook off the thought and enjoyed myself for another hour, then decided to leave.

Banks

Seeing Heaven, with that clown ass nigga, made my blood boil. I missed her so much, it was starting to drive me crazy. My mama was right. I was in love, and she just kept pushing me away. I couldn't blame her though, I had played games with her, fucked with her heart and turned out to be the same nigga, her ex-husband was. That wasn't my intentions.

I planned on heading home and just giving her some space to clear her head, after I popped up at her house the other night. But, something was telling me to pop up one more time. If I wasn't able to convince her, I'd never hurt her again, then I was done with the whole situation. I couldn't make her forgive me, but I was sure as hell about to try.

I pulled up to her house an hour, after she'd left the party. I used my key to get inside, remembering this time, that I hadn't given her the key back. I heard the water running in the shower and her singing as usual. I didn't want to barge into the shower and scare her, so I waited patiently in her room. I sat down on the bed, then ten minutes later, she walked into her bedroom. Her mouth dropped when she saw me. She stopped dead in her tracks and placed her hand over her chest.

"Carter, what the hell!" She yelled and picked up a bottle of lotion from the dresser. She threw it at my head and I ducked. "You scared, me! What are even doing in here?"

I stood up and started walking over to her, but she put her hand up. "You need to leave. You can't be here."

I held up her key. "This is how, I got in Heaven, but I'm not leaving until you talk to me."

She sucked her teeth. "We are done, I don't understand what you don't get. You cannot play with my heart anymore, I won't allow it."

I watched, as she walked over to the closet and grabbed her robe, then quickly dropped her towel and threw it on. I stood in my same spot, trying to figure out what to say. She was putting up a fight, but I wasn't giving up that easily.

"Go." She pointed in the direction of the front door. "You can't be here, okay." She tried to push me, but I grabbed her hands. We struggled against one another, until I finally pinned her up against a nearby wall.

I released her arms and closed the space between us, by placing my arms on either side of her and pressing my body slightly into hers.

"Don't fucking push me away, Heaven! You know you want me to be here. You need to stop being so stubborn and listen to me." Her breathing was heavy, as she stared up into my eyes. I could see her breaking down, beneath my touch. I licked my lips, and continued. "Baby listen to me, please. I need you in my life. I'm sorry for any hurt, I caused, okay? I am in love with you, I want to be with you."

She turned her head and lightly pushed me away. I could still see her pain, it was written all over her face and expressed through her body language. She barely wanted me to touch her, and I hated that. I grabbed her chin and made her look at me. "Talk to me, Heaven."

Heaven

"Heaven!" Chance yelled through the halls.

My heart started beating faster, I just felt this would end badly. Chance had gone to pick up some food, so I quickly showered waiting for his arrival, but instead Banks popped up. Here he was spilling out his heart to me, telling me how much he loved me, when Chance walked in.

I quickly moved away from, Banks, which caused his eyebrows to rise in confusion, as I patted my face, removing any trace of tears.

Chance walked over to my nightstand, to sit the food down. He then, turned to look at the two of us and shook his head. I could already sense what he was thinking, since this was the third time he'd encountered, Banks.

Chance tried to be cordial. "What's up, bruh?" He said to, Banks, who gave him a head nod. He purposely walked over to me and leaned down, to kiss my forehead. "You good?" Chance asked, which must've pissed Banks off because he shoved him backwards into the wall.

"The fuck is you asking her if she good, for? I know, you see me standing right the fuck here, of course she good, nigga!"

"Oh my, God! Stop!" I yelled, as I attempted to step in between the two.

When Chance, charged at Banks I was shoved out of the way and hit the floor with a loud thud, due to my feet still being a little wet from my shower. I quickly hopped up onto my feet, but by then the two of them were tussling and punches were being thrown.

"Banks, Chance, Please stop!" I yelled, but my pleas fell upon deaf ears.

Banks was definitely winning, throwing blow after blow, but some way somehow, Chance, was able to put him into a headlock.

"Fuck is yo' problem, nigga? I don't know you from a can of paint and you come up in here starting shit." Chance said, through gritted teeth, as Banks struggled to get out of his chokehold.

I was afraid, because I didn't know what, Chance, was capable of and also, because I had never seen this side of him. He always seemed so calm, as if he couldn't hurt a butterfly.

I was frantic and didn't know what to do. They had absolutely no reason to be fighting each other, because just as Chance said, they didn't know each other from a can of paint.

I tried to wedge myself between the two of them. "Get off of him!" I yelled as, Chance, locked eyes with me.

He continued to hold, Banks, so I slapped him with all of my might, which caused him to release his hold. As soon as, Banks, was free he tried to bum rush, Chance, but I stood firmly in my spot, not budging with my arms stretched out.

"Both of you are behaving like, little ass children! Why are you even fighting to begin with?"

Chance stood in front of me, glaring at me, holding the spot where I'd slapped him, as Banks stood behind me breathing heavily.

Ignoring my question, Banks spoke up. "You got about two seconds, to get the fuck up out of here. Or I'm gone put some bullets in yo' dumbass, without hesitation."

Chance chuckled, as he wiped a few droplets of blood from his busted lip. "Whatever man." He looked at me. "You have my number, call me when you're ready, for a real man. I don't play games. I damn sure ain't about to be fighting, niggas, over you." I remained quiet, not knowing what to say.

Chance walked past Banks, purposely bumping shoulders with him, as they mean mugged one another. As soon as the front door opened, then slammed shut, I was finally able to release a breath. I didn't realize, I was holding. With one hand on my head and one on my hip, I turned to, Banks, who was wiping blood from his lip, that was also busted.

Chance looked all banged up and would probably be all bruised up in the morning. He was practically eating the punches Banks was throwing at him. Hell, his eye was already swelling up, when he left. Banks on the other hand, only had to deal with his lip.

"What the hell is wrong, with you, huh? First, you didn't want me. You got back with your ex, broke up with her, popped up to my house, then we had sex. I saw you at that stupid party, then you popped up over here again, and you had nerve to fight my company."

He sucked his teeth. "Man, fuck that, nigga."

I watched, as he removed his ripped shirt, leaving him shirtless, then sat down on the bed, to remove his shoes. I could tell that he was worn out.

"Please explain, Carter." It was a habit, I had to call him by his name, whenever he pissed me the fuck off.

"There ain't shit to explain. I'm tired of playing these games. You're not about to walk around here, acting like a nigga, didn't mean shit to you. What we have is a real connection. Yes, I fucked up, but damn I'm apologizing twenty-four fucking seven, give a nigga a break!" He said, as he glared at me with a sour look on his face.

I sighed deeply. "Listen, I do care about you, okay! I never said, I didn't."

He latched onto my wrists and pulled me in front of his seated position on the bed.

"Okay, so prove it." he said. "If you care about me, give me another chance. I don't want to be just your friend, or a friend with benefits, like I real deal love you. I swear to God, I do. I hurt you, I know that it did. I just—" He paused, and reached up to pull my chin, to look at him, since I had my head slightly turned away from him. "Look at me, baby."

I looked at him, I could see the sincerity in his eyes. "Come here."

I sat on his lap and he tried to kiss me on the cheek. Forgetting that his lip was busted, he winced in pain. I quickly, stood up letting him know, I'd be right back.

I went into the kitchen and slipped some ice cubes into a zip lock bag, so he could ice his lip. When I returned, he was leaned back on the bed, using his elbows to hold him up.

God, as much as I wanted to hate him, he looked so fucking sexy. His eyes were on me like a hawk. I crawled onto the bed and straddled him. His hands immediately went to my exposed ass since I didn't have on any panties underneath my robe. I leaned forward and placed the ice to his lip causing him to sexily scrunch up his face, as I held it in place.

"Thank you, baby." He mumbled, as his hands slowly made their way up to the front of my robe.

Once he untied it, my breasts and freshly shaved pussy were put on display.

"You're welcome."

"Heaven, for real, though. I meant everything, I said. I want to be yo' man. I want you to be mine. You hear, me?"

I wanted to respond, but my thoughts were interrupted, when he sat up abruptly and flipped me over. I was now on my back and he was between my legs. I giggled slightly.

I smiled after hearing those words come out of his mouth. "Yes, I hear you. I just want you to know, you did hurt me, but I'm willing to give us a try."

'*Girl, you better get yo' man! Stop playing and get your man.*' I thought to myself.

He started cheesing wide as hell but stopped instantly after remembering his busted lip. He grimaced in discomfort, once again.

"Keep the ice on your lip, babe." I said to him scooping up the makeshift ice pack, I'd made, but he took it from my hands and laid it down next to me.

"It's okay, don't worry about me, right now."

I sat up on my elbows and gave him a knowing glance. I knew what he had up his sleeve.

"Oh yeah? What should I be worried, about?"

He stood up momentarily, and I watched, as he removed his pants and boxers. He was down to his birthday suit. He climbed back on top of me, as his dick started to brick up.

"As your man, I want to please you all night long, so we can make up for lost time."

I playfully swatted his arm, then playfully rolled my eyes, trying to fight the smile tugging at my lips.

When he positioned himself at my entrance "Okay," was all, I managed to say.

"Damn, you're wet already, babe." He wasn't lying. After watching him beat Chance up, I was turned on in more ways than one, and after he confessed his love to me, my pussy was like a faucet.

"Oh my, God." My toes curled instantly, and I gasped, sucking in as much air as I could when he unexpectedly plugged deeply inside me.

My legs wrapped around his waist and my arms were around his neck, as he took his time and made love to my mind, body and soul, for the rest of the night just as he said he would.

Tamara Butler

Chapter 22

Heaven

My hands began to sweat as, Banks, pulled up to his mother's house. He'd convinced me to meet her today, and as his girlfriend, I felt it would be a good idea to meet. We'd have to meet sooner than later, but the way my heart was beating, I was silently cursing myself for not saying no. I was a nervous wreck.

It was his mother's birthday, and although, he made it seem like it wasn't a big deal to meet her. I felt otherwise. Once he came around to open my car door, letting me out, I looked at the lovely two-story home decorated in white and yellow. The yard was filled with tulips and Lilly's. There was a white picket fence surrounding the home. I watched as, Banks's, little cousins ran around playing a round of freeze tag.

"Let's go home." I blurted out.

He chuckled. "But, we just got here. What's wrong?"

"I don't know, I'm nervous. My stomach is bubbling, bae."

He glared at me with a confused expression, on his face. "Maybe you gotta take a shit, baby."

I playfully pushed his shoulder.

"What?" He laughed, once more as if I was telling the world's funniest jokes. "Yo' stomach is bubbling and you're trying to say, it has nothing to do with needing to take a shit?"

"I'm just anxious, that's all."

"Listen, my mother has a smart-ass mouth, but that's only with me. I'm sure, she'll love you, okay?"

"Okay." I said wanting to get this dinner over with.

We walked up the driveway, hand in hand.

"Awe shit is that my favorite, nephew?" An older man, with hair on his sides but not on the top of his head, walked over to us. "Come over here and give me a hug, nephew!

"Hey, uncle Dee. This is my girl, Heaven." Banks said as he pulled back, after hugging his uncle.

Uncle Dee sipped on his beer and cheesed, while showing that he had missing teeth. "She's a bad one, nephew, looking just like the singer, Ashanti." I watched, as his beady eyes roamed all over my body. "You thick like her, too!" He yelled for no reason in particular.

He was rather loud, but I plastered a fake smile on my face, hoping we'd walk away from his somewhat drunken uncle.

"Unc, chill out."

"What? She thick and pretty, looka them thighs and ass she——"

Banks cut his eyes at him. "Unc, just chill."

Uncle Dee apologized, but only because, Banks looked like he was going to snap. I was sure his uncle didn't want that. "Okay, I'm sorry, lil' lady."

I smiled sweetly, at him as Banks lead the way inside of his mother's house. Banks looked back at me, I gave him a nervous smile, as we walked through all of his relatives in the living room, stopping to greet them, ever so often.

"Mama!" He yelled, not really knowing where his mom was.

"I'm in here boy, stop yelling in my got damn house." She yelled back.

"See what I mean?" Banks whispered, causing me to snicker.

We walked towards the back of the house, towards the kitchen. His mom was setting up the dinner table. It was just about time to eat.

She had a wide smile on her face when they made eye contact. He leaned in and hugged his mother placing a tender kiss on her cheek. Standing at four-eleven, his mother was very short, but she had a whole lot of mouth. She was a beautiful, light-skinned woman, who was clearly an advocate for black don't crack. She had long dark brown bundles that hung down her back, a few moles on her cheeks, and chinky eyes. His mom was rocking some pink Giuseppe heels, along with an all-black strapless dress, that had the back out, but it wrapped around her neck. She looked like she worked out. Although her makeup was flawless, I could still see the scar from her car accident faintly. All in all, she was gorgeous.

"Hey, suga, how you doing?" She stared at Banks lovingly, with one hand on her hip.

"I'm doing good, mama. Can't complain." He grabbed her by the hand and spun her around in a circle. "What the hell do you have on, Ma? Where's your sweater."

She playfully swatted his chest. "Gone on now. It's my, birthday. Let me live a little."

I chimed in wanting to be a part of the conversation. "You look great, happy birthday."

Banks playfully tapped his head. "I'm sorry, where are my manners. Ma this is my girlfriend, Heaven.

I was shocked when she latched onto me, to pull me into a hug. "I'm so happy to finally meet you, thank you so much for coming to, my birthday party."

"You're welcome, nice meeting you, as well." I said, as I stepped back from our hug.

"Aye, y'all stop all that running." Banks yelled to his little cousins, but they ignored him and continued to run around.

"No, let them play. They'll get tired faster and fall right to sleep, after dinner." A woman stated, as she walked into the kitchen, with a baby boy on her hip.

"What's up, cuz?" Banks greeted, before they shared a brief hug.

"Nothing much, trying to survive with these bad ass kids. They are getting on my fucking nerves."

"Watch your mouth." Banks's mother chimed in giving her the eye.

"Sorry auntie."

The room grew quiet, as this mystery woman looked me up and down, like she had a problem. "Who's this?" She looked, at Banks, then pointed at me.

"Oh, Heaven, this is my cousin, Deena. Deena this is my girlfriend, Heaven."

I waved at her, she tooted her lips up. She was being a bitch, to me for no reason, but out of respect for his mother, I decided to play nice. "Hi nice to meet, you."

"Oh, she's cute." Deena said, but I could tell, she was being sarcastic. "Whatever happened to, Lakenya? She was perfect for you." Deena blurted out, with a smirk.

I was just about ready to tell her jealous ass to kiss my ass.

I looked at, Banks, waiting to see what he was going to say. "Really Deena, Lakenya and I didn't work out. I'm with, Heaven, now."

His cousin began to laugh. "I just wanna know, what happened. Lakenya is my girl, I introduced y'all. The two of you, were all in love and shit and——"

Banks cut her off mid-sentence.

"A'ight, Deena, that's enough. Stop with all this rude shit. This is my girlfriend, I don't give a fuck, what kind of ties you still have to, Kenya, we not together. Since you're, so hell bent on bringing her up shit, you go be with her gold digging ass then!"

Deena rolled her eyes and started to pat her baby on the back, as he began to cry. I was starting to think, this was a bad idea. I didn't understand the shade, Deena, was throwing, but my mouth was just as nasty, so if she kept trying me, I was going to set her straight.

"Whatever." Deena said, as she walked out of the kitchen, acting likr nothing had just transpired.

I decided to change the subject. "Would you like help setting the table?" I asked his mother.

"Yes, I would, thank you so much."

"C'mon baby. Let's go get our bags and put them upstairs first." Banks suggested.

I turned to his mother. "I'll be right back."

"Okay, sweetie, I'll be right here."

I followed him out of the kitchen, back to the car, then to a small little guestroom upstairs. We planned to stay the night, because he really wanted to spend some time with his mother, and make sure she didn't turn up too much. We'd be leaving the first thing in the morning.

Once upstairs I flopped down on the bed. I laid down and stared at the ceiling.

"You tired, baby?" Banks asked, after he closed the door and sat down on the bed, next to me.

"No, I'm just thinking."

"Look, my cousin and I are very close, we grew up as best of friends, so she's territorial over me. But, trust me, I'll never let her, or anyone disrespect you in front of me. Okay?"

I shook my head in agreement. "I'm glad you stood up, for me." I slid a little bit closer to, Banks, on the bed and pulled him closer by the back of his head. He smirked when I started pecking his lips.

"I always got your back, baby, never forget that." He pulled me a little closer and slipped his tongue in my mouth.

His hands began to roam a bit and he tried to slide them under my dress as our kiss intensified. I pulled away, breathlessly.

"Babe I have to finish helping your mom, downstairs I don't want her to think, I'm a liar."

He ignored me and started to kiss on my neck, as he massaged my pussy through the thin material of my panties.

I giggled. "Baby did you hear me?"

He mumbled against my neck. "I need you, right now, too." He grabbed my hand and placed it on top of his dick, that was standing at attention. "Can I have, my pussy, real quick? Just let me put the head in." He lifted his head from the crook of my neck, when we made eye contact, we both started to laugh.

"Really babe? That's not going to do shit, for you." I stated matter-of-factly. A sudden knock at the door, interrupted our conversation.

"Carter?" His mother called his name through the door. We quickly adjusted ourselves.

"Come in!" he yelled.

When his mother stuck her head in the door, she smiled widely at me. I returned the smile, then she directed her attention towards Banks.

"Yes ma?"

"Carter it's time to eat, but your cousin done invited, that damn ex of yours up in here. I don't want to ruin, my birthday, by going to jail, so you need to handle it."

Her words made me frown, I was sure Deena, had invited her on purpose.

"I'll handle it, ma."

She walked away leaving the door open. I didn't even want to leave the room. I did not want to deal with his ex for the millionth time. Reluctantly, Banks kept reassuring me, he was going to take care of it, so I reluctantly made my way downstairs. Once in the kitchen everyone was practically already sitting down. We stood by the nearest wall, trying to figure out where we were going to sit.

"There's a chair right there for you, Heaven." Deena said, attempting to sit me all the way at the other end of the table, far away from Banks. I shook my head, she had me fucked up.

"It's so nice to see you, Lakenya." Deena was trying to rub the shit in, but it wasn't bothering me one bit.

"It's nice to see all of you here. All of my family under one roof, I'm glad everyone could make it." Bank's mother said, trying to change the subject.

She winked at me, which caused me to smile, she obviously didn't like, that bitch, Kenya either.

"Kenya let me talk to you real quick." Banks's voice was calm, yet stern.

She rolled her eyes and scoffed, putting on a damn show with her over the top ass.

"No, I'm good, right here."

He reached over and grabbed her arm tightly, making a few people stop what they were doing to stare.

"What the fuck. Get off of me, Banks." She snatched away from him and tried to regain her composure.

"I'm done playing, Kenya, get up and get the fuck out for real." I could see the veins on the side of Banks's neck popping out. He was furious.

She smirked, pushed back her chair and stood up slowly. "That's how you gonna treat, the mother of your unborn baby, huh?"

My eyebrows rose quickly, at the mention of an unborn baby. I pushed him from behind, since I was behind him, he spun around to face me quickly.

"The fuck is she talking about." I screamed. Although, I did not want to be yelling all up in his mother's house, it was too late for that.

Lakenya rubbed her belly, with a satisfied look on her face. She was gloating.

"Oh, I'm sorry, boo. I thought he would've told you by now."

I put my hand all up in her face, to silence her, and she pushed my hand away. I jumped at her stupid ass and she flinched.

"Stop talking to me, girl. I swear, I'm about to beat yo' ass again!"

Kenya chuckled. "Oh, please! He left me to be with you, but failed to mention, I'm going to be around a lot longer than expected. So, get used to seeing me, bitch, for as long as you stay with his ass! I'm not going anywhere."

"Kenya chill out." Banks finally jumped into the conversation. "I don't even know if that's my baby, or if you're even pregnant. So, don't come up in here trying to start shit, with my girl, in my mother's house on her birthday. Don't nobody want you here, and no one asked you to be here, so again, get the fuck out."

"What are you going to do?" She sneered, stepping closer to Banks. "You gonna physically put me out?"

It was quiet for a few moments. "No I'ma put you out, bitch!" I latched onto her hair and yanked her forward, until she fell into the floor.

She threw her hands up and waved them all around, attempting to block my hits.

"Someone get her off of, me! I'm pregnant" She managed to say, after I delivered blow after blow to her face.

Banks yanked me off of, Lakenya, and I had a hand full of her tracks. One of Banks's family members helped her up off of the ground. Her hair was all over the place and her makeup, especially her lipstick was smudged. She looked like a damn fool. I was breathing hard as hell, trying to catch my breath.

"You ain't tired of getting your ass beat, hoe?" I spat as Banks drug me outside. I could hear, Kenya whimpering, but I could care less about her at the moment.

Once we were out of the kitchen, Banks, put me down once we made our way to the patio.

I didn't waste any time questioning him. "Why didn't you tell me, there was a possibility, that bitch is having, your baby? I'm your girl, you didn't think, I needed to know that shit?

He wiped his hand over his face and took a deep breath. "Listen baby, I'm not trying to keep anything from you. I just didn't want to have you mad over this shit, like you are, right now. I don't know for sure, but you know I'ma get a DNA test."

When I didn't respond he continued. "You wanna leave?"

"I mean, I definitely ain't tryna stay here, Carter!" My words were laced with venom.

I was livid, and on the verge of beating his ass next. I just didn't want to be in his presence, at the very moment. I needed to be alone.

****

"Babe you sleeping?" I asked, as I shook, Banks a million times.

I knew he had to be sleeping like a baby, after I fucked him to sleep. Mad sex is definitely, the best sex. He'd talked me into staying after, Lakenya left, we were able to enjoy the rest of his mother's party, after I apologized to everyone. Deena was pissed about the whole ordeal, so she left with all of her kids, but that didn't stop the party. We all ate, drank and enjoyed ourselves, without all of her negative energy.

"Baby, I'm thirsty. Can you go downstairs and get me something to drink?" I said, as Banks stirred in his sleep.

"Yeah, okay, baby in a minute." He said lazily, not even opening his eyes.

I was sure, he was sleep talking because a minute, turned into ten minutes, quickly. I sighed loudly, then stood up, throwing on my black silk robe. It was almost one-clock in the morning, but my mouth was parched. I made my way downstairs careful not to make any noise.

I searched the cabinets for a cup until I found one. I quickly, poured myself some water and spun around to see his mother standing in the doorway.

I gasped and placed my hand on my chest. "Oh my God, you scared me."

She chuckled. "I'm sorry, sweetie. What are you doing up so late?"

She walked over the pantry to retrieve some cookies. I watched as she sat down at the kitchen table to enjoy them.

I held up my cup. "I got a little thirsty."

"Come sit down with me for a moment, suga."

I was silently kicking myself, for not staying in the room. I did as I was told, she smiled at me, before offering me a cookie.

"I can tell the way, that he talks about you, that he's in love. I couldn't be happier. I know you two haven't been dealing with each other for long, but trust me, it's possible to fall in love in such a short period of time. Hell, I fell for Banks's father in four months."

I smiled at her kind words.

"You know, my son is an amazing man, even though he doesn't always make the best decisions. That Lakenya girl was horrible for him. He knew that deep down inside, he was never in love, but he had love for her. With you he's in love."

I was taken aback, by what she said, but flattered at the same time.

She placed her hand on top of mine. "Excuse my French, but don't let that, bitch or any other bitch, try to steal what you all have. These hoes see him, they see dollar signs. I can tell you're different. I can see the love in your eyes. The way that you fought that girl—" she chuckled. "I don't condone fighting, but she had it coming!"

"She definitely did. I just don't want to lose him over some BS. How can I compete, with another woman carrying his first child?"

"That's the thing. You don't need to compete, you've already won"

We continued to chat for another fifteen minutes, or so until we decided to head back to bed. I tried not to think about the whole baby situation, but even after climbing back into bed with Banks, it stayed on my mind. Even after some bomb sex, I was still angry.

Banks

She Fell in Love with a Real One

I was pissed as fuck at, Kenya, for showing up to my mom's place and starting shit. So, I popped up at her crib the next day, to have some words with her. I banged on her damn door, so fucking hard, you would've thought, I was the police. She opened the door about two minutes later.

As soon as the door opened, I started going off. "What the fuck is wrong, with you? Why would you——"

She placed her hand over my mouth, shutting me up, or at least attempting to. I pushed her hands away and stormed inside of her place. I didn't even get to say anything, because she started talking a mile per minute.

"You know what, Carter? I deserve so much more than you give me. I am carrying your, baby." She began to pout, folding her arms over her slightly protruding belly. "You let that bitch, put her hands on me, in front of your mom and whole family. I was so embarrassed!"

"I didn't let her do anything, you shouldn't have told her, that was my job and you went about it, the wrong fucking way."

She shook her head "You're foul, Carter, real foul. You act like you don't care about our, baby." She rubbed her belly slowly, never breaking eye contact. She had a little pudge but nothing major.

I shook my head. "I'm not saying too much of anything, right now. Neither one of us know if that's really, my baby." I pointed to her belly and she scoffed.

"What the fuck ever, Banks. You and I both know, that we fucked raw so——"

"Man, Kenya, I ain't come over here to argue with you. I came over to tell you, to leave me the fuck alone, at least for, right now. I know you're trying to ruin my relationship because you told her first! I never got a chance to. I'm not getting back with you. So, you basically did all of that shit for no reason. I'm more than willing to take the DNA test when the baby gets here."

"So, you gone do me, like I'm some hoe off the street. I have feelings too, you know." She tried to grab my arm, so I couldn't leave, but I backed up.

"Lakenya stop fucking tripping. It's for the best, and don't come at me, with no bullshit about having feelings. Were you thinking about my feelings when you left me, and I begged you for a second chance? You left me at my lowest point, didn't give a fuck about my pleas." Silence was bestowed upon us. "That's what I thought. Remember, what I said." I threw up the deuces sign, while exiting her apartment.

"Fuck you!" I heard her yell.

Obviously, she was upset, but I didn't care. Shit, I was upset, too. I'd take care of the baby if it was mine. But, I was praying like hell, God didn't stick me with, Kenya for the rest of my life. She was a mistake, I regret ever meeting her ass.

I hopped in my whip and sped off towards the studio. I had a lot on my mind and needed to release some stress in the booth. I also needed to take some time to myself, to figure out how to get back on, Heaven's good side.

We just made things official, and with Kenya telling her about the pregnancy before I could, I knew she felt, I was lying and keeping things from her. She was pissed at me, she hadn't looked at me since yesterday. She spoke when I asked her things, but the conversation was vague and dull. With her birthday being tomorrow, I definitely had some tricks up my sleeve. I was hoping, this would make her forgive me and put all of this shit behind us. I was nervous as hell about what I was about to do, but nothing could change my mind. I prayed, tomorrow everything would go as planned.

Shelby

I was nervous wreck, it was all due to simply, just think-ing about what I was about to do. This could land me in jail for many years, but it was worth a try. I would do anything to protect my child, my son, and my world. I'd never been

278

married, never had a consistent relationship and never had anyone love me, the way my son, Naheem, loved me. He was truly all I had in this world.

I glanced at the clock on my nightstand and shook my head. It was almost showtime, I hadn't the slightest idea of what I wanted to say yet. My hands were clammy, my armpits were a little sweaty, I even felt my heart speed up faster and faster, with every second that passed.

'Shelby man up and stop being, a little punk. Grow some fucking balls.' I said to myself, trying to give myself a pep talk, but even that didn't really work.

The doorbell rang, so I grabbed the liquor bottle on my dresser and took two shots of Hennessy. I also sprayed on some body mist and headed for the door immediately after.

'Act natural, Shelby, just be yourself, then once you get him drunk, just come right out and say it.'

I swung the door open and came face to face, with the person who had my son's fate in the palm of his hands.

"Good Evening, Judge Carson." I smiled widely, spreading my arms out to hug him.

"Oh, nonsense Shelby, you don't have to call me judge, when I'm off the clock." He chuckled, placing a tender kiss on my cheek.

"I'm sorry, it's a habit—but please come in."

I stepped to the side and allowed Carson into my home. We were old college buddies, I'd always called him by his last night. No one ever really called by his first name.

"Smells good in here. What are you making? He strolled into the kitchen.

Just as I assumed he would and crowded around the pot on the stove.

I pointed to a chair in the kitchen. "Here sit down."

He smiled prior to following my directions. I walked over to the pot and gave it a stir, but I made sure to put on the sexiest walk, I had. I was sure the Judge's eyes were wandering. Hell, at the age of forty-seven, I still looked good and managed to slip into a sexy all-black dress, that had high slits on both sides and the top wrapped around my neck exposing my back.

I glanced over my shoulder, just to make sure he was looking, sure enough he was licking his lips.

"I'm making steak, with white rice, corn on the cob, cornbread and for dessert, I thought you might enjoy my banana pudding."

He smirked. "When did you learn how to cook?" he joked.

"Oh, please—don't act like, you don't remember me having people line up outside of my dorm, to get a plate. You used to be in that same line." I joked, which caused the two of us to reminisce.

"You know what—you got me there." He sat back and loosened the tie he was wearing. "You used to put your foot in that food, back in college."

I swatted him with my oven mitt. "Trust me, I remember your greedy butt, used to always try to skip everyone. Those were good times. I was pissed when someone snitched and got me shut down, after a whole semester of business." I thought back, to how I always wanted to go to school, to be a chef, but with, Naheem. I wasn't able to do much as a struggling single mother, so that dream never got fulfilled.

"You look very nice tonight, Shelby. I hope I'm not being too forward." He blurted out, shifting the conversation in the direction, I wanted it to go in. He looked nervous.

"Oh, this old thing?" I spun around in a circle giving him a full view. "I just threw this on, but thank you, Carson, I appreciate that."

I fixed him a plate, as well as myself and sat the plates down onto the table. "Anything to drink? Hennessey perhaps?" I was trying to get this fool drunk.

"No, I'm actually a recovering alcoholic, so I'd prefer some water please." He smiled sweetly, at me.

'Damn Shelby, this is going to be hard.' I thought to myself.

"Oh, my God, Carson, I'm so sorry. I didn't know." I pled hoping I didn't mess things up with him.

I poured him a tall glass of water and set it in front of him. He quickly took a sip.

"It's okay, you didn't know. Back in college we used to turn up, but I'm a very different man now. I've also given my life to Christ."

I almost wanted to scream inside. This night was already turning out horrible. I sat across from him and we held hands momentarily, as he said grace. Once he was done, we continued to chat, ever so often between bites.

"I was so surprised to see you at Golf Land the other day. It's been years since I've seen you." I purposely did my research and popped up on his ass, pretending, I played Golf, just to reel him in.

"I know, Carson, it seems like forever. But, I love Golf, I used to play all the time with my son, Naheem, but he's gone now."

"Gone?" He questioned. "I'm sorry to ask, but did he pass away?"

I shook my head, "No, uh—he's actually locked up. I just miss him, so much." I placed my hand over my face and mustered up as much tears, as I could to put on a show for this man.

"Oh, my goodness Shelby, I'm sorry to hear that." He stood up and walked over to me, so that he could rub my back.

"No, it's okay. I'm just hoping and praying, tomorrow with his sentencing he gets off easy. I'm hoping for one-year of house arrest and about one-year of probation. This has all been so stressful, I just want, my baby back."

He stopped rubbing my back, momentarily. "Tomorrow? Your son wouldn't happen to be, Naheem Holmes, would it?"

I nodded, "Yes, he's really a good guy, he just made some mistakes. I'm praying for him to come home, I miss him dearly." I continued to sob and put on a show, but unfortunately, he saw right through me.

"I uh—I have to go, Shelby." He turned to leave, and I quickly dropped down to my knees.

"No, please don't go, Carson. Let me please you, the same way I did in the past. I—I can make you feel good." I tried to unbuckle his pants, but he quickly pushed my hands away.

"Stop!" I fell backwards on my ass as he took off for the front door, but I was right on his trail.

"What's going on with you, Carson, why are you acting like this?"

He stopped walking mid-stride and turned to me, with a grimace on his face.

"You are what's wrong, with me. I'm no fool, Shelby. I thought you wanted me here to catch up on old times. Instead you telling me about your son, knowing that, I'm the judge for that case tomorrow."

"I had no idea, Carson, I swear!" I lied, right through my teeth.

"You know we can both go to jail for this, right? You expect me to reduce his sentencing down to house arrest, just because we used to sleep together in the past? Because we have history together, you expect me to just lie?"

I didn't know what else to do so I started to beg. "Please Carson, I beg of you. My son has his whole life ahead of him. If you could please, just help us, I would be——"

He held up his hand, abruptly. "I have to go, this conversation is over!" He said sternly.

As he was leaving, I yelled out, "I know about, Marjorie!"

He stopped walking, and when he turned around, all of the color in his face was gone, he looked like he saw a ghost.

He marched over to me, matching the movements of those in a marching band. He latched onto my arm, slamming me into the door. "What the fuck, did you just say?"

His whole demeanor changed, he seemed like a different person, then who was just sitting in my kitchen, claiming he gave his life over to, Christ.

I smiled widely. "I know about that young girl, you were fucking. I do my fucking research, trust me judge if you want to keep your title. I'd suggest, you help me. That girl was only seventeen, you're no different from my, son!" I said through gritted teeth. "I think it's crazy how a young girl stepped up saying she was having sex, with you. Then all of a sudden, she practically disappears from the face of the earth. The charges were dropped, due to no evidence."

"Bitch, do you know who you fucking, with?" His eyes were cold, and his jaw was clenched tightly. I could also see the veins in his neck-popping out. "You think, you're about to blackmail, me? You got me fucked up, keep your fucking mouth closed, or I'll close it for you." Was all he said as he walked off.

"Do as I say, we won't have a problem!" I yelled, but he kept walking and my heart started beating fast.

I closed the door and flopped down onto the couch. This was not supposed to happen, he left without me knowing if he was going to help me or not.

'Shelby what the fuck, did you just get yourself, into?'

****

The Next Day

I sat in the courtroom, just a few feet behind, my son. I could not focus at all. I felt sick to my stomach, my head was killing me, from staying up half the night drinking liquor. My head hurt from thinking about my encounter with Carson.

I knew, that '*I turned my life over to, Christ*' talk was a bunch of bullshit. He hadn't changed, he didn't fool me a bit. I knew shit about him, I shouldn't, but it wasn't my fault the bitch he was fucking ran her mouth like a fucking faucet. That's why I always said, you couldn't trust anyone, not even the muthafucka you slept with.

Casey, his on again off again girlfriend, was an acquaintance of mine from work. Imagine my surprise, when we went out for drinks and she spilled every bean there was to spill, about her so-called man. She knew everything and had never told a soul, but she was pissed off and fed up with his bullshit. So, after about five Blue Motherfuckers, she was torn up from the floor and answered every question, I had. The next morning, she couldn't remember much, but from what she did remember, she made me vow not to tell anyone. However, my son needed his freedom, so I threw that info in Carson's face.

My thoughts were interrupted, when the bailiff began to speak. "All rise for the, Honorable Judge Carson!" Everyone rose to his or her feet.

In walked Carson and for a second, I swore that our eyes met, but maybe I was just being paranoid. He took a seated position at his bench and everyone was told to take a seat so that he could continue.

"Case number F-four, seven, eight, three, nine, two, eight, zero, five, State of Florida vs. Naheem Holmes." He adjusted his thick ass bifocals up onto his face, a few times before he said, "Let's go ahead and begin."

Naheem looked back at me and gave me a nervous smile. I returned the gesture, prior to mouthing '*I love you.*'

I felt myself begin to sweat once more, probably more than I was sweating last night. Judge Carson went on and on about the consensual sex, that took place between, Naheem, and that dumb ass little bitch and how it was wrong, no matter if it was consensual or not.

I kept tuning in ever, so often. "You are an adult over the age of twenty-one, you knew exactly what you were doing. This young lady ended up with child and——"

My thoughts interrupted his speech. If you asked me, he was up here being the biggest hypocrite of all time. He was up there yapping his gums for at least ten minutes. Once he finally finished his whack ass speech, he asked Naheem, to stand for his sentencing.

I was literally on the edge of my seat, not breathing. I forgot how to breathe, and it felt like I had the bubble guts.

Naheem stood up slowly, it hurt me to see his hands restrained with cuffs. I'd seen him in them multiple times, but it was just something I'd never get over seeing.

"Naheem Holmes, I'm sentencing you to one-year house arrest, one-year probation, and you have to be registered as a sex offender there's no if, ands or buts about that. You are also not to contact, Shania Lenard, at any point."

My heart literally sank into the pit of my stomach. My blackmailing actually worked.

"Man, what the fuck! This is some bull shit your honor, and you know it!" I glanced over at Shania's family and rolled my eyes.

Her father was the ringleader of anything that had to do with their family. He was obviously pissed about the outcome, but I could care less. His daughter was a whore sleeping with a married man, she knew what she was doing end of discussion.

"I will not stand for this, Mr. Lenard, do I need to detain you?" Carson said, which shifted everyone's attention back over to Shania's family.

Her dad stormed out of the courtroom, as his wife and two small children trailed behind him. Shania was nowhere to be found, which I wasn't surprised about, but either way, my son was free.

There was a permanent smile on, Naheem's face as Carson asked to have, Naheem, removed from the courtroom, so he could head back to the prison and be processed out. That process wasn't always a quick one, but I was jumping for joy on the inside as his sentencing hearing came to an end. I quickly made my way to my car and waited at a coffee shop nearby the jail, waiting for, Naheem, to call and tell me, he was ready for me to come and get him.

About two hours later, I received a text message from an anonymous number, but I already knew who it was.

Random number: I did what you asked, now keep your mouth closed bitch, or you'll be in a body bag sooner than you think!

I shook off the eerie feeling that washed over my entire body and quickly deleted the text message. I was a little scared, but I didn't plan on telling anyone about this, so technically that message didn't apply to me.

I finished up my Latte and headed to the jail, to pick up, Naheem, after getting that call, I was so desperate to receive.

With his arms stretched as wide as they could possibly go, Naheem, practically jumped on me.

"You were right, ma, I trusted you. Now look at me. Ya' boy is a free man." He beamed kissing me on the cheek.

"I told you." I beamed. "Ya mama always has your back son, don't ever forget that." I told him, right as we got into the car.

My mind was all over the place, but I kept my cool. I didn't need, Naheem, thinking something was up. I just really hoped, I didn't regret fucking with Carson. He seemed like the wrong person to cross. I didn't want to find out anytime soon, what he was really capable of.

Chapter 23

Heaven

I felt the constant vibrations of my phone, as it vibrated underneath me. I let out a yawn, stretched and fished for my phone. Took me awhile, to find it tucked deeply underneath me on the bed, but I finally retrieved it.

"Hello." I said lazily, not really wanting to talk to anyone.

"Happy birthday!" Renaissance sang into the phone.

"Aww thanks, boo."

"No problem, you know you're my girl. I couldn't miss wishing you a happy birthday, on your special day."

"Well I appreciate it, but there's nothing happy about it." I said, thinking about the foolishness, Banks, put me through with his so-called baby mama.

"Why not?" Renaissance said, genuinely concerned for me.

"Nothing, forget what I said."

"Okay, well what's your plans for today, bae?" She sounded more excited than I was, it wasn't even her birthday.

"Nothing, I was just going to sit at home and watch some T.V. or something." I was telling the truth. Today felt like any other day.

"That's boring, Heaven. Let's go to the beach, go shopping, get some drinks, and go to the spa, or something. I don't know." She threw out ideas, but I decided to decline her offer.

"Nah, I'll pass on that. I'm just not feeling it, this birthday."

"Okay, well if you change your mind, you know I'm down for whatever." She always was, so I knew she wasn't fronting.

"Okay, Hun, will do."

I bid, my best friend goodbye, then hopped up to brush my teeth and take a much-needed hot shower. On my way to the bathroom, I heard a loud sound coming from the kitchen. It sounded like someone dropped a bunch of pots and pans.

I poked my head inside and saw Banks in an apron slaving over a hot stove.

"What's going on?" I said, as I sat at the island on a tall bar stool.

"What? I don't get a good morning?" He said, as he placed a plate in front of me filled with butter pecan pancakes, eggs, grits, and sausage. He also sat a small bowl in front of me filled with strawberries, pears, grapes, watermelon, and pineapples. He even made mimosas.

"Good morning, but what's going on Banks?" I was confused as hell.

"You thought, I forgot your birthday?" He smiled widely, but his smile soon faded away when, I snapped on him.

"Why are you doing all this?" I glanced around the kitchen and noticed a bouquet of roses on the dining room table as well as a few balloons.

"You deserve it." He flashed, me a quick smile and grabbed ahold of my hands.

"Don't touch me." I pulled away from him, he cut his eyes at me.

"I'm just trying to understand, why you're not appreciative of this breakfast, I fucking spent hours to make. I woke up early, to get all of this shit for you." He pointed around the room at all of the gifts and decorations.

"So, what, I didn't ask you to."

"Bae really? You're really about to start an argument, with me, on your birthday?"

"No one is arguing with you, Banks." I rolled my eyes at him. "You fixed me a breakfast, like I'm supposed to be so damn grateful, drop down to my knees and suck ya dick, or something." I was annoyed, and just wanted to be alone to be honest.

"What the fuck is wrong with you, Heaven?" he inquired.

My face twisted up like a rubix cube. "Why didn't you tell me she was, pregnant?" I needed answers.

He exhaled deeply and stepped closer to me. "I told you." He peered down into my eyes and I looked away. "I fucked up, I'll admit that. I didn't want to say anything, until I was sure she was pregnant by me, but you're right. As my woman, I should have told you. This whole thing is my fault. I never really got closure and felt like just maybe there might still be some love there. I realized I was never really in love with her, I just had love for her. We broke up, because I realized, I'm in love with you and I apologize baby for all of this."

I sighed. "I just need to be alone."

I walked out of the kitchen and headed straight for the restroom. I was definitely hungry, and the breakfast looked and smelled amazing, but I didn't want him to know that. After brushing my teeth, I stripped down to my birthday suit and hopped in the shower.

"Sweet lady would you be my—"

I rolled my eyes when I heard slow music blasting throughout the house. He knew I was a sucker for R&B music. Not even five minutes after being in the shower. I rolled my eyes, when I heard the bathroom door open and close. I was hoping, Banks came into the bathroom to wash his hands or to pee, but instead he got into the shower with me. I spun around and came face to face, with the man I loved and hated at the same damn time.

"Carter if you need to shower, wait until I'm done."

"I'm not getting out."

"Okay, fine I'll get out and once you're done, I'll finish. Excuse me." I tried to get out of the shower, but he grabbed my arm. I yelled, "Let me go boy!"

I was annoyed and just about ready to karate chop him in the neck.

He gazed into my eyes and licked his lips. "Do you love me?"

I shook my head and sucked my teeth. He had to be joking. "What? See now you're just doing too much."

He scoffed, but I didn't care, I was dead serious. "How, just answer the question, Heaven."

I pointed to the two of us and then to the showerhead. "You really wanna have this conversation, right now? In the shower?" I looked at him with a puzzled look on my face, trying to figure out what he was thinking.

"I just want you to say yes or no, it's not that hard."

I tried to push past him, but he pushed me back softly up against the glass shower door. I arched my back once it hit the cold door.

"I just need to know, where your head is at." He moved his hands to place them on either side of my face. "Yes or no."

I looked away from his piercing gaze and he stepped closer to me. My heart began to beat fast. His hands dropped down slowly, as he lightly applied pressure around my neck. I sighed deeply as my eyes slowly closed.

"Huh?" He said with his lips on top of my lips. "Answer me."

"Move." I said softly, as my eyes slowly opened. His eyes were apologetic.

"Baby, please don't ever stop loving me." His hands slid down to my breasts, as he massaged my nipples slowly.

I released a moan and at this point, Banks, knew that he had me right where he wanted me. He pecked my lips a few times, as I wrapped my arms around his neck to deepen the kiss. He slipped his tongue inside and our tongues lightly massaged one another.

"You love me." He said in between kisses.

I nodded, wanting him to stop asking such a foolish question. He lifted me up, I instantly wrapped my legs around him. We made eye contact. Careful not to drop me, he eased me down slowly on to his long, hard dick causing me to gasp loudly.

My pussy was so wet for him. He used one hand to hold onto the wall, as his other hand rested around my waist. He bent his knees and began to pump in and out of me, as I matched his thrusts by rocking my hips against him.

I screamed as I felt him lose his footing. "Don't drop me." I said breathlessly.

He put me down and turned off the shower. We both got out and dried off quickly, Banks was eager to get back inside of me.

"Bend over." He said, I did as I was told.

I bent over the bathroom counter, as Banks slid back into me. I instantly closed my eyes. He felt so good as he pumped in and out of me slowly.

Our breathing increased as he picked up speed.

"Harder." I managed to say, as I bent over a little more and tooted my ass up in the air, as high as it could go.

I could feel his balls slapping my pussy, with each stroke. He latched onto my hair and gripped it with one hand and used the other hand to wrap around my neck.

"You know you're never going anywhere, right?"

"Ye—yes—ahhh shiiit!" I reached back and placed my arm on his bare chest, trying to push him back, but he moved my hand out of the way.

"Nah, don't run." He said, as his grip on my hair got tighter.

"Let me turn around, babe."

Banks pulled out for a moment, allowed me to turn around, and hop up on the bathroom counter. We locked eyes, as I leaned back on my hands and lifted my legs into the air. I smirked, as I opened my legs giving him a clear view of my freshly shaved pussy. I watched his dick jump in anticipation. He licked his lips, as he watched me spread my pussy lips to stick my freshly manicured finger inside. My juices were all over my finger when I pulled it out. I stuck my finger into his mouth and he savored my juices as he sucked and licked my finger clean.

291

With my legs still up in the air, he pulled me to the edge of the bathroom counter. He then took his dick and slapped it against my pussy.

"I want it." I whined.

"What? Tell me what you want, baby." He said, as he put the head in and then pulled it back out.

"Put it in." He repeated, his actions by sticking the head in yet again and pulling it back out.

"You want this dick?"

I shook my head up and down, with lust written all over my face.

Unexpectedly, he slammed into me as my hands quickly latched onto his shoulders and I sunk my nails into his skin. I was sure, he'd probably have bruises when we finished. I could feel him all up in my stomach, as he fucked me. Banks dug all up in my guts. He must've been looking for gold.

"I wanna cum on that dick."

He pushed my legs back further, as he picked up speed. My hands traveled up his shoulders and latched onto his neck, as he fucked me, so hard my back slammed into the counter with each thrust. I was sure my back would have a bruise afterwards as well. He stuck out his tongue, I leaned forward to capture his tongue in my mouth. I sucked on his tongue as he deepened the kiss periodically pulling away to bite on my bottom lip.

"Where you want this nut?" He said in between thrusts.

"Put it in my mouth" I said as his eyes light up. "Oh fuck!" My body began to shake from my orgasm, as my toes curled, and my body stiffened.

"You ready for it?" He questioned, breathlessly, as I managed to shake my head.

Right as he was about to nut, he pulled out quickly and I stuck my tongue out. I caught his nut and swallowed, then the two of us struggled to catch our breath.

"Now get yo ass in there and eat that breakfast." He said, in between kisses. I weakly smiled up at him.

****

After breakfast, we laid on the couch wrapped up in each other's arms. The sound of his heart beating as I lay on his chest, was soothing. I was damned near on my way to la la land, because after two more rounds of sex, I was exhausted.

"Can I say something?" He questioned, as I looked up at him.

"Sure."

He took my hand and kissed it, intertwining our fingers together.

"I'm sorry." He blurted out. "I want us to always be together. I love you, I can't be without you."

"I could have told you that, I knew all along." I smirked.

He mushed my head playfully. "You ain't know shit." he chuckled.

He pulled me into a hug and placed a bunch of sloppy kisses all over my face.

"Okay, Banks, that's enough." I gave him a disgusted look, as I wiped my face with the palm of my hands and wiped it onto his shirt. "You play so much."

"But, you like it, though." He said, as I rolled my eyes.

This was the perfect start to a birthday.

Chapter 24

Heaven

"Where are we going, baby? I squealed, when I almost tripped in my four-inch red knee high Fendi boots.

Banks said, he had a surprise for me. He didn't want me to see the surprise, so he blindfolded me. I was literally talking the smallest baby steps ever. I was afraid he was going to have me walking into a wall or falling flat on my ass. I put my hand out to feel around, I squealed when he popped the back of my hand, the same way you pop a child.

"Ouch, bae really?" I whined, as I heard him chuckle.

"Just let me guide you. You ready?"

I didn't say anything, I just clutched onto his arm tightly.

"Okay, slide to the left, now slide to the right, criss cross. Everybody clap your hands."

I was so annoyed with, Carter, this fool really had me doing the Cha Cha slide. I reached up to snatch off my blindfold.

"You play too much, I'm taking this off."

He was laughing so hard, he could barely breathe. "No, don't take it off yet." He removed my hands quickly. "I'll stop playing."

I released a deep sigh, as we took a few more steps and he helped me up some steps.

I was nervous, but anxious at the same time.

"Okay, baby remove your blindfold."

When I opened my eyes, I saw a bunch of familiar faces. "Surprise!" Everyone yelled, I turned to Banks and practically jumped into his arms.

We were in a gorgeous ballroom, filled with pink and gold balloons, all of the dinnerware was gold, white roses were the centerpiece on every table, there were ice sculptures, gorgeous crystal chandeliers hanging from the ceiling and a huge banner that said Happy Birthday, Heaven & Nevaeh.

"Awe baby you did all of this for me?" I puckered up my lips and he pecked them a few times.

I couldn't hide the wide ass Kool-Aid smile on, my face. His smile was just as wide, if not wider than mine. As I wiped my lipstick from his lips, Renaissance, walked over with her arms spread wide.

"Happy birthday, bae." I gave her a side eye, moments before Skye walked up cheesing from ear to ear.

"Both, of y'all knew about this and didn't say anything?"

Skye threw her hands up. "I mean, boss man told me not to say anything?" she declared.

I looked at Renaissance who simply shook her head.

"He ain't tell me shit. I'm glad, he didn't because you know, I can't keep a secret for too long."

I laughed because she was right. The three of us shared a hug. Everyone then began to swarm around, me like a crazy pack of wolves wishing me, a *Happy Birthday* and showering me with hugs and kisses. Banks's mother was there, a few of my old friends from high school and college, and family members. I was still shocked, he managed to put this together, for my sister and I. The two of them were like oil and water, they just didn't mesh well, but he knew she'd feel left out if he threw the party only for me. Nevaeh was nowhere to be found. I made a mental note to call her as soon as, I made my way through the crowd and greeted everyone.

My sister must've had twin intuition and knew, I was thinking about her, because as I scanned the crowd once more we locked eyes and I waved her over. As soon as she was in my presence, I practically jumped on her causing her to giggle.

"Happy b—birthday to us, bitch!" She yelled, I could smell the alcohol on her breath.

Her words were slurring, so I already knew she was drunk. "Yes, happy birthday to, us." I agreed pulling her in for a hug once more.

"This venue is all that and a bag of chips. I wonder how much, Banks, spent on this shit. She looked around at the scenery then back at me. "I hope yo' nigga don't expect anything from me, since he threw us a double party."

My sister always had to ruin things with the stupid things that she said.

"Huh?" My eyebrow rose in confusion, as my head cocked to the side. "What do you mean?"

She chuckled. "I mean the nigga, don't even know me, but he breaking bread on me." she shrugged. "He probably wants a threesome, with us, every nigga wants to fuck twins. I wouldn't mind."

I shook my head and stepped closer to her. "I don't know how much you drank tonight, Vaeh, but you're tripping real hard."

Her eyebrows rose, and her face held a smug grin. "Chill sis, I was just saying."

"I don't need you to be just saying anything."

My breathing increased, as we stared at one another, me staring more intensely than her.

Although she was drunk, she had no reason to be saying the shit she was saying. She knew, I didn't play about my man. I wanted to say more but was startled when our friends and family bombarded us, as they brought out two huge cakes to sing Happy Birthday.

"Happy Birthday to you, Happy Birthday to you, Happy Birthday dear Heaven and Nevaeh, Happy Birthday to you!"

I couldn't do anything other, then smile. I was truly happy and at a loss for words.

"Make a wish, baby." Banks said cheesing from ear to ear.

I closed my eyes and made a wish, prior to blowing the candles out. When I opened my eyes, everyone was practically shoving their cellphones into my face. I looked at, Bank's mother who was crying, Nevaeh's mouth was wide open, and Renaissance was fighting back tears.

I looked behind me and was shocked to see, Banks, down on one knee. My breath got caught in my throat, my mouth instantly hung open, and my heart was beating so fast.

"Babe what are you doing?" I placed my right hand over my mouth when he grabbed my left hand.

I had so many emotions running through my head. I was afraid, that this was a joke, nervous that he might change his mind halfway through the proposal and happy that I was possibly getting another chance at love after what happened with, Naheem.

He smiled up at me to ease his nervousness. "I—this is different from anything I've ever done, before. I have never truly been in love. I have never had someone see the good in me. I have never wanted to be with someone for the rest of my life, until I met you. My heart beats fast every time you walk into a room. I can't stop thinking about you, when you're not around. I love the way you laugh, the way you walk, and just everything about you. I am in love with you. I——"

Banks began to choke up on his words as I watched him get teary eyed. For the first time ever, I saw a softer side of him. I reached up and wiped his tears away.

"Take yo' time!" Everyone laughed, as Banks's homeboy, Lance, began to yell things out.

"It's okay, baby take your time." I reassured him, as I wiped away a few tears falling down my face.

He opened a black velvet box, with the biggest and prettiest engagement ring, I'd ever seen. I was no jeweler, but it looked really expensive.

"Will you marry, me?"

I quickly nodded my head. He slipped the ring on my finger, and then stood up, quickly practically attacking my lips.

"I love you, I love you, and I love you." He said, repeatedly against my lips.

I wrapped my arms around his neck, to pull him in closer as people crowded around us snapping a thousand photographs.

"I love you, too. Thank you for making me the happiest women on earth." I couldn't stop the tears from falling, as our friends and family asked to take pictures of my ring and us of course.

I had the biggest smile on my face, as we posed for pictures with my hand out as, Banks, stood behind me with his arms around my waist showering my cheek and neck with kisses.

"I'm so happy for you. You deserve it." Skye said, giving the both of us a hug.

Renaissance chimed in. "Yes, I'm so happy for the two of you, too. Finding love is a beautiful thing, and girl that ring is big as hell, you must have that bomb cat between those legs." Renaissance joked, which caused me to swat her on the arm, "What, I'm just telling the truth." she laughed.

"But, for real though, I have been waiting for this moment, to see you happy again." Renaissance said.

I fanned my eyes. "You're going to make me cry, again."

"You have always been like a sister to me. I want what's best for you." Renaissance kissed my cheek and embraced me in a hug. "Congrats sis."

The two of us were pulled in many different directions as everyone came up to us to say congratulations.

I smiled when Bank's mother walked up smiling from ear to ear, with her arms spread wide. "Welcome to the family, beautiful." She wrapped her arms tightly around me and gave me a big hug. When she pulled away, she looked me in the eyes and said, "Remember, what I told you? You've already won."

It made me feel good to know, that his mother liked me, and was on my side, after the whole baby situation with his ex, but I was prepared to stick by his side no matter what.

299

Nevaeh

I sipped on what might have been my third Hennessy and coke, as everyone gushed over my sister and my man. Well technically he was hers, but you know what I mean. He should have been mine. I still didn't understand, why he chose her over me, we look the exact same. I shook my head and tossed back that drink, as Lance walked over to me and took a seat. I scoffed, and he smirked when I looked over at him.

"The fuck do you want?"

He reached over and slid my drink away from me, which caused my eyes to widen.

He shrugged off my comment. "You need to chill on the drinks"

"You need to go find that, bitch, you were fucking and leave me the hell alone."

He sighed. "Yo' why you so bitter?"

I chuckled and folded my arms with furrowed brows. He couldn't have been serious"

"I'm far from bitter, I'm just not in the mood for your BS tonight. I have been avoiding you all night, for a reason, then you come and sit your ass down over here, like we're the best of buds trying to give me life lessons. I'm good, trust me."

"You're not. Your words are slurring, you been acting slutty all night."

I cocked my head back. "How the hell would you know?"

He exhaled deeply. He seemed to be annoyed but really, he was the one that was annoying me.

"You got this little ass shit on, then you out here pushing up on different men, you gave your number to like four niggas up in here." He shook his head. "Get yo' shit, I'm taking you home." He tried to grab my arm and I pulled away.

He glared at me. "I'm not about to fight with you, get your stuff and let's go, don't make me say it again."

I rolled my eyes but did, as I was told. I didn't want to cause a scene. I tried to take one last sip of my drink, but he snatched it away and slammed the glass down onto the table. I exhaled and stood up slowly, careful not to trip since my legs were wobbly.

He grabbed me by the hand and helped me walk around to a few friends and family members to bid them goodbye.

Once I stopped in front of my sister to tell her, I was leaving some bitch walked in being extra loud, which caused everyone to turn and see where the ruckus was coming from.

"Well, well, well, what do we have here? she yelled.

She had her hair tied up and was dressed in sneakers, black leggings and an oversized shirt. She definitely wasn't coming to the dinner party. She was dressed like she was ready to fight.

"Umm excuse me who the hell are you?" Renaissance chimed in.

"Mind yo' business bitch, I don't know you, and I don't care to." As she stepped closer, I realized it was Imani, Lance's wife.

He dropped my hand quickly, like it was on fire.

Renaissance rolled her neck. "It's my best friend's birthday you are not about to come up in here and—"

Renaissance's words were cut short, when Imani marched directly over to, Lance, and slapped him across the face, so hard, I was sure he'd have a bruise.

She was breathing hard and Lance held the spot, she slapped, then he stepped closer to her. I looked around and everyone stood back watching the scene unfold.

"You still fucking her, Lance? She pointed at me

"Nevaeh what's going on?" Heaven asked, and although her moment was just ruined, by this woman. I still was her sister, and she was always ready to fight.

Imani looked back and forth between the two of us, obviously a little confused about who was who. I looked at my sister, who looked like she was just about ready to take her shoes off. Then I looked back over at Imani.

"I don't know this, bitch." I stated pointing at, Imani.

Imani laughed. "You do know me, so don't act like you don't. I already told you to close yo' legs to married men. I told you to stay the fuck away from my man, but you ain't listen, so I'ma have to beat yo' ass again, hoe!"

She tried to charge at me, but Lance jumped between the two of us. "What the fuck are you doing? He yelled at her. "Take yo' ass home, Imani, I'm not playing!"

"No, you know what nigga, fuck you. You text me all the time, late at night asking for us to get back together. Yet, I had to follow you just to find out, you still fucking this bitch, so you know what, I want a divorce."

"Let's go somewhere private and talk about this."

She shook her head. "No, you've already made your decision, obviously." She meaned mugged me.

He tried to grab her arm, but she snatched away from him.

"I wanna work this out with you, baby, don't do this shit here."

"Fuck you! Fuck the both of, y'all."

She walked away, just as quickly as she had come and like a fool, Lance followed her. I shook my head, and then excused myself quickly. I had to run to the bathroom to throw up, my sister was hot on my trail.

I practically knocked people over trying to get to the bathroom. Tears ran from my eyes as I threw up everything in me. My sister holding my hair, interrupted my thoughts.

"Are you, okay? What's going on with you?" She asked, with a voice full of concern.

"I'm fine." I flushed the toilet and wiped my mouth, with a piece of tissue, she handed me.

"You don't look fine." She stared me in the eyes. "You're coming home with me, I want to make sure you're okay."

She Fell in Love with a Real One

I wanted to decline her offer, but she insisted and wouldn't take no for an answer. The party that was already ruined had ended so Banks, Heaven, and I got in the car and made our way to her house.

Heaven

When we got to my house, I was startled to see that almost all of the lights were on. I figured, I'd just left them on by accident when I was rushing out of my place earlier. Both Banks and myself held up Nevaeh who was pissy drunk. As one arm held my sister up. I used the other to stick my key into the door and kicked it open with my foot.

My eyebrows rose, when I smelled an aroma and heard music playing throughout the house. My heart started beating faster immediately, thinking that someone must've broken in and made their self at home.

"Babe, I think someone is here." I said, in a frantic voice, as he three of us stepped a little further into the house.

There were also rose pedals on the floor, that spelled out '*I love you*' which raised a big red flag in the back of my mind.

"Hold her real quick, baby." I held my sister up, as Banks, pulled a gun out of the waistband of his pants. "Stay behind me." He commanded.

A male figure emerged from the back room, causing myself, and Vaeh, to scream. Her drunken ass didn't know what was going on and had only screamed because I did. My mouth dropped instantly, when I realized who it was.

"Nigga, who the fuck are, you!" Banks yelled, as he pointed the gun at him.

"Wait baby, it's okay! I know him!" I said, in a feeble attempt to get, Banks, to put his gun down.

"You know him? Who the fuck is this?" He questioned me, still holding his gun up.

"I'm her fucking, husband! Who the hell are you?" Naheem, stated proudly, disregarding the fact that he and I were one step away from divorce.

"I'm her, Fiancé!"

TO BE CONTINUED...
She Fell in Luv with a Real One 2
Coming Soon

Submission Guideline.

Submit the first three chapters of your completed manuscript to ldpsubmissions@gmail.com, subject line: Your book's title. The manuscript must be in a .doc file and sent as an attachment. Document should be in Times New Roman, double spaced and in size 12 font. Also, provide your synopsis and full contact information. If sending multiple submissions, they must each be in a separate email.

Have a story but no way to send it electronically? You can still submit to LDP/Ca$h Presents. Send in the first three chapters, written or typed, of your completed manuscript to:

LDP: Submissions Dept
Po Box 870494
Mesquite, Tx 75187

DO NOT send original manuscript. Must be a duplicate.

Provide your synopsis and a cover letter containing your full contact information.

Thanks for considering LDP and Ca$h Presents.

Coming Soon from Lock Down Publications/Ca$h Presents

BOW DOWN TO MY GANGSTA

By **Ca$h**

TORN BETWEEN TWO

By **Coffee**

BLOOD STAINS OF A SHOTTA **III**

By **Jamaica**

WHEN THE STREETS CLAP BACK **III**

By **Jibril Williams**

STEADY MOBBIN

By **Marcellus Allen**

BLOOD OF A BOSS **V**

By **Askari**

LOYAL TO THE GAME **IV**

By **T.J. & Jelissa**

A DOPEBOY'S PRAYER **II**

By **Eddie "Wolf" Lee**

IF LOVING YOU IS WRONG… **III**

LOVE ME EVEN WHEN IT HURTS

By **Jelissa**

DAUGHTERS OF A SAVAGE **II**

By **Chris Green**

TRAPHOUSE KING **II**

By **Hood Rich**

BLAST FOR ME **II**

RAISED AS A GOON **V**

By **Ghost**

ADDICTIED TO THE DRAMA **III**

By **Jamila Mathis**

She Fell in Love with a Real One

LIPSTICK KILLAH **III**
By **Mimi**
WHAT BAD BITCHES DO **II**
By **Aryanna**
THE COST OF LOYALTY **II**
By **Kweli**
SHE FELL IN LOVE WITH A REAL ONE
By **Tamara Butler**
LOVE SHOULDN'T HURT
By **Meesha**
CORRUPTED BY A GANGSTA **II**
By **Destiny Skai**
SHE FELL IN LOVE WITH A REAL ONE II
By **Tamara Butler**

Available Now
RESTRAINING ORDER **I & II**
By **CA$H & Coffee**
LOVE KNOWS NO BOUNDARIES **I II & III**
By **Coffee**
RAISED AS A GOON I, II, III & IV
BRED BY THE SLUMS I, II, III
BLAST FOR ME
By **Ghost**
LAY IT DOWN **I & II**
LAST OF A DYING BREED
BLOOD STAINS OF A SHOTTA I & II
By **Jamaica**
LOYAL TO THE GAME
LOYAL TO THE GAME II

307

Tamara Butler

LOYAL TO THE GAME III
By **TJ & Jelissa**
BLOODY COMMAS I & II
SKI MASK CARTEL I & II
By **T.J. Edwards**
IF LOVING HIM IS WRONG…I & II
By **Jelissa**
WHEN THE STREETS CLAP BACK I & II
By **Jibril Williams**
A DISTINGUISHED THUG STOLE MY HEART I II & III
By **Meesha**
PUSH IT TO THE LIMIT
By **Bre' Hayes**
BLOOD OF A BOSS **I, II, III & IV**
By **Askari**
THE STREETS BLEED MURDER **I, II & III**
THE HEART OF A GANGSTA I II& III
By **Jerry Jackson**
CUM FOR ME
CUM FOR ME 2
CUM FOR ME 3
An **LDP Erotica Collaboration**
BRIDE OF A HUSTLA **I II & II**
THE FETTI GIRLS **I, II& III**
CORRUPTED BY A GANGSTA
By **Destiny Skai**
WHEN A GOOD GIRL GOES BAD
By **Adrienne**
A GANGSTER'S REVENGE **I II III & IV**
THE BOSS MAN'S DAUGHTERS

308

She Fell in Love with a Real One

THE BOSS MAN'S DAUGHTERS II

THE BOSSMAN'S DAUGHTERS III

THE BOSSMAN'S DAUGHTERS IV

A SAVAGE LOVE **I & II**

BAE BELONGS TO ME

A HUSTLER'S DECEIT I, II

By **Aryanna**

A KINGPIN'S AMBITON

A KINGPIN'S AMBITION **II**

I MURDER FOR THE DOUGH

By **Ambitious**

TRUE SAVAGE

TRUE SAVAGE II

TRUE SAVAGE **III**

DAUGHTERS OF A SAVAGE

By **Chris Green**

A DOPEBOY'S PRAYER

By **Eddie "Wolf" Lee**

THE KING CARTEL **I, II & III**

By **Frank Gresham**

THESE NIGGAS AIN'T LOYAL **I, II & III**

By **Nikki Tee**

GANGSTA SHYT **I II &III**

By **CATO**

THE ULTIMATE BETRAYAL

By **Phoenix**

BOSS'N UP **I , II & III**

By **Royal Nicole**

I LOVE YOU TO DEATH

By Destiny J

I RIDE FOR MY HITTA

I STILL RIDE FOR MY HITTA

By **Misty Holt**

LOVE & CHASIN' PAPER

By **Qay Crockett**

TO DIE IN VAIN

By **ASAD**

BROOKLYN HUSTLAZ

By **Boogsy Morina**

BROOKLYN ON LOCK I & II

By **Sonovia**

GANGSTA CITY

By **Teddy Duke**

A DRUG KING AND HIS DIAMOND I & II

A DOPEMAN'S RICHES

By Nicole Goosby

TRAPHOUSE KING

By **Hood Rich**

LIPSTICK KILLAH **I, II**

By **Mimi**

BOOKS BY LDP'S CEO, CA$H

TRUST IN NO MAN

TRUST IN NO MAN 2

TRUST IN NO MAN 3

BONDED BY BLOOD

SHORTY GOT A THUG

THUGS CRY

THUGS CRY 2

THUGS CRY 3

TRUST NO BITCH

TRUST NO BITCH 2

TRUST NO BITCH 3

TIL MY CASKET DROPS

RESTRAINING ORDER

RESTRAINING ORDER 2

IN LOVE WITH A CONVICT

Coming Soon

BONDED BY BLOOD 2

BOW DOWN TO MY GANGSTA

Tamara Butler